Journey to the Hopewell Star

Hannah D. State

Cover art by Irfan Budi
Published by Glowing Light Press, NB, Canada
For inquiries, contact: glowinglightpress@gmail.com
All rights reserved
ISBN: 978-1-7772542-0-9

If you enjoyed this story, we encourage you to write a review at www.amazon.com and help spread the word!

In loving memory of my mother, Barbara Novak, who was a writer, and who inspired me with her love of words.

For the children who desire and deserve a better world.

"Nothing can dim the light which shines from within."

Maya Angelou

1

Curled up on the couch in front of the fire, Sam Sanderson watched the snowflakes dance around outside. The clouds drifted and dispersed, shades of gray and black swirling through the night sky. A moment later, a piercing light broke through. She caught the moon gleaming at her, an eye in the sky, observing and holding her captive to its brief radiance. The trees swayed, casting eerie shadows across the fields. The wind howled and rattled against the window. Tonight, they expected a storm.

In the kitchen, Sam's grandfather, Walter, was busy tidying up and calibrating their meals. The TitusTech 2000 3D Multi-Print Cooker was a small device, half the size of a regular convection oven, and almost every home had one. It cut down meal preparation by hours, and you could customize it to print hundreds of different meals. Her grandfather had purchased this one two months ago, and it had taken a while to understand all of its features.

She glanced at her grandfather; his face was heavy with concentration. As he got older, simple tasks took longer. His movements were slower these days, and more labored. Where once he could vacuum the house in less than an hour, it could now easily take him all day.

How long would they be able to manage living on the farm? She didn't say it often enough, but she wanted to stay here. She liked her homeschooling, and she dreaded the day she would attend a public school. Her grandfather seemed to know this too.

The cooker began to whistle, indicating it was ready. Pip, their small white terrier, turned his head toward the source of the sound and howled along.

On the ledge above the fireplace rested a photo of Sam's parents. They were young, in their mid-twenties at the time. Her mother wore a white dress with lace, her hair the color of caramel, flowing down past her shoulders. Her father dressed in a suit with a blue tie. His blue eyes contrasted against his dark brown hair. His warm smile softened his features.

Sam wondered when she would see them again. It had been nine months since they left on a government mission abroad. The actual work always remained a secret. They never went into detail about it, so it wasn't exactly clear what they did. If she asked about it, they never explained it in simple terms, always leaving her feeling frustrated and in the dark. They usually changed the subject to focus on Sam.

However, she knew for certain of their accomplishments as highly-regarded scientists in the field of physics; their publications lined the bookcase in the den, along with framed news articles and degrees which hung on the walls. The picture of them brought back memories, and a sudden pang of sadness rose up in her. That was all she wanted for her birthday this year: for them to return home safe and sound.

"Hurry, Grandpa! It'll be on soon!" She was referring, of course, to the TV show *Jeopardy!* They always watched it in the evenings before bedtime, and her grandfather knew all the answers. Well, most of them.

"Be there in a minute," he replied.

A loud popping noise startled them both. He jumped back and a look of horror spread across his face.

"Grandpa, what was that? Is everything okay?" Sam got up and quickly headed toward the kitchen. She looked at the floor, the walls, the ceiling, littered with hundreds of shards of glass and chunks of food.

"It's the darn cooker. It exploded!"

"Can I help?"

"No, no, there's too much glass. How about you go and take Pip outside while I clean this mess up?" He grabbed the dustpan and broom and began to sweep, muttering under his breath.

Sam made her way to the hallway closet to gather her coat and boots. Without hesitation, Pip made his way to the door and took a seat in front of it, wagging his tail.

It was too much work. She didn't want to get all bundled up just to take him out for a few minutes, with the weather so blizzardy out there. She'd just open the door a crack, then call him back in when he'd finished his business. Simple as that.

As Sam opened the door, a blast of icy air hit her face, startling her senses. Shivering, she grabbed a scarf and wrapped it around her face and neck. Pip made his way out into the cold as she watched from the doorway. He looked quite brave, his ears perked up and his face held high as he bulldozed through a small mound of snow.

The wind howled louder and fiercer as the snow continued to fall quickly, blanketing the fields and houses in the distance. The sky grew dark now, and Sam couldn't see much else except some lightning in the distance, which seemed odd. It was extremely rare to have thunder and lightning at these cold temperatures while snowing, and yet, there it was.

"Pip, I think we'd better get back inside." As she called him, she saw her breath in the frigid air. She imagined transforming into a large dragon, blowing fire onto the land, melting the snow with her powerful breath. The steam whirled from her nostrils and mouth into the frosty air.

But when she drew in more air, Pip ran away.

"Pip! Come back!" She must have frightened him! "Pip! Where are you going?" It was no use. He ran awkwardly through the thick snow toward the barn.

She zipped up her coat, pulled her scarf higher to cover her face, and ran frantically toward him. He'd freeze to death out there!

With each step she took, her boots sank into the snow. The relentless wind howled and blew her red hair every which way without remorse. Its forcefulness created an invisible wall that she tried to push against. The icy snow hit her face like a thousand pinpricks. Next time, she'd keep him on a leash.

The barn, just a few meters ahead, reflected the ghostly pale moonlight, creating an eerie effect against its darker surroundings. It creaked and groaned, its walls shaking and rumbling under the pressure. Above her, storm clouds swirled. Flashes of white light streaked across the sky. Sam shuddered as she heard the loud, sharp crack of thunder, the sound reverberating in her bones as it trailed off but continued to rumble close by.

She made it to the barn and noticed that the latch had come off its hinge. The door stood ajar. Inside, the animals trembled and cowered. She looked around and heard the loud rustling of hay as the animals scurried about, anxious and on edge.

She sensed it too, in the pit of her stomach.

* * *

Walter swept up the glass. What had led to this? Probably a faulty part. It wasn't the first time the piece of TitusTech technology had broken down. He sighed, thinking about his own foolishness to have purchased one in the first place. He should have known. They didn't make things like they used to. What a waste! And no warranty on this one. It seemed like they designed their products to break down quickly so that people kept buying them. And it wasn't like anyone else made them, either. TitusTech had a stranglehold on the market.

He emptied the dustpan into the waste bin and took a deep breath. The thunder rumbled outside, growing louder, deeper. He couldn't remember a storm this bad in all of his sixty-five years. He allowed his mind to wander, his thoughts turning to past memories here in this home.

He remembered the time spider eggs had hatched in Sam's room during the night. He'd walked in to find her covered in spiders. Instead of reacting with fear, she'd remained unusually calm, and went to sleep in the guest room with no fuss while he swept hundreds of tiny spiders off the ceiling and floor.

That was one of the worst nights he could remember. But Sam didn't think twice about it. Even today, as his thoughts moved back to the present, he considered her reaction when the cooker exploded. She'd reacted with practicality and expediency, asking if she could help. Her sensibility would serve her well in the future.

Walter emptied the last of the glass into the waste bin, standing a bit too quickly. He waited to catch his breath, his head dizzy. A sharp pain seared across his chest. He rubbed it with one hand, using the other to steady himself. His mind raced. Was he having a heart attack? No, couldn't be. Just indigestion. He took some deep breaths, but the pain blazed again. He panicked and stretched his arm over his head. He waited a few seconds, then took another deep breath. This time, no pain. He relaxed his muscles.

But what about next time?

With no services nearby and the farm so isolated and remote, even emergency vehicles would have a tough time accessing their home, especially in the winter months. It would be better to live in a larger city with better access to health care, in case something happened.

This year, he decided, would be the last year at the farm.

He wiped a damp cloth along the counter, making sure to pick up any remaining splinters. His thoughts turned to his daughter and son-in-law. He needed to see them again. It had been so long since he last heard from them. Initially, the assignment was only supposed to last three months, but it kept getting extended. Tomorrow would be the first time they weren't all together to celebrate Sam's birthday, and this was especially hard on Sam. Walter didn't want to think the worst, and instead pushed those thoughts aside.

Flustered, he remembered Sam. What was taking her so long to return? He looked outside the window, catching a glimpse of her running toward the barn. Now, what was she doing, running out there in this cold? She would freeze to death. With that, he grabbed his coat and boots and ventured out into the night.

2

Sam couldn't remember a storm like this, ever. Inside the barn, she listened intently as the walls and foundation creaked and groaned from the weight of the wind pushing against them. The door flapped open, swaying in the wind and banging against its hinges. A high-pitched whistling noise came from the metal roof, the wind billowing across its body, ready to rip it off its beams.

She turned on the light and watched as it flickered and then dimmed, emitting a faint greenish hue. It took a moment for the light to disperse across the barn, and for her eyes to adjust. She looked around the pens, trying to spot Pip. Her eyes scanned the barn and she found Peggy, her potbelly pig. She'd dug a hole within a block of hay and curled up under it for protection, shaking gently.

Sam knelt beside her, trying her best to comfort her. "It's okay Peggy, not to worry. The storm will pass soon."

As she cradled Peggy and stroked her soft ears, Sam gazed down and noticed something odd. Splattered on some hay, she spotted a few drops of dark blue liquid. She looked up at the ceiling, wondering if the roof had sprung a leak, but saw nothing out of place. So, where did it come from? What was it? She reached out her hand and touched it, rubbing it between her fingers. It had the consistency of blood. Disgusted, she quickly wiped it off on nearby hay.

Then she heard a faint sound. Not a cry, but more of a groan.

"Who's there?" She set Peggy down inside her snug block of hay and stood up, looking around in an attempt to pinpoint the source of the sound. She tried to shake the unsteady feeling growing inside her. "Come out where I can see you."

In the corner of her eye, she spotted something moving just a few meters away. A moment later, a figure emerged from the shadows. It looked like a boy, around her age, only he had blue skin, flowing brown hair, and golden eyes.

Out of fear, she grabbed a pitchfork and held it out in front of her.

"Who…wh…what are you?"

He wore a black metallic suit covered in strange, gold hieroglyphic markings. The suit accentuated his form, jutting out horizontally along his shoulders, making him appear strong and well-protected. Parts of the suit included additional plated enhancements, made of what looked like reinforced material, like armor. Only, it didn't look like anything Sam had seen before. It glistened in the light, almost as if the suit were alive and contained some kind of energy. His suit was tattered along his right shoulder and arm, and Sam could make out his body underneath, if only barely. His torso looked oddly muscular for a boy of his age. He held a helmet in one gloved hand. Despite the suit, he didn't look properly dressed for the winter months. In fact, he looked quite out of place here.

Impressed with the suit's features, she wondered where he got it. Maybe she could convince her grandfather to get her one for Halloween too, even though it wasn't for another ten months. "Nice costume. Where did you get it?" The words slipped out of her mouth before she could think. Even after she said them, she couldn't make sense of why this boy would be dressed up in a costume and blue makeup, in her barn, in the middle of winter.

She inched forward to get a better view, her curiosity growing stronger. He pushed his hair back with one hand, and she noticed his large, pointed ears.

Her mouth dropped open, but she couldn't find any words.

He took a step back, his body shaking. "I'm sorry, Sam! Please, don't hurt me." He appeared genuinely frightened as his eyes pleaded with hers.

Looking into his eyes, she experienced a deep sense of calm, but also marvel. Specks of golden dust collected and welled like small pools in his eyes. She sensed he was in some sort of danger. But why? Where was he from, and how did he arrive here?

She tried piecing her thoughts and the situation together, but it was disjointed in her mind. Sure, she had seen many shows about the possibility of intelligent life on other planets, and she suspected that other beings existed in the universe. Scientists now had ways of traveling farther than ever before in the galaxy. Her parents had been part of planetary missions in the past, but to witness a being from another planet here on Earth made her even more curious than before. How did he know her language, let alone her name?

Suddenly, Pip ran in front of her and barked at the stranger, snapping Sam out of her thoughts and bringing her back to her senses.

Did this stranger pose a threat? She kept her distance, just in case. Her hands felt permanently glued to the pitchfork. She stood her ground and narrowed her eyes. "How do you know my name?"

He shifted uncomfortably, looking as though he'd done something terribly wrong and felt ashamed of himself. "Your parents...they sent me to deliver a message, and bring you a gift." He stretched out his hand, and in it was an envelope.

Sam took it quickly with one hand, still holding on to the pitchfork in the other, and tore it open.

"And I failed horribly. I'm really sorry! I wasn't supposed to be seen. It was supposed to be a quick drop-off and then I would go back to my planet, but unfortunately, as I was landing, the lightning storm nicked my only method of transport!"

Sam couldn't believe what she was hearing and seeing. Holding the note up to the pale light, she instantly recognized her mother's handwriting. The note was brief:

My dearest Samantha,

As you are reading this, I hope you and your grandfather are safe and warm by the fire. Your father and I wish we could be there with you to celebrate your 12th birthday. We are entering the final stage of our project and are close to finding the key. It is a very dangerous mission and unfortunately, I can't tell you much more. We miss you very much and are thinking of you every day. We hope to see you soon. In the meantime, here are some gifts from our travels. Never be afraid to follow your dreams and make your own adventures! Be safe, my love, and we will write more when we can. Please give your grandfather a big hug from us.

Lots of love,
Mom and Dad

Confused and somewhat skeptical, Sam decided that she needed to ask more questions. "Why wouldn't they deliver this message themselves? Why would they send a..." She hesitated. "A *boy* to deliver the message?" Her mind raced to find a logical explanation. If he really knew her parents, she would need to test this somehow. But how?

"It's...complicated."

"You'll have to do better than that."

8

He shifted on his feet and bent down, setting the helmet carefully on a block of hay. "They were passing through our star system, and they stopped on my planet to fuel up their ship with perilium from our moon. They couldn't stay long, and needed to be on their way for an important mission. That's when they asked me to do them a favor by dropping off these gifts for you. So, I did."

She thought about his answer for a moment. It made sense, perhaps. It was a logical explanation. She realized her parents couldn't interrupt their mission, but they had found an opportunity to reach out to her nevertheless, through this boy's actions. He must have been on very good terms with her parents. Why else would he travel all this way to deliver these gifts?

Silence permeated the air until he spoke again. "You referred to me as a boy, but I'm not a boy. Actually, I'm ninety-seven years old on my home planet."

"*Ninety-seven?*"

"We age much slower on Kryg, compared to Earth."

How was that even possible? He looked so young. And he didn't even meet her in height, she realized, as she stood a couple inches taller than him. She was considered short for her age.

"I don't understand… How could you age so slowly on your planet?"

He shifted his eyes downward, focusing on a block of hay. He slowly took a seat, holding a hand up that suggested he needed to rest. "Time is a funny thing, Sam. Common humans haven't quite grasped its possibilities yet."

"Why do you refer to me as a *common* human? What else is there?"

"I want to tell you more, it's just that—oh no!" He held his hands to his temples and closed his eyes. His eyelids twitched, as if he was locked in a trance of some sort.

"What?"

"That reminds me. They're going to wonder where I went, if I stay here too long. I've already broken my planet's laws by letting you see me. My Elders won't be pleased with my lack of competence. Please, I need to get back to my planet as soon as possible, before they find me."

"Before who finds you?"

"Your leaders. They'll take me prisoner. I've already broken more than one planetary law. My name is Boj, by the way."

"*Bosh?*"

"Yes. Well, in your language it's spelled *b-o-j*, but the *j* is soft, more like a '*sh*' sound. It's hard to find an equivalent among languages sometimes." He suddenly yelped in pain.

"You're hurt, Boj!"

Blue blood flowed down his arm. She gasped, realizing it was the same blue liquid she'd seen on the hay earlier.

"Just a second. Grandpa keeps a first aid kit in here. I'll go get it." She quickly returned with the kit and applied pressure to the wound with a bandage. Her hand brushed against his skin and it felt smooth, like silk. "It looks pretty deep."

"I'll be okay. Thank you, Sam."

"Why would my leaders take you prisoner?" Sam asked. "You haven't done anything wrong."

"I've just made myself vulnerable, is all. I shouldn't have crashed here in the first place."

Sam sensed he was evading something. Maybe to protect her? She still didn't understand the situation, but if he knew her parents and he needed help, she could probably trust him. He certainly didn't look threatening—in fact, he looked quite defenseless, and in a lot of pain. She tried to place herself in his shoes. After all, if she were stranded on another planet and needing medical attention, wouldn't she feel the same way?

"Well, how do we get you back to your planet?"

"There should be a device in there." He pointed to a small black chest, then reapplied pressure to his wound. "They—your parents— sent you gifts, including a klug. It's a transport device. It's the only way to get me home."

Sam's gaze shifted toward the chest in front of her. She opened it carefully. Inside were various objects: a book, a pair of mittens, a golden necklace with an amber amulet, a spyglass, a key, and her mother's space pen. She picked up the space pen, admiring its chrome finish. When she first saw it years ago, she remembered wanting to have one too. Her mother told her it could be used upside down and the ink wouldn't dry up. Sam gazed at it further, noticing the inscription: *Be brave, and follow the light inside you. Love, Mom.* The fact that Boj had delivered her mom's space pen helped assuage Sam's initial suspicions.

She glanced down again at the other gifts, and something else caught her eye. It was her father's meteorite, the one he usually took on his trips abroad for good luck. Shaped like a crescent moon, though somewhat jagged at the edges, she remembered the day he'd found it a few years ago while they were collecting seashells along the beach. She picked it up and rested it in her palm, feeling the weight and density of it. Boj had delivered this gift to her as well. Her trust in Boj increased and she began to speculate that Boj's intentions were perhaps good-natured.

She continued rummaging through, gazing at other items she'd never seen before. "What am I searching for, again? A glug?"

"A klug. It's a small metallic ball with a light source inside. It's the only transport device on Earth that will be able to take me back to my planet."

"Is this it?" Sam asked, holding a small glowing ball in her palm.

"Yes! Now, the thing is, only *you* can activate it. It works with your fingerprints. Everyone's fingerprints are different."

Sam suddenly realized what this meant. "So, if only I can activate it, that means I would have to go with you…to your planet?"

Boj nodded. "It's not that bad. Really."

Sam blinked a few times, feeling the adrenaline course through her veins. She suddenly felt sick to her stomach. What were his motivations, really? Was everything he'd said true? Would it even be safe to travel to his planet? She would be taking a great risk if she went.

"It's similar to Earth in a way, but different. You'll see." He smiled, his eyes full of optimism and hope. "Anyway, we don't have much time."

"How does it work, exactly?" Sam examined the klug, feeling its coolness against her skin. On closer inspection, she noticed a series of faint, but detailed hieroglyphics.

"The klug acts like a wormhole."

"Wormhole?"

"Yes. It's like a tunnel through space-time, connecting two points that are far away. It's a shortcut through the universe. We'll be traveling many light-years. The gravitational pull within a wormhole and the bending of time and space makes the journey very fast. Also, my planet orbits its sun slowly compared to Earth, but spins very quickly on its axis. Because of the time differential, once you come back, even though we can spend days on Kryg, only seconds will have passed here on Earth. You'll be right back where you are now."

The explanation assuaged her fears somewhat, even though she still couldn't wrap her head around it all. Inside, she felt a certain exhilaration about traveling to another planet, not knowing what it would entail. Was it pure recklessness? Maybe. But she also worried about her parents, and needed to find out more. Perhaps she'd be able to find a further clue to their whereabouts.

"How do I activate it?" Beads of sweat collected on her forehead.

"Just hold it in your hand, press the red button with your thumb, shake it a couple of times, and say '*Kryg*'."

She hesitated. Despite Boj's connection to her parents, she felt she was missing something important. Could she really trust Boj, someone she'd just met? Sam thought about the letter from her mother. She looked at the note again. It was definitely her mother's handwriting. It seemed she had genuinely trusted Boj to deliver these gifts. And if she trusted him, then surely Sam could trust him too, right?

Sam looked into Boj's eyes, which shone like the inner core of the klug. His eyes had a certain gentleness about them. He too looked nervous about the situation, but also thankful and kind-hearted. He reached out his hand, pleading with her. She took it and grasped it tightly, hoping she was doing the right thing. She just wanted to survive the journey, get him home to his planet, and return to Earth so her grandfather wouldn't worry.

She followed Boj's instructions. She pressed the red button with her thumb and heard a small clicking sound. She felt a slight heat from the device against her thumb, and light emerged from the inner core, shining outward. It produced a tingling sensation, like the device was scanning her fingerprint, and she could feel it creating a connection with her. She shook it as Boj had instructed, and something moved inside. It made a sloshing sound, like it contained some type of liquid within one of its inner compartments. The device buzzed in her palm and she felt its energy magnifying. She whispered "Kryg", and after a moment, the whirring grew louder. She felt a force emanating from the center of the klug, emerging and pulling her closer, like a black hole's gravitational force attracting objects into its vicinity. The force grew stronger, seconds later encapsulating them both.

She tried to focus on a single point, a stationary object, but felt the room spinning around her. She fell down a deep, dark tunnel that looped in different directions. Her body was weightless, sliding along an invisible current. It pulled her further and faster down its path. She tried to call out, but the sound bombarded her eardrums and reverberated. Her stomach lurched. She tried steadying herself with her hands, but the gravitational pull affected her senses. She couldn't tell which way was up. A moment later, warmth surrounded her. She opened her eyes and found herself lying in a field with the prettiest yellow flowers glowing and floating everywhere.

"Am I dead?" she asked in awe.

Boj laughed. He was seated beside her, then brushed himself off and stood up, extending his hand. "No, Sam! This is my planet, Kryg. Welcome!"

Sam took his hand for balance and got to her feet, though a bit wobbly, and looked around in astonishment. "These floating flowers are so beautiful! I've never seen anything like them!"

"They're called kylies. They're more like weeds here, but they're necessary to our survival. You see, they help filter our air."

Sam took in a deep breath, the air smooth against her skin. Its fresh scent, like a combination of mint and lavender, filled her lungs, and instantly she felt relaxed and at ease.

Boj continued. "We have more water vapor in our atmosphere, so the air is not as dry as it is on Earth. We make sure to keep it clean because, like humans, we rely on it to survive."

At the mention of Earth, Sam jolted back to the present situation. "Are my parents here? Do you know when they're coming back?"

Boj's expression turned solemn. "Unfortunately, no. They're still on a mission in another solar system. They only visited briefly with the task of delivering their message to you, but then they went on their way."

His explanation sounded familiar. Had she asked him this same question before? Feeling dizzy, Sam stumbled along, disoriented.

"How about we go to my home by the lake, so I can make you a meal and you can rest? You've seen quite a lot of travel and excitement for one day, and traveling by wormhole can be overwhelming the first time."

Sam was conflicted. "Thank you, but I really should be getting back to my home. Grandpa may get worried if I stay too long, and he'll wonder where I am."

"Not to worry. But as I mentioned before, time is slow here. You could stay here a few weeks, and when you went home, only a few seconds would have passed on Earth. You would be right where you were before we left."

"Well, I suppose I could at least stay a few days. I'm tired from all the travel."

"Glad to hear!"

As they walked toward the lake, her steps felt lighter. In fact, she could leap a few feet higher than she could on Earth. "There's not much gravity here, is there?" she observed, admiring the landscape.

"Indeed!"

"This is fun!" She leapt into the air and landed a few meters ahead. "It almost feels like I'm flying!"

Boj chuckled. "We take these things for granted, sometimes. It's nice to have human visitors who appreciate our way of life. It's very unusual to have humans on our planet."

"Why is that?"

"Well, it's forbidden. The Elders don't allow it. Only a few have ever visited us."

Sam wondered why this was, and if there would be repercussions now that she was here. But before she could ask another question, Boj gestured to a dome adjacent to a large lake.

"Here we are."

Inside, the main room's light and airy ambiance drew her in. It reminded her of a giant greenhouse, with plants and trees situated around the room, some flowers, nuts, and what looked like berries. She watched as Boj snipped leaves from a nearby plant and placed them in a bowl. He then poured a yellow liquid from a small container and began stirring the leaves carefully, soaking them fully in the liquid. The leaves grew larger in size. Boj then removed his bandage. Sam cringed as she watched the blood flowing again. Boj gently placed the leaves over his wound. The leaves stuck well on their own, as if they had some natural adhesive property.

"Is that to…stop the bleeding?" she asked.

"Yes. These are kaloi leaves. They act as a natural coagulant. They also contain minerals and antibacterial agents to speed up the healing process," Boj replied matter-of-factly, then continued. "Should be back to normal in a few minutes."

It didn't seem long at all, considering how deep the cut had been.

Boj then collected some berries, flowers, and fruits in a bowl and set them aside. It looked like he only used vegetables, fruits, and some sort of puffy grain in preparing his meal.

Sam watched as he pressed a button near the edge of the rectangular table and a large vat emerged from a compartment within. Inside, she noticed a purple cabbage-like vegetable in liquid. Was that used as some sort of preservation for the food?

He pressed another button, and a cylindrical machine rose from the center of the table. It looked like a tube, stretching from one end to the other, and acted as a conveyor belt. He placed the ingredients inside the machine at one end, and a few moments later they emerged from the other, fully chopped and steaming hot.

"Please, have a seat. It'll be ready in one minute."

It felt good to sit down. Her legs had been wobbly from the wormhole, but she was feeling more at ease. The smell of cooking food made her stomach rumble.

Boj gently removed the leaves from his arm. To Sam's surprise, the bleeding had stopped, and it looked like his arm was now completely healed. There were no markings or any evidence that he'd been hurt. He went to the counter at the other end of the room, discarded the leaves into a bin, and washed his hands. He then returned with two plates and spoon-like utensils, and began dishing up their food. "Please, eat up before it gets cold."

Sam took a moment to admire the rainbow of colors. "You don't eat meat, do you?"

"No. My people are vegetarians. We respect all creatures, and reduce suffering as much as possible. It's our way of life."

She ate what looked like carrots, peas, rice, and beets. Everything was sweeter and more flavorful than their earthly counterparts. The purple berries the size of apples had a juicy, fleshy texture, like the inside of a cherry. She bit into one, surprised by the smooth center. It tasted just like caramel, soft and chewy.

"What are these called?" she asked, taking another bite.

"Karamelon berries," Boj said.

If she could live on karamelon berries, she would happily eat them all day. She hesitated, noticing the purple flowers on her plate.

"It's okay, you can eat those too. They're called klynes. They're named after our moon. They're quite nutritious, and guard against many diseases."

Sam tried to figure out what on Earth she could compare it to. It wasn't sweet, but it wasn't sour, either. It didn't taste fruity, but she had trouble placing it. The flower melted on her tongue.

As Boj chattered on, she gazed across the lake to the trees floating on the water and the rolling hills in the distance. The landscape was pristine.

"That is called Kassa Lake. It's called that because on our planet, we have insects that light up at night, like there's a kassa inside them, or what you would call a 'fire' inside them. That's where they go in the evenings, and if you watch tonight, you'll see what I mean."

Sam considered this for a moment. "We have insects on Earth that glow at night too, but we call them fireflies."

"Ah, yes, fireflies. They're very similar to kassa insects. But kassa insects can change their colors."

Sam looked forward to seeing the kassa insects change color later that night. But for now, a question continued to gnaw at her. "Why are humans forbidden here? I can imagine many humans who would love to visit your planet. It's so beautiful, and there's so much to learn!" Despite her eagerness, she felt exhausted, like she'd suffered a significant time change that had finally caught up to her. Boj seemed to sense her weariness too.

"I will tell you a story about it later. But first, you really must rest. Traveling by wormhole for the first time can cause your body to feel heavy and disoriented. The food I prepared tonight contains nutritious properties, which act like medicine. It will help restore your energy, but in order to do so, it will make you tired first."

She yawned as Boj explained it further. She felt the effects on her body already. Her eyelids drooped and it took all her energy just to keep them open. After the delicious and satisfying meal, she could now use a rest. "Thank you for the meal, Boj, it was really good."

"Of course." He stood up and gestured to the hallway. "There's an extra room down the hall, on the left. If you need anything, just call out."

She made her way down the hall. Too tired to take in much detail, she was relieved when she found the bed in the corner of the room. She pulled across the sliding door and shifted the locking latch into place. Feeling like she hadn't slept in days, she let the weight of sleep pull her into its darkness.

3

Sam awoke feeling groggy and disoriented. She sat up, her heart racing at the sight of the strange surroundings. For an instant, she'd forgotten she was on another planet, and it took a moment to get her bearings as the memories flooded back. The bed she lay on consisted of a strange green, spongy fabric—was it synthetic or natural? She couldn't tell. Nevertheless, its material was irresistibly comfortable, and she realized it adjusted to the contours of her body as she changed positions. She ran her fingers along the edge of the silver blanket. She let out a gasp. It was surprisingly silky smooth and warm, even though it was as thin as the aluminum foil her grandfather sometimes used to cover dishes. She wondered whether the material existed on Earth.

Her bed was positioned along a jagged wall made of black stone speckled with gold flakes. She touched it, feeling its coldness. To her right was a small open area—what looked like an atrium—with some simple wooden blocks strewn about the room. A seating area, perhaps? She got out of bed. Despite the darkness and coolness around the sleeping nook, she instantly felt the temperature rise by more than a few degrees as she entered the atrium, the soft light filtering through the windows providing a gentle warmth. She looked out across a lake filled with turquoise water. She wanted to explore more of the room's features, but stopped when she heard footsteps and muffled voices coming down the hall.

She tried to listen, but they spoke in a different language. It sounded like Boj's voice.

A few moments later, Sam heard a knock on the door.

"Good morning, Sam." Boj's voice carried through the door.

Sam shifted the latch and slid open the door to let him in. Boj entered the room along with another being, a woman with striking silver eyes. She stood a full two feet taller than Boj. Her light blue, wrinkly skin contrasted with her long, white, thinning hair that went down to her shoulders. Boj wore a simple brown robe, but hers was adorned with metallic accents. Like Boj's, her ears were pointed, however Sam also noticed small cylindrical protrusions extending from them that moved synchronously in different directions.

"Sam, please meet our Elder, Onnisa."

"It's a pleasure to meet you." Sam extended her hand. Onnisa paused for what seemed like an eternity. She then reached out in greeting, her hands much smaller than Sam's, but containing a multitude of long, spindly fingers, maybe twenty of them per hand, each as thin as copper wire and cool to the touch. Sam gasped as she felt an initial shock of energy and a tingling sensation like pins and needles in her hand. She looked down as sparks of blue light traveled between their hands. It took much effort to hold herself steady, for she had an urge to retract her hand from the sudden burst of current. At the same time, different memories flooded her mind, including images of meeting Boj, and their conversations. It felt as though those memories were being accessed and shared with Onnisa, somehow. When she'd held Boj's hand traveling to Kryg, it was different. She hadn't felt the same strange connection.

Onnisa finally pulled her hand away, and Sam realized they probably didn't have the same greeting gestures as people on Earth. She wondered whether she'd crossed a line by offering a handshake. Perhaps they were too polite to correct her. She looked to Boj for an explanation. To her surprise, he looked gloomy.

As if anticipating her thoughts, he said, "Here, it's customary to bow heads together rather than shake hands in greeting. I'm sorry, I should have explained it first."

Before Sam could respond, Onnisa swiftly turned to Boj. "I will speak to you later about your transgressions. I need to consult the other Elders before determining your fate."

"Yes, Onnisa. I'm truly sorry."

Sam wondered about the sudden tension between Boj and Onnisa, and what transgression Onnisa was referring to. But before she could question further, Onnisa continued.

"I believe she is the one. Only, it happened much sooner than we expected."

"Yes." Boj's eyes lit up.

Sam had about a thousand questions going through her mind, but she was unsure which to ask first. Instead, she waited until Onnisa spoke.

"Boj tells me his ship was destroyed on his way to deliver something to you, and that you helped him return to Kryg. Is that true?"

"Yes."

"Is it true that you traveled here by klug?"

"Yes, it's true."

"And why did you?"

Sam thought hard. She didn't necessarily have to bring Boj back to his planet. She'd just met him. She remembered her initial fear about the situation. But when he'd spoken to her, she'd believed his words and felt sorry for him. "I wanted to help Boj. He told me the klug was the only way to bring him back to his planet, and that only I could bring him back because the klug somehow…would only respond to *my* touch. It was part of a chest of gifts my parents gave me, and if they trusted Boj with this, I wanted to trust him too. I felt sorry for him, being so far from his home, so I did what I could to help." She also worried about her parents, but kept this to herself.

Onnisa's demeanor changed. She appeared more hopeful, but concerned nonetheless. Boj, however, could not have looked more ashamed of himself.

"Did Boj tell you it is forbidden for humans to travel to Kryg?"

"Yes, but I'm not really sure why."

"There is a prophecy. But before I tell you this, you must understand that once you return home, you are never to tell anyone about Kryg. Do you promise?"

She remembered Boj telling her the same thing. Confused but abiding, Sam replied, "Yes, of course. But why? Why can't anyone else from Earth come here?"

Onnisa formed her words slowly, and Sam thought that maybe she was trying to determine which parts to tell her. "It has to do with a prophecy between our two planets. But I will begin by explaining something else. You see, life itself is a gift, and planets support life that work in symbiosis. But planets are finite. They only survive if the elements and beings within them work together. Over time, the planet Earth has been overcome with many burdens on its natural systems—overpopulation, pollution, and global warming. This has in large part been fueled by greed. Humans have put incredible stress on their living environment, and it is a threat to the sustainability of the planet. In the last one hundred years, there have been thousands of species extinctions. One million more are threatened with extinction as humans continue to exploit the land, and as the population increases over time, it demands more resources. If humans ever came to inhabit our planet in their multitudes, there is a risk that our world would be…ruined."

At the thought of this, Sam frowned. "But not *all* humans are horrible and greedy," she contended, looking to Boj for any clues as to why they would devise such a harsh rule. He remained silent.

"You are right. And there is a prophecy that appears to have come true since you arrived here."

Boj spoke softly,

"A red-haired girl will help a friend.
Her mind is sharp and her heart is pure.
She travels to Kryg in a wormhole bend.
She is the key to finding a cure."

Confused, Sam shifted on her feet and crossed her arms. "I don't understand. A cure for what, exactly?"

Onnisa spoke slowly, yet a momentum carried her words. "A cure for your planet. Your people." Her eyes gleamed magnificently in the light, and at the same time, Sam couldn't help but laugh at how matter-of-factly the words came out of her mouth, as if it were a simple solution to a massive problem. She laughed at the ridiculousness of the situation, and how naive she felt. Surely they didn't require a girl to help them when they had all this specialized technology. How did they even know how to speak human languages? Obviously they were more advanced than humans, and no doubt they had the wrong person in mind for this task.

Sam tried to control her nervous laughter before responding. It seemed to unsettle Onnisa and Boj. She took a deep breath and exhaled. "I don't think so. I mean, I can't save my planet! I'm just a child! And besides, no one would listen to me anyway. I don't even know *how* to save it. Until now, I didn't even realize it was dying. I think you have the wrong per—"

Boj cut her off and continued.

"She is our Elder, our new queen true.
She will find the Hopewell Star.
To her we owe our gratitude.
Support her, allow her to grow and go far."

Onnisa spoke softly. "Earth is one of a kind. From our own exploration, we have never found a world like it. But it is under threat. And the same is true for our planet, Kryg. It is much older than Earth, and our sun is dying. Past Elders have said the Hopewell Star will extend the life of our sun. If you can find it, you will save Earth *and* Kryg. That is the prophecy."

Sam paced, considering the implications. It was a lot to ask of someone. Although she felt compassion for the Krygians and wanted to help them, it felt so beyond her capabilities.

She wiped her sweaty palms along her sides and shrugged. "I'm sorry, but there must be some mistake. I don't know how to do this. It must be someone else."

Onnisa glanced at Boj, and he nodded. It was as if they were having a private conversation. Sam felt left out. Boj pointed to her hand.

"Yes," Onnisa agreed. "I see she has the mark."

Sam's impatience grew with the silence, feeling as though she was missing some vital information.

"Sam, could you please hold out your hands?" Onnisa asked.

Sam obliged, but wondered what information she sought, and if her hands could really provide any clues.

Onnisa studied her hands, holding them gently and turning them over in hers. Again, Sam felt electricity between them, like her thoughts were open and oddly transparent. Onnisa examined the small scar on Sam's right hand. It formed the shape of a heart. Boj recited the next verse.

"She carries the mark of a heroine's heart.
Her action is daring and brave.
The life she saves is due in part,
To her benevolence in the way she behaves."

Onnisa gently ran one of her fingers over Sam's scar. Immediately, Sam had a flashback to the day at the river a couple of years ago when she'd taken Pip for a walk. Pip had pulled the leash out of her hands to chase a flock of geese, and to her surprise, ran right into the water. When she tried to call him back, it was too late. The current carried him along the bank and further out. Without thinking, she ran into the river after him. Although a shallow river, the force of the water rushed against her body, trying to throw her off balance. An experienced swimmer, she had cut through the waves, keeping her focus on Pip as the current carried him faster and faster downstream. Soon she caught up with him and pulled him out of the water, carrying him to the bank. She remembered how he'd continued to move his legs in a swimming motion even though he was safely in her arms.

"It's okay, Pip. You'll be okay," she had assured him. As they made their way back home, she'd noticed a cut on her right hand. She wasn't sure how it had happened, whether she had cut herself on a rock, or something else. She wrapped it with her scarf and went with her grandfather to the hospital, where she received six stitches. It was the nurse who had first noticed its unusual heart shape, and since then it was a constant reminder of that day at the river. Thinking about it now, Boj's words seemed to make sense.

She carries the mark of a heroine's heart.

What were the chances of someone else having the same heart-shaped scar as a result of saving a life? She didn't want to consider what would have happened if she hadn't gone in after Pip. It was just a matter of course. She hadn't thought twice about it, and she would no doubt do it again, if she had to.

Onnisa did not have to ask about the scar. Sam knew, looking into Onnisa's eyes, that she'd seen Sam's memories, just by having touched her hand. It was a special ability, one she didn't know could exist—until now. Onnisa looked at Boj, and he nodded.

"The future queen will travel to Kryg,
Her spirit as bright as the sun.
Only a girl of pure spirit and heart,
Can reverse the damage done."

"There is only one way to prove the prophecy." Onnisa looked directly at Sam. "Your spirit must be judged by the great Mukalakatakalakum."

Judged? Sam didn't like the sound of that. "The Mukalaka—what, now?"

Onnisa turned to Boj, her light blue skin suddenly changing to gold. Sam gasped, amazed they had the ability to change their skin colors so easily. And then she remembered that several creatures on Earth—like some octopuses and lizards—had a similar ability, and wondered what it would be like if she could do the same. She was so fascinated by this, it took her a moment to recognize the heaviness that permeated the air.

"Boj, you transgressed Krygian law when you lied to this human girl. Klugs adapt to the fingerprints of *anyone* who first touches it. You could have returned to Kryg on your own. We could have corrected this and recalibrated the device for proper dispatch. But no. Instead, you compelled her to come with you. You will be punished for your crime, and if I am not mistaken, interfering with the proper dispatch of a klug is punishable by death."

Her words sparked a terrible anxiety in Sam. "Wait, *what*? Death?"

Boj continued as if he'd already accepted these circumstances. "I understand, Onnisa. I'm truly sorry. But I knew of the prophecy, and when I saw her…"

Onnisa cut him off. "And yet you took this risk, knowing the potential consequences?"

"Yes." He looked to Sam, his head hung low. "I'm sorry, Sam, for lying to you."

Although she was somewhat miffed, she couldn't allow them to sentence him to death. "It's okay. Really. I forgive you, Boj," she replied, and then added quickly, "I would do it again. Please, Onnisa. Boj doesn't deserve to die." Why was the penalty so harsh? It seemed extreme. Had she made a huge mistake coming here in the first place? What worried her also was the idea of having her spirit judged. What would that entail, exactly? Would it be painful? What if she wasn't the one? Would she still be able to go home?

Boj's golden eyes filled with tears. "I don't deserve your kindness, Sam."

Without skipping a beat, Onnisa spoke sternly. "Boj, I will confer with the other Elders to determine your fate. For now, you and Sam will prepare for your journey to the Mukalak caves."

"Yes, Onnisa."

"I will provide you with further instructions when it is time for you to leave."

"Of course."

Sam watched as Onnisa extended her hand. Boj hesitated for a moment and then obliged, reciprocating the gesture. As they touched hands, sparks flowed through them for a few moments. Were they sharing memories this way, just as Onnisa had done with her? They leaned and touched their foreheads together. Onnisa straightened up and lowered her head toward Sam. Sam did the same.

Onnisa exited the room swiftly, leaving them in silence. Sam contemplated the next stage of their journey together. A mix of emotions swirled inside her: anxiety about Boj's fate at the hands of the Elders; determination to help him, and to save his life if it came to that; nervousness at the prospect of having her spirit judged; uncertainty about her mission and what was expected; and her biggest fear of all—not succeeding.

* * *

Onnisa couldn't understand how Boj's mission had gone so horribly wrong. For one thing, Boj demonstrated carelessness in his ship's navigation, heading straight into the thundersnow. It was a rare phenomenon on Earth, but Boj should have known to avoid it.

The other thing that really gnawed at Onnisa's mind was the fact that Boj did not follow explicit instructions from the Elders to keep the klug and the chest of gifts separate. There were two specific, scheduled drop-off points. First, to deliver the gifts to the girl, and second, to deliver the klug to a discrete, undisclosed location to be discovered by its true, chosen owner. If Boj had placed the klug in the chest for convenience, that was one thing, but to place it there on purpose, intended for the girl, was something else entirely. She needed to explore the details further.

The other Elders would know what to do.

Onnisa made her way down the winding pathway toward the center of the community. Communities were structured in a similar curving pattern across Kryg. The center contained the Hub of activity, where commerce, law, health, and educational facilities were located. Spiraling outward were a series of domed residential complexes and greenhouse clusters, which offered a more natural setting. They allowed for privacy, quietude, and peacefulness. Onnisa hardly ever visited the Hub. She found it too noisy and befuddling, and preferred her residential abode by Kassa Lake.

She noticed the residents staring at her as she made her way closer to the community center. Everyone looked excited, whispering to each other as she passed. Many residents stopped what they were doing, as if they already knew something was up. Word traveled quickly. She did not like being the center of attention, but as an Elder it proved difficult to hide from it. She bowed her head and exchanged pleasantries with the residents as she passed through. She nodded in greeting and picked up her pace.

She didn't have time for this.

Eight minutes later, all five of the Elders, including Onnisa, arrived hastily in the Reflection Room. Located in a circular stone building at the center of the community, it was designated sacred quarters; its sole purpose was for discussing important matters pertaining to ancient Krygian law. Only the Elders had access to this space.

Light poured in through the window, casting an eerie glow among the members. Everyone took seats around the room, lighting their individual fires. In turn, the fires spread along the floor gutter toward the center of the room, where a single flame grew large and flickered, signifying the meeting had commenced.

Onnisa chose her words carefully. "I call this meeting in light of the arrival of a human girl on our planet, and because I have received information that suggests transgression of Kryg's ancient laws."

The others murmured in unison, denoting their concerns and excitement at the news.

Dytanis was the first to respond. "Has the prophecy come true, Onnisa? In regards to the human visitor?"

"I cannot say for certain. Her spirit will need judgment from Mukalakatakalakum. However, I have seen the mark on her, the one that the prophecy speaks of."

More whispers erupted from the other Elders. Boku, the eldest of them, spoke next. "What of the transgressions you speak of, Onnisa? In the name of Krygian law, I request translucence."

Translucence was the process of sharing memories through hand-to-hand contact. The gift of translucence was a trait one was born with, and not many Krygians possessed this ability. It was customary at times like these, where the urgency to transmit facts and information was integral to making a collective decision. Information through any other means—including telepathy—was subject to modification, and thus not suitable for this type of meeting.

Initially, Onnisa feared telling them, for she knew that transgressing certain ancient Krygian laws meant death to the transgressor. But as an Elder, it was her duty to bring such matters before the others for discussion. She wondered if there existed another way, perhaps a less serious punishment they could agree to.

She slowly extended her arms to those adjacent to her. Everyone clasped hands, and Onnisa's memories of the events flowed like an electrical current between them all. Once they completed the transfer, Onnisa looked around to see looks of great concern among the Elders.

Dytanis spoke first. "Boj is young among us. He made his first trip alone to Earth's star system. He acted with no restraint, yet I for one do not believe he deserves this punishment. Does the law allow room for leniency?"

Ajisav spoke next. "No, it does not, Dytanis. He interfered with a klug's proper dispatch. As we all know, that is punishable by death."

More murmurs erupted among the Elders. Onnisa realized they were having as much trouble digesting the news as she had.

Ajisav continued. "His errors were numerous! He flew into a rare lightning storm—something he should have known better than to do. When his ship crashed, he failed to follow proper procedure in notifying authorities on Earth. He revealed his Krygian form to a common human. He lied to a common human about the possibility of being taken hostage from a human authority. He also lied about the klug's properties. He meddled in a very serious operation, which has caused much disruption. Because of his failings, we will never know whether the girl acted of her own free will."

Onnisa decided now was the best time to voice her opinion.

"The girl has already made a connection with Boj. They've formed a bond, and she trusts him. She has made a favorable impression, and has already objected to his punishment. If we carry out this sentence, we might lose her confidence. It may affect the likelihood that she carries out her tasks in fulfilling the prophecy."

Everyone murmured to each other, considering what was at stake. Dytanis shifted in his seat. "Is it true then, Onnisa? Is she the one?"

Onnisa continued. "The only way to tell for certain is with judgment from Mukalakatakalakum. If he determines that she is the one, then what has transpired was meant to be, as part of the prophecy. As queen, she and only she would have the power to grant an exception to the rule of Krygian law. It will be entirely in her hands to spare Boj's life, and her right to do so."

Ajisav remained silent for a few moments, tugging on the material of his metallic robe. "The implications are severe, Onnisa. We do not know how this has affected the prophecy. What if the girl is not the one? Will she keep her travels to Kryg a secret? Suppose other humans find out? Boj has led them *both* on a dangerous path."

Waiting for the silence in the room to take over, Onnisa treaded carefully. "Boj knew the risks. He knew the prophecy. He wanted more than anything to find the girl and seek out the truth, a way of finding the Hopewell Star. In his mind, he acted not out of discord to Krygian law, but the contrary. He tried to bring the prophecy to fruition, and in doing so, crossed the line."

Ajisav cleared his throat. "Even if Boj's intent was virtuous, Onnisa, law is law. The Kantak tribe will surely question it, if punishment is not dealt accordingly. My concern is that we risk the Kantak tribe challenging our decision and overthrowing the long-standing rule of ancient Elders."

Boku continued the train of thought. "If she is not the one, then Boj will be sentenced to death, as per Krygian law. A quick and painless death at the hands of Mukalakatakalakum by soul extraction. The girl will be spared and returned to Earth with her memories of Kryg wiped clean."

Silence fell over the room. The idea of Boj's punishment terrified Onnisa. She didn't like the circumstances nor the options, but what was to be done? Was there anything they had missed leading up to this? They needed to find out more about the circumstances of Boj's mission before coming to a consensus.

Her thoughts turned to Boku. As the eldest and most respected among the Elders, Boku knew better than anyone what was at stake. He had a separate, covert mission as an Elder: to obtain information about the Kantak tribe, to determine their intentions, and to bring forth any potential threats to the attention of the Elders. The Kantak tribe threatened the Elder system of rule, and they did not believe in the Hopewell Star prophecy. If the Elders did not uphold Krygian law, or made an error in their decisions, they risked the Kantaks' rebellion, and civilization would fall into disorder. Their society would collapse, violence would rise again, and the disruptions would serve as a distraction from their ultimate mission to find the Hopewell Star and restore light to their sun. One small mistake along the way would mean Kryg's destruction.

Sika had not said a word during the meeting, and surprised everyone when she did. "It is important to understand why Boj made so many errors after training so extensively. Boj sought and received permission for that mission. Permission is only granted once the trainee has passed all tests. Compared to other missions, it was a simple one. A couple of quick drop-offs at pre-determined locations. First, a gesture of thanks for the parents of the girl. And second, correct placement and dispatch of the klug. If Boj successfully passed his training tests, this would prove his capability, so why did he fail? Have we overestimated his competency? Have we overestimated the effectiveness of our tests?"

"The tests are irrelevant in this matter, now," Dytanis said. "What's done is done."

Sika continued to probe the issue at hand. "I disagree. We must explore all aspects of this case if we are to understand fully what happened. In the name of Krygian law, I request translucence pertaining to the events, including Boj's preparatory training leading up to the Earth mission."

Murmurs of agreement passed between the Elders. Boku, who had been in charge of Boj's preparatory training, opened his hands to those adjacent to him, and soon, Onnisa saw the images flash in front of her.

The training had gone well, and Boj had exceeded his instructor's expectations on multiple fronts, passing all tests with flying colors. To her dismay, she understood that Boj had been so determined by the prospect of upholding the prophecy that it blinded his sensibilities. So much so that he was willing to suffer the ultimate sacrifice. It wasn't long before the Elders realized this too, and everyone agreed that punishment was necessary.

"Boj will take the girl to meet Mukalakatakalakum," Onnisa said, trying to hold herself together. She hoped Boj was right about the girl. After all, his life was in her hands. "The girl will go first. Once she has left the cave, Boj will meet his fate."

The Elders agreed on the plan.

"This resolves the problem of the Kantak tribe," Boku said. "If she is the one, then the prophecy is true, and they have no challenge to make. If she is not the one, the proper punishment will be carried out, and they cannot challenge it."

With that, Onnisa called for consensus among the Elders. All agreed to move forward as discussed. She ended the meeting with the customary phrasing, "This meeting is now adjourned. In closing, I thank you for your insight and discussion. In the name of the prophecy, may the light continue to shine bright inside you." She quickly left the sacred quarters, feeling anxious and tired, and wondering how the future would unfold.

* * *

Ever since talking with Onnisa, Boj looked dispirited. He remained quiet and oddly distant as he prepared their meals for the journey, as if focused on something more important. Sam felt better when he finally broke the silence.

"You will need to address Mukalak by his full name, Mukalakatakalakum. Can you say it, Sam?"

"Mu-ka-la-k-ata-k…huh?"

"It's what your people refer to as a palindrome—the name can be spelled the same way both backward and forward."

"Oh!" Sam took a moment to consider the spelling in her mind. Then she tested the letters again on her tongue. "Mu-ka-lak-ata-kal-ak-um."

"Yes, that is good. That is important because we do not want to offend him."

Sam practiced the word a few more times so she could memorize it. Was this meeting going to be difficult?

"What if I'm not the one, Boj? What if my spirit's no good?"

Boj quickly responded. "I believe you can do this, Sam. Worrying only wastes time and makes us doubt ourselves and our abilities. If you can learn to believe in yourself, it will be okay. I promise. Now, we just need to take it one step at a time. I can tell you what to expect, but I don't know everything. Not about this. Onnisa will provide more instructions before we leave." He packed the items into a small handbag. They made their way outside the huts.

As if anticipating this action, Onnisa stepped forward to greet them. Sam waited as Onnisa gave Boj instructions in the Krygian language. As she spoke, Boj's expression changed. At first, he cast his eyes downward, his brow furrowed, concentrating on something. Then, as he looked up and met Onnisa's gaze, his eyes widened in determination and hope. Onnisa held out her hand and Boj took it. As Sam watched, sparks of energy and information flowed between them. A few moments later, Onnisa broke the connection and they bowed heads. Sam noticed that Onnisa's demeanor had also changed. Earlier that day she had spoken in harsh tones with Boj, and with hardened and exacting eyes. Now, her quieter tone complemented her softer manner. Onnisa's eyes searched Boj's for understanding, as if she were validating his choices and providing him acceptance and support. There was something else, though Sam couldn't determine what. As Sam bowed heads with Onnisa, she noticed Onnisa's eyes were filled with tears. Onnisa quickly left before Sam could say anything.

"What was that about, Boj?" Sam asked as he quietly led her up the pathway toward the caves.

Boj hesitated and looked uneasy. "It's…complicated. I'm sorry. All I ask is that you please stay focused on the task at hand." As he continued, he took what looked like a thermos out of his bag, opened it, and touched the glowing, neon yellow liquid inside. He then smeared the substance across a tree trunk. "The caves are easy to find. It won't take long, but I need you to focus on where I place these markings, okay? If something happens to me, you can find your way back. Do you understand?"

Sam suddenly felt sick to her stomach. The thought of having to make her way anywhere on this planet without Boj rattled her nerves. More than that, she felt Boj was guarding a secret between him and Onnisa, and that his life was in danger. Was it because of her actions? Onnisa had mentioned a penalty of death, but why would they give such harsh punishment for a simple mistake he'd made? Even though Boj was ninety-seven years old, he still looked like a boy, young and innocent. Surely they couldn't sentence him to death! And Onnisa said something else about determining his fate. What did that even mean?

She knew if she prodded further it would only make him upset, and she didn't want that. Instead, she stated her expectations of their journey. She wanted to remain hopeful, despite the circumstances. "Okay, but we're going to return down this path together. I like having you by my side, Boj. I need you telling me things I don't know about this planet. So that's what we'll do after seeing Mukalakatakalakum. Okay?"

Boj didn't respond. Instead, he continued marking the trees in silence. Soon they entered an open grassy area with large boulders jutting out at different angles from the ground. They made their way around the boulders and Boj led her to a hill. They started to climb. The angle was such that you couldn't see much beyond the top, given the steep slope. Sometimes Sam's curiosity got the better of her. "What is he—Mukalakatakalakum—like, exactly?"

After what seemed like an eternity, Boj answered. "I have never met Mukalakatakalakum. Not many have this honor. The Elders have met him as part of their initiation ceremony, including Onnisa. All I know is the cave where he lives is very dark. He's nocturnal, I think, and is blinded by natural light. He sees things…differently. Not in the way you or I could see—or understand, for that matter."

As they approached the top of the hill, Sam saw mountains and caves in the distance, maybe a kilometer away. They took a moment to catch their breath. Boj pulled out a couple of meals he'd prepared. Initially they ate in silence, taking in the view of the landscape. Boj was particularly quiet. It was only when Sam asked questions that he obliged in answering them.

"Why is it the water in the turquoise lake doesn't float away due to the low gravity?" Sam asked.

"That's a good question. Even though Kryg is smaller than Earth and there's less gravity, our planet still has mass and an atmosphere, so things don't just float away or evaporate into space. But we've made some changes over time, like you see here. Most of the water on this planet is in fact groundwater. We have a pressurized synthetic atmosphere using a specialized magnetism device in different parts of the planet to secure resources in place. The technology—the magnets— are actually hidden around the lake to keep the water in one place above ground, and to give the illusion that the lake is a naturally-occurring phenomenon. But it isn't. It's purely for aesthetic purposes. It's a common technology we use, and it's woven into the fabric of our communities."

"So the lake is artificial, then?"

"Yes. In fact, many parts of the planet are artificial now. But it wasn't always that way. When we were a younger civilization, we made the mistake of using up most of our planet's molten-iron core material to aid in space exploration. Over time, the core cooled down and contracted and gradually our planet shrank in size, reducing in mass, and as a result the gravity decreased. Since then, we've learned a lot and now, most of our resource extraction comes from other uninhabited planets or celestial objects, like our moon, to avoid this issue."

"How interesting!"

"It's been a long process, but we've started to rebuild our planet, adding mass from other resources in space, like asteroids. Kryg has changed and evolved through trial and error, but it isn't as pristine as it once was. It's also why we value Earth so much. Compared to Kryg, it's quite rustic, and has a natural beauty, parts of it unaltered by humans. But as you know, that is changing quickly."

Sam nodded, but didn't know what else to say. She let the silence descend over them and allowed her thoughts to drift as she pondered these new insights.

Soon they arrived at the mouth of one of the caves. Boj stopped, staring up at the gaping entrance. Sam focused her gaze upon a series of markings; strange symbols like hieroglyphics were engraved into the rock along the edge of the cave opening. She peered inside, the darkness foreboding. How would she navigate this?

"Remember what I told you," Boj said.

"You mean—you're not coming with me?"

"I can't. I'm sorry. Once you leave the cave, I'll meet with him separately. Now, remember what I said about addressing him. Once you are inside, listen to his voice and he will guide you through the cave. Do not worry, Sam. I'll be waiting here for you. Now, go. There is no time to waste."

Sam took a step inside, unnerved and a bit shaky. Nevertheless, she had come this far. What were a few more steps to go?

Inside, darkness enveloped her. All she heard was her loud breathing, her footsteps echoing on the stone floor. She held her hands in front of her and took small steps, worried she would bump into something.

"Oh great Mukalakatakalakum." She hoped she'd said it correctly, her voice quivering as she continued. "It is I, Sam Sanderson, a girl from planet Earth. I was given instructions by Onnisa and Boj to come to meet you." She realized she spoke so softly she didn't expect to receive a response. Hesitant but determined, she took a step further into the cave. She looked back, but Boj was now out of sight. She didn't know which way to go.

A booming voice reverberated around the cave walls. "Come closer into the darkness, so that I can see you better."

As she ventured deeper into the cave, she came across phosphorescent plants that illuminated the cave walls. At least now she could get her bearings somewhat. She shivered as a large shadow moved along the wall in front of her, an outline of a spiked creature five times her size, with massive claws.

She froze, and her heart skipped a beat. She considered the options in front of her. There were three tunnels, the middle one being the darkest and most unsettling. She took that one.

The deep, low voice growled. It sounded much closer now. "Ah, such beautiful music I hear, but what a repulsive smell. It could only be from a... *human*!"

Taken aback and confused, Sam unfurled her arms and let out her breath. Why was her human scent so disgusting to him? She felt compelled to continue, to explore further. "Mukalakatakalakum!" She whipped out his name before she could stop herself. Growing irritated with the circumstances, she continued more confidently. "I come in peace and request your judgment of my spirit...please." She stopped and listened carefully. There was movement—something approaching rapidly. She suddenly felt vulnerable. Perhaps it was a bad idea to come here. She tried to steady her breathing and clasped her arms around herself in a tight hug. One last hug, standing still, bracing for a terrible fate. But it was no use—her body shook uncontrollably.

A warm hiss of air flowed above her. She felt the creature's heat and realized it was towering over her.

"Do not be afraid," the creature said. "Onnisa sent you?"

"Uh...yes," Sam managed to respond, now able to control her breathing. Without her sight, she found it exceedingly disconcerting. Without thinking, she went into inquisitive mode and blurted out, "Please, tell me about your abilities. What do you see? Is it true you can see my...my spirit?" Her fascination with the creature seemed to take over her own sensibilities. Would he be offended by such direct questions?

Although she couldn't see him, she felt his presence sizing her up. To her surprise, he didn't hesitate in responding. "Yes. Yes, I can. I see *all* light and sound waves emitted from different beings and objects. Yours is a very bright multicolored light. It is so strong it is almost blinding. I have never seen anything like it before."

"You say you can see *all* light and sound waves from different beings and objects?"

"Yes. Each object—like a rock or plant—contains energy, just as each being contains energy. Onnisa's is blue, and radiates slowly. Yours radiates quickly, and at a very high frequency of sound waves. Its music is beautiful. Soothing. It is not often I come across a human, but when I do, the frequency is low and the light is usually very dim. I see only one or two colors, at most. Never a rainbow, like yours."

Only a moment ago she'd been terrified, filled with dread. Now, she found herself fascinated. The creature's abilities—in particular, the ability to see so much light within such darkness—was incredible.

As if sensing her curiosity, the creature lurched, shuffling toward her in the dark. "What is it that you seek?"

Sam cleared her throat. "I've come—I've come to seek the truth. I want to know if I am the one the prophecy speaks of. Onnisa said I need to find the Hopewell Star. But what is it?"

"Ah, the prophecy. Yes. It speaks to the history of our two worlds, Kryg and Earth, and their interconnectedness. Let me tell you more about the past so you understand."

"I would like that, thank you."

"Long ago, a great war was waged within the galaxies. Many planetary civilizations and factions competed for power over different parts of each galaxy. As Kryg grew in age, so did its civilization and technologies. Its citizens explored and occupied many different planets, including Earth, to ensure continuity of their people."

Sam gasped. Were Krygians living among them? It wasn't completely unlikely. Krygians and humans shared similar features.

As Mukalakatakalakum spoke, images appeared in her mind like she was watching a movie. "As time moved on, the Krygians witnessed the destruction of Earth by its own people. Some tried to intervene, but it only got worse. To protect both planets, a star was created by another civilization known as the Rigellians, a lizard-like race of beings in the far reaches of the galaxy."

An image flashed in her mind of the Rigellians with massive hexagonal eyes and sturdy, scaly green bodies.

Mukalakatakalakum paused and continued. "Thanks to the Rigellians, this star would bring harmony to the people of both planets. They wanted Kryg and Earth to work together toward peace. Although Earth was much younger than Kryg and its people had much to learn, the Rigellians knew that over time there would be people, including a special one, that could reverse the damage done and restore order to the galaxy."

Mukalakatakalakum continued as Sam listened intently. "Unfortunately, the Rigellians have since disappeared, and with them, the star itself. No one knows its location. The universe is vast and strange, and you are but a young girl."

"But what *is* the Hopewell Star? How was it made?"

"Ah, these are good questions, and I do not know for certain. It was made at a time when humans began building their weapons and machines, polluting the air and water, and the population grew in large numbers. Its secret will only present itself to me once my spirit goes there. My ancestors believed that once we pass away, our spirits return to the stars, to be reborn again. If it looks anything like the light that radiates from inside you, it will be a wonderful place. I never thought I would meet a girl with a pure spirit in my lifetime. It truly is an honor."

"How do you know my spirit is pure? Can you see it?"

"The light that shines inside you shows me. You may tell Onnisa what we've discussed, and you may go as you please, Queen Samantha. You are the true chosen one."

Sam was taken aback. No one had ever addressed her like this before. It made her feel strangely uncomfortable, but more than that, it made her feel like she had a significant and daunting task ahead of her, one that she could not ignore. The title was like a calling; she now had a responsibility and a duty to protect both worlds. Their fates rested in her hands. Her actions could inevitably change the course of history, for better or worse. If she succeeded, it would restore the light and bring peace and well-being to both planets. If she failed, the repercussions could be disastrous. She didn't want to think of the consequences. She felt anxious but determined. Now that she had an obligation to live up to her title and her responsibility to both worlds, she could not—would not—let them down.

"Now, you must go," Mukalakatakalakum continued. "Your friend Boj is waiting."

Sam wondered how Mukalakatakalakum knew that Boj was even there. Then she remembered what Boj had said about going back to Onnisa if anything happened to him. She didn't understand how, but she knew—his life was in danger. She had to do something.

"May I make one last request before I leave, oh great Mukalakatakalakum?"

"As you are our new queen, yes, you may."

"I request that you spare Boj's life. I know he's made mistakes and broken Krygian law, but I also know he realizes it was wrong. I have forgiven him. I don't wish any harm to come to him. He doesn't deserve such harsh punishment."

"Ah. You have proven yourself, Queen Samantha. Truly, you are a girl of pure spirit. Only the queen may grant an exception and spare a life. Boj is lucky to have you as a friend. I honor your request. You may both go back to Onnisa. Please send my regards to her. And may the light continue to shine bright inside you both."

"Thank you." Not knowing when she would be back, she added, "I am forever grateful." With that, Sam left the way she'd come, steadying herself and making her way slowly toward the mouth of the cave where the light sparkled outside. Her eyes had trouble adjusting at first, and she shielded them from the bright light.

She found Boj sitting on a small boulder. She ran to him, telling him everything. She couldn't read his expression at first. With his head hung low and his face downcast, he slowly looked up to meet her gaze, his eyes full of hope and gratitude.

"Thank you, Sam," he said at last. "I—I don't know how to repay you. I'll be forever in your service."

"I don't want your service, Boj. I just want your friendship. And…for you to be honest. I appreciate the time we've spent together on Kryg, but there's still a lot for me to learn." She thought about her responsibility now that she was queen, as well as her upcoming mission, the uncertainty of it, and what else might be involved. "I really could use all the help I can get."

"Yes. Of course."

* * *

Sam and Boj returned to the huts, and Onnisa was glad to see them both. Sam was surprised to learn that somehow, Mukalakatakalakum had sent a message to Onnisa before they arrived. She knew exactly what had transpired before Sam could tell her.

Onnisa gave her specific instructions. "I will continue to be your advisor and guide." Her eyes shimmered in the light. "Now, in fairness to you and your family, you will continue living on Earth as if nothing has happened, but your work will be to uncover the Hopewell Star, no matter how long it takes. For the time being, your task is *not* to rule the day-to-day operations here on Kryg. It would be counter-productive. The Elders will take care of those operations and govern as we have done in the past. Your sole purpose is to find the Hopewell Star. Do you understand?"

"Yes, Onnisa." The task of finding the Hopewell Star seemed more urgent now. It made sense to allow the Elders to continue running the day-to-day operations. After all, she didn't know much about their society or their laws, and if she spent too much time on those things, it would detract from her main mission. But was there something else, a clue, in Onnisa's words? Perhaps she was to return to Earth because her experiences there would prove useful in some way. Regardless, if she didn't get back to Earth soon, her grandfather would wonder where she was.

"Good. Now we shall go for a walk outside and get some fresh air."

As they left the stuffy room and made their way outside the hut, she was surprised to see so many residents. They stood waiting to see them and greet them. They parted to create a pathway for Sam.

Boj protected her as he walked beside her, shielding her from the multitude of Krygians gathering around. "Don't be nervous. They want to meet their new Elder, their new queen."

They made their way down the path. Cheers grew louder from up ahead. Sam stopped in her tracks when she saw it: a massive, open-air amphitheater with tiered stone rows and a stage that hovered in midair. A ramp led up to the stage.

Sam followed Onnisa and Boj toward the ramp, her palms sweating. She glanced out into the rows upon rows of Krygians and guessed there were maybe two thousand eager spectators. The Krygians bowed and knelt as she passed. They showered her with flower petals. Onnisa led them up the ramp to a floating altar the size of a stage. A few other Krygians took their seats, and Onnisa gestured for Sam to do the same. She took a seat, somewhat awkwardly. The altar moved slightly under her feet, like a floating dock propped up by a cushion of air. She tried not to lose her balance.

Onnisa opened a thin black box the size of a laptop sleeve. Inside rested a circular band of shining translucent material covered with small jewels that glowed brilliantly, as bright as light itself. Onnisa crossed the stage to Sam and gently placed the crown on her head, the halo of light radiating above her.

"May the light continue to shine bright inside you," Onnisa said quietly to Sam. Then she turned to address the crowd. "To Queen Samantha. May she rule in peace. May she find our Hopewell Star. She is always welcome on Kryg. All hail our new queen!"

The crowd repeated these words and bowed. Sam was taken with their graciousness and kindness, and bowed her head in acknowledgment.

It looked like they expected her to say something in return. The blood drained from her face at the thought of giving a speech. What would she say? She took a breath. "As your new queen," she began softly, feeling silly and unsure of herself.

"Speak up! We can't hear you!" shouted someone from the crowd. Boj gestured to Onnisa, who gave him a small device that started spinning quickly.

"Just a moment." Boj stepped in and placed the device a few feet in front of Sam. It hovered silently and magnified her words so everyone could hear, near and far.

Sam took a deep breath and cleared her throat. "As your new queen," she repeated, "I thank you for this honor!" She realized she'd never delivered a speech before, let alone one to an entire community. Terrified, she turned to Boj, who smiled and encouraged her to continue. "I promise to try my best to please you, and to find the Hopewell Star, to help save both Kryg and Earth."

Everyone clapped and cheered. Feeling grateful once the ceremony ended, Sam wanted to enjoy the rest of the day without feeling she had to prove herself further.

Later that evening, she joined the Krygians and took part in a large feast and bonfire by Kassa Lake. It wasn't long before the sun set, casting pink streaks of light across the sky. The purple moon shone magnificently among the stars. As Boj had mentioned, the kassa insects congregated and flew over the lake in different formations, their lights glowing brightly in a multitude of different colors. The fiery reds and oranges took turns dancing around the beautiful turquoise blues and calming greens, culminating in a wonderful mosaic that lit up the lake on this special evening.

As Sam watched the show, Boj said, "The kassa insects communicate with us using their colors."

"They communicate? *How?* And how do you know it's intentional? What are they saying now?"

"Just keep watching."

She wasn't sure what to look for. The colors seemed random, like dropping a handful of different colored sprinkles on a cupcake. And then...

The kassa insects swept over the lake quickly in the form of a rainbow, twisting and turning through the air and over the water. Sam couldn't believe what she was seeing.

"Their formations depict our language in the form of hieroglyphics," Boj said as the insects formed different geometric shapes. "Earth is interesting because it contains a multitude of languages, whereas ours is universal among all Krygians. It even extends to other species."

"I see!" Sam replied. She wondered what it would be like to be able to talk to the animals on Earth! What would they say to her? If she could, she would ask them all sorts of interesting questions, like what did they think of humans? Did they believe in some sort of afterlife? How did they view their own life spans compared to those of species who lived longer? What were their creation stories? Did they have dreams? And if so, what were they?

For those creatures that had shorter life spans, would their time on Earth be different for them? She thought of Pip, and whether he would think his shorter life span was unfair. Maybe he just made the most of every moment. Or was time viewed differently among species? Would each second last longer to Pip?

She would also ask difficult questions, like how has their environment changed in their lifetimes, and how are they coping with these changes? She thought of polar bears and how sickly and thin they looked in pictures, their once-stable ice flows now melting, and going without food for long periods of time. How did they feel about humans taking over the planet, destroying their habitats and murdering species? They were probably disgusted, much like the way Onnisa regarded humans. That was why they weren't allowed to live on Kryg. If species had universal communications, maybe they would form alliances. Maybe they would demand humans change their ways.

Despite humanity's destructive patterns and greed, Sam thought about cases where animals intervened and risked their lives to save humans. Why? Why put themselves in harm's way? Humans could learn so much from other species that could help them solve problems and become more tolerant as a society. If only they listened.

"So, what are they saying to you now?"

"Well, they acknowledge you as their new queen…and…" He paused. Suddenly, the insects swooped down to where Sam stood, hovering close to her. Initially she closed her eyes in fear, but then opened them slowly, only to find their bright-eyed, sweet-looking faces looking back and smiling at her, buzzing happily. The insects studied her closely, and swiftly formed another shape over the water. Everyone gasped and admired in awe as they saw the face of Sam glowing over the water.

"They are honored to meet you, and…they wish you all the best in your journey."

"Thank you," Sam called out to them. After the insects finished their declarations and the crowd began to disperse, Onnisa joined Sam and Boj on their walk back to the huts. Sam yawned, tiredness taking over her body. This was probably the most exciting day ever, but it was also time for some much-needed rest.

* * *

The next morning, feeling rejuvenated, Sam greeted the same crowd with joy and sadness. She was leaving. But she promised to return and visit soon.

As she was getting ready to leave for Earth, Boj approached her.

"I would've offered to fly you back to Earth, but the Elders have grounded me. They took away my flying privileges for now. I really made a mess of it on my last flight."

"Oh. I'm so sorry, Boj."

"It's okay. It's only temporary, and it's a small price to pay. It could've been a lot worse."

Sam agreed. "I'm really glad that...well, that things worked out the way they did, and that you're still alive."

"Me too." Boj then presented her with a small gift. He opened the box to reveal a floating kylie flower encased in a shimmering material. It looked like glass, but she figured it was probably some Krygian mineral. "So you remember us while you're away on your travels."

"Thank you, Boj. I truly appreciate the hospitality from you and your people, and I promise to return to visit soon." With that, she shook the klug and uttered the word "home". The scenery spun around her. The force pulled her into the wormhole's grip, and she found herself twisting and turning, falling into darkness.

4

Sam awoke in her bedroom to the smell of eggs and toast wafting up the stairs. She looked at her clock. It was nearly ten. She'd *really* slept in! She was about to get dressed and head downstairs when she stopped and stared in awe at her dresser. Resting on the top, she recognized the floating yellow flower encased in the translucent container. The kylie flower. Her heart skipped a beat. Her experience was real. It wasn't a dream. The gift from Boj now resting on her dresser proved that. But…was it *all* true?

"Good morning, Sam!"

She jumped at the sound of her grandfather's voice. He stood at the doorway.

"I made a special breakfast for the birthday girl. It's downstairs, when you're ready."

"Thank you, Grandpa. When did I fall asleep? I thought I went to the barn last night to get Pip?"

"You did." Her grandfather spoke slowly, as if trying to piece together the events. "It's funny. When I got there, you were fast asleep on the hay, and Pip was lying next to you to keep you warm. I didn't understand until I saw the chest of gifts and the letter from your parents. I guess the postal service must have delivered it earlier in the day while we were out. Although, I'm not sure why they delivered it to the barn instead of the house."

Sam wondered what to make of it all and switched the subject quickly to avoid further questions. "Grandpa, have you ever heard of something called the Hopewell Star?"

He stopped and thought for a moment. "Well now, I don't think so. There are the Hopewell Rocks, but a Hopewell Star…? I've never heard of it. What is it?"

"I don't know. I just…I think I heard it somewhere."

Her grandfather shrugged and noticed the unusual flower on her dresser. "Well, now. That's quite a pretty piece. Where did you get that?"

Sam had to think fast to cover up the truth. "Oh, that. Just a gift from a friend."

"Well, let's have breakfast. Then we can talk about school."

"*School?*" A wave of anxiety and excitement ran through her.

"Yes. Well, I was thinking for some time now, and if you agree, I think it might be best if you go to a public school this year." He paused when she frowned. "I mean, only if you want to. But I do think you're ready. There's so much I just can't teach you, and so much more you could learn there."

"I understand, Grandpa. But what if the kids don't understand me? What if they don't like me?"

"Now, there's no reason to worry about that. You have a good soul, Sam, and a right head on your shoulders. Just remember to keep your chin up, and I will always be here for you. Always. Now, how about you get dressed and we can talk about it more after breakfast?"

"Thank you, Grandpa. That sounds good! I could really use a meal after all that..." Sam wanted to say *travel,* but then she would have more explaining to do. She decided it was better to focus on the present. "Excitement. All of that excitement last night."

Her grandfather looked like he was about to ask something else, but stopped himself. He nodded in agreement and left the room.

Sam got ready and made her way downstairs, her stomach rumbling. She realized with delight that he had made her favorite breakfast from scratch: French toast with maple syrup and strawberries on the side. She ate more than usual, to her grandfather's amazement, helping herself to seconds and thirds.

"My goodness!" her grandfather exclaimed. "Anyone watching right now would think I hadn't fed you in the last week!"

Sam tried to slow down. "Sorry, Grandpa," she replied between mouthfuls. She couldn't contain her excitement. She looked forward to opening her gifts, but mostly she was eager about the prospect of starting at a new school, and the adventures she would go on.

When she felt satisfied and couldn't eat any more, her grandfather smiled and said, "I think it's about time now for gifts. Go on."

They made their way to the living room. A small package lay on the coffee table, enfolded in an assortment of wrapping paper scraps from previous occasions. Her grandfather always looked for opportunities to avoid unnecessary waste. The effect was a multitude of colors and mishmash of designs, bringing back memories of past family occasions, including ones they'd celebrated with her parents. She smiled, admiring the fancy blue ribbon on the top. She opened the first present carefully to reveal a beautiful notebook bound by a wooden cover with an intricate engraving of a lush garden, birds, and deer on the front—somewhere to write down her thoughts, ideas, and adventures.

"Thank you, Grandpa. It's perfect!" She smiled and gave him a big hug. He gestured her toward a large and awkwardly-shaped gift standing upright next to the window. It was wrapped in ugly brown burlap, the same type he used to shelter the cedars out back. She admired his frugality and resourcefulness. She didn't give a second thought to the wrapping. She knew whatever was inside would be more important and thoughtful. What could it be?

Her grandfather coaxed her gently. "Well, go on."

She removed the burlap. It only took a few moments for her to realize what it was. She gasped. A *telescope!* She stared at it in awe.

Her grandfather broke the silence. "I've heard you talking about it for quite some time now," he laughed.

Her face lit up. "I love it!"

Even though her parents couldn't be with her to celebrate, Sam was happy to share the day with her grandfather. She was grateful for a lot of things, but especially for his love and support.

* * *

When the evening arrived and it was time to go to bed, Sam should have felt tired from a long day. Instead, she lay wide awake, wondering about school next September and when she would go back to visit Boj. She gazed again at the kylie flower that sat on her dresser. She was convinced it was not a dream. It had felt too real, and the gift from Boj validated that.

It felt so real, and yet, so odd at the same time.

She wondered about the Hopewell Star. What was it, exactly? The universe was so vast, and it would be easy to get discouraged looking for it. It was like looking for a needle in a haystack. It could be anywhere!

Outside, the stars shone brightly in the cloudless sky. Sam got out of bed and decided to try out her new telescope. First, she directed it toward the moon. It took some minor adjustments to get it aligned and into full view, but as it came into focus, she saw its craters clearly and magnified in the night sky. She saw the face in the moon, but when she increased the magnification, it captured more detail. The surface was rugged, gray, and dull. It wasn't vibrant or colorful like Earth. It reminded her of a ball of clay, something malleable and impressionable. Was it like that all the way through to its core, she wondered? Or maybe it had a heated core like Earth and kept it well hidden. Inside, a light flickered, and she sensed a soft warmth bubbling up inside her. As she closed her eyes and started to drift to sleep, an idea floated through her mind, almost fleeting. She saw a deep well filled with light, a light similar to the colored lights of the kassa insects. She remembered their faces, bright and full of hope.

Hope.

Well.

Hopewell.

This well was deep and bottomless. How would she fill it?

She yawned. Maybe when she went to school, she would learn about things that she could not yet fully understand, and hopefully she would gain more knowledge, and perhaps wisdom too, to help her succeed in her journey. And maybe she would make friends there who could help her find the answers. She wondered about this and her eyes felt heavy. She could only hope.

She tried to keep her eyes open for a few more moments, thinking about this new idea, but it was late, and it wasn't long before she drifted peacefully into a deep slumber.

5

A late-summer heat wave slowly but persistently crept into the small town of St. Stephen, New Brunswick. The dry spell, which lasted weeks, imposed everyone and everything to slow down. The city advised residents to stay in air-conditioned buildings in order to cool off, and to keep well hydrated.

Sam would give anything to travel back to Kryg on days like these. She'd thought about Kryg a lot recently. The Krygians had given her a mission to find the Hopewell Star, but she didn't really know what to do. She didn't even know what the Hopewell Star was, let alone how it could save their planets. Onnisa was clear that Sam should not return to Kryg to govern, that she should instead focus on finding the Hopewell Star. But what if she couldn't do it? It seemed daunting and hopeless, and she didn't know which direction to go.

Since her journey to Kryg, time on Earth seemed to crawl along. Sam became less and less focused on her home studies and, to her grandfather's dismay, cooler and more distant. She feigned interest in the subject matter, but it wasn't as pressing as her search for the star. She needed to find a clue—anything that would help her on her journey. What did school matter when she had an obligation, a *duty* to protect Earth and Kryg?

She'd never asked for this responsibility. And not being able to tell her grandfather made it awkward. She had to explain it as something else. But she had made a promise to Onnisa and Boj's people never to tell anyone about Kryg. No matter how many books she read or how many hours she spent positioning her telescope, she felt she was not getting any closer to the truth.

As Sam lay on her bed wondering about school coming up in a few weeks, she had trouble shaking her anxiety. Her grandfather mentioned too often now that it was time she go to a public school to be with other children her own age, and that there were things he couldn't teach her. Even so, she would miss their way of life on the farm, and taking care of the animals. She always looked forward to her grandfather's lessons in biology and astronomy. She always looked forward to hikes with him in the woods, picking berries and herbs and making exotic teas. She would have to say goodbye to all of that in a week, when they moved everything to their new home in Moncton.

She had packed up most of the belongings in her room into boxes, yet there were a few loose odds and ends lying about. Standing in the middle of the large room, taking stock of what little remained, it felt empty to her now.

The nightmare she'd had since her return to Earth proved to be a recurring one. It frequently woke her up, and she tried hard to make sense of it. It always began with her entering the Mukalak cave by herself, just as she had done before. But instead of darkness, the cave contained flickering lights casting shadows, and she heard muffled voices. Then she saw them: beings that didn't look like the other Krygians—they were thin and tall with markings on their faces. They teased Mukalakatakalakum, and she gasped when she saw his form. He was massive—twice the size of a grizzly bear—with large sunken eyes, mangy black fur, and bulky spikes sticking out from his back and arms, his claws swiping at his offenders. The light blinded him so he could not see what was happening. She watched as the beings struck him over and over with the glowing sticks they carried. He cried out a horrible sound. She ran to Mukalakatakalakum and a bright yellow light emerged from him. It entered her body and she screamed. That's when she finally woke up.

She'd had the dream three times now, and each time she woke, she felt the same unbearable sadness in her soul. It affected her deeply, and she could not shake the grief and hollowness inside.

Something terrible had happened.

But what was she to do? She was here and they were there. She was isolated and helpless.

Beads of sweat collected on her freckled nose. She wiped them away with her sleeve. In her hand she clasped a small locket. She held it up to the sunlight and clicked it open, studying the photos inside. Her mother and father were in one frame, with her as a baby in the other. She wondered where her parents were now, and what type of mission the government had sent them on. She had last heard from them on the eve of her twelfth birthday when their letter had arrived, apologizing that they wouldn't make it home to see her, and promising to visit soon. Months had passed without any further news from them. In a few weeks she would be starting classes at her new school. Where were they?

She felt lonelier now than she had in a long time. Her eyes shifted to the translucent case resting on her bureau. She watched the beautiful kylie flower inside, a gift to her from Boj. The flower shined brightly in the afternoon sun. As she gazed at it, she noticed something strange. It looked like it was *moving*. She went to inspect it more closely. As she peered into the translucent container, she noticed one of its petals had turned brown. It broke away from the stem and fell to the bottom, shriveling and turning to a cloud of dust before her eyes.

It struck her in a way that she could not describe.

I really don't have much time.

* * *

Onnisa called another meeting of the Elders. Three days had passed since the Earth girl's departure, and there was much to discuss. The sun's dimming over time would pose certain risks to the population. Their technology offered temporary solutions, but they would not last forever. There was bound to be panic, and they needed to take action to preserve order among the citizens.

She wanted to believe Sam would be successful in her journey to find the Hopewell Star, but they needed a secondary plan, as a precaution if the first one failed. She required the discretion and trust of the Elders to put it in effect. She was also interested to learn more about Boku's secret dealings with the Kantak tribe. While they still presented a threat to the stability of the Elder way of governing, she needed to assuage her fears.

Everyone took their seats swiftly. All the Elders were present and looked just as eager to discuss the matters at hand. Onnisa did not hesitate. "I call you all to this meeting to discuss recent governing changes, and for an update on the state of Kryg's citizens."

Sika spoke up without hesitation. "As Elder of Health, I must report that the state of well-being of Kryg's citizens continues to deteriorate. The solar reflection technology we implemented to heat the planet is unstable, a temporary solution at best. As our sun continues to dim, we must adapt if we are to survive. I visited Oru village very recently, where I witnessed many young ones suffering severe respiratory illnesses due to the cold. There were a number of deaths, and the pace only continues to quicken."

"How long do we have, Sika?"

She hesitated before responding. "Perhaps forty years, if we are lucky. In fifty years, Kryg will be completely uninhabitable."

Murmurs and gasps erupted among the Elders.

A darkness swept over Sika's face. "I fear the cooling effects of our dimming sun has altered the genetic properties of our plant life, including those that we use for healing purposes. They are no longer as potent as before. In order to counteract this, I have gathered the seeds and placed them in different stations across communities that contain artificial atmosphere. Even so, this takes up resources, and what will happen once people find out the plants we require no longer survive in the wild? We cannot let people panic, but we must look for solutions."

"Surely the queen will find the Hopewell Star before this happens? If the prophecy is true." Dytanis's question came out more as a statement.

"We can only hope," Sika said.

"Agreed. I do not doubt she will find it," Onnisa responded, steadily eyeing the other Elders around the room. "Nevertheless, we require a secondary plan. In case Queen Samantha fails in her mission, we must seek out a secondary habitable planet and form an emergency planetary evacuation plan. We will use it as a last resort."

"What you are proposing, Onnisa, is dangerous," Ajisav said. "If the Kantak tribe finds out we are seeking other habitable planets…they will not be happy. It will add fuel to the fire, and inflame their idea that the prophecy does not exist. They will resort to overthrowing our governing system."

"We must not let anyone know," Onnisa responded carefully. "It will be a secret mission. Boku, what are your recent dealings with the Kantak? Please, speak freely."

Boku shifted in his seat, his eyes wide and fearful. "I am afraid the Kantak are not happy with the recent events. They refuse to acknowledge the girl as their new queen. They have noticed the community health issues and blame our governing. They are using this to recruit members to their cause."

Onnisa sighed. It seemed the Kantak tribe always criticized the Elders' ways and never offered any solutions in these difficult times. Before she could request the Elders' acceptance of the secondary plan, Boku continued.

"There is something—perhaps alarming—I should add. They

spoke hateful comments about Mukalakatakalakum, believing he was mistaken in his judgment that the girl was the one. As you know, Mukalakatakalakum passed away last night, and the burial ceremony commences tomorrow evening. I fear the Kantak are behind Mukalakatakalakum's death."

Onnisa was horrified by this news. It was a great sin to commit murder, but murder of a Mukalak creature, one of the most revered creatures on Kryg, was beyond understanding. The words stung in Onnisa's heart as she heard them. Her fellow Elders looked just as confounded and distressed. "Thank you, Boku. I will request that you continue your search. We must know who committed this heinous act."

"An act of treason," Sika said, a tear slowly rolling down her face. "Such hatred in those spirits."

"This is taboo," Dytanis added. "I have never heard of this happening before in all of Kryg's history. If this is true, the traitors must be punished."

"Agreed," Ajisav said. "Darkness is coming. I fear a great evil is upon us."

Boku nodded. "I will do my best to seek out the truth, my respected Elders. In the meantime, I concur with Onnisa's assessment and recommendation. We must seek out another habitable planet, and do so with discretion."

"Do we have agreement?"

All of the Elders nodded, and Onnisa continued. "Thank you. I will ask that we meet again soon and continue to work in upholding order as much as possible. This meeting is now adjourned."

The meeting ended rather abruptly and Onnisa took the evening to reflect and grieve, and focus on what needed to be done next.

6

A large maple tree stood in the front yard as they approached their new house from the quiet street. A tire swing hung from one of its branches. Sam's grandfather parked the car in the driveway, adjacent to a basketball net left by the previous owners. The house—a two-story detached dwelling—looked well kept from the outside, judging by the fresh coat of paint and clean windows. A small garden lined the path to the porch, filled with lupins and daylilies.

Her grandfather looked pleased. "You'll be able to walk to school. It's only a few minutes away."

"That's good," Sam replied quickly, although she still felt nervous thinking about the first day. "It also means I can walk home for lunch."

Did her grandfather realize how difficult the first couple days would be on her?

"Let's go inside and get settled while we wait for the movers," he said, changing the subject. "You can take a look around your new room."

"Sounds good."

As they made their way up the steps, her grandfather stopped.

"Actually, why don't you take Pip inside and wait for the movers? I have to go to the hardware store for a few things."

Sam nodded as he gave her a key to the house.

"I'll be back soon."

Although it wasn't as hot that day as the previous week, and although the car windows were rolled down, Pip barked and pawed at the car door, anxious to explore his new territory.

"Don't worry, Pip. We didn't forget about you!" She opened the door and grabbed the leash and a bag of groceries they'd picked up on the way there. She waved goodbye to her grandfather as he backed the car down the driveway and drove off. As she headed toward the house, she sensed a strange presence lingering close by. She examined the exterior of their neighbor's house. Its roof was partially sunken on one side and the paint on the trim was peeling away. A crack ran up the side of the foundation. The steps leading up to the front porch were uneven, and a separate ramp curved to the side, allowing separate access to the entryway. Sam's eyes rested on the front lawn, its grass overgrown, unkempt and strewn with dandelions. When she glanced up at a dirty window on the second story, she was surprised to see a boy watching her, his face expressionless, almost cold. It sent a shiver down her spine.

Pip tugged on his leash so hard it twisted her hand and she dropped the bag of groceries. She grumbled and kneeled down, picking up the items one by one and placing them back in the bag as Pip barked furiously beside her and ran around in circles.

"What's wrong, Pip?" She had never seen him so flustered before. Once she put the last item—an apple—in her bag, she sighed. "Okay, let's go."

She glanced up at the window again, but no one was there. A white curtain was pulled across, now swaying in the breeze.

* * *

By the end of the first week, most of the boxes were unpacked and Sam and her grandfather slowly settled in. Her new room was cramped compared to her old room at the farm, barely half the size. With no closet, she folded her clothes and managed to squeeze them into the bulky bureau in the corner.

She'd placed her telescope in front of the large window overlooking the backyard. She missed seeing the dark sky at night out at the farm. Here in the city, light pollution affected the image, and with more structures it had taken her a while to position the telescope just right so that it wasn't obstructed by trees or wires.

She spent most of the morning in their backyard playing fetch with Pip. The tennis ball was soggy now and losing its form after having been chewed on for hours. Pip waited patiently at her heels. She threw the ball toward their large cedar, hoping to hit its trunk with her aim, but was off by a few inches.

The backyard was mostly grassy and contained a few trees and shrubs. Her grandfather had promised to plant a vegetable and herb garden later in the month.

It won't be as large as the one we had on the farm, but it will be something. You'll see, he'd assured her.

She missed the farm, and her life there.

Pip returned a minute later and dropped the ball at her feet. She picked it up and threw it absentmindedly while looking over at the house next door. It looked quiet and desolate compared to the other houses on the street. She hadn't seen the strange boy since the day they'd moved into their new home. Still, she couldn't shake the feeling, the prickling on her spine and back like an odd presence, that someone was watching her.

On the next throw, in an effort to confuse Pip, she aimed the ball so it would rebound off the roof of the shed and bounce back to her. She threw the ball hard, but instead of striking the shed it went further, over the wall and into the neighbor's backyard. She would have to retrieve it. Would they get angry at her for trespassing? On second thought, if she was quick, maybe they wouldn't even notice.

Sam darted across the lawn toward the gate on the neighbor's property, hoping she wouldn't get caught. She found the ball under some rose bushes near the back. She ducked down to retrieve it, being careful not to get pricked. Her hand reached the slimy ball. On second thought, she should have just left it there. As she stood up, she caught sight of a little girl in the window. She was maybe five or six, and watched Sam intently, her expression curious.

Sam smiled, held up the ball, and waved.

To her surprise, the girl waved back.

Sam ran back to the gate and closed it gently behind her. Pip barked impatiently on the other side.

* * *

Sam noticed her grandfather's tense jaw and inquisitive eyes as she walked through the door. He sat on the couch reading the newspaper. The recent headlines were troubling. A number of prominent scientists had gone missing—including a few working for the government. He creased his eyebrows in a stern expression of concentration. He often looked like that when troubled. Sam guessed he was worried for her parents' safety.

He looked up from the paper and caught her gaze. "Where were you?"

"Sorry, Grandpa. I—I was playing ball outside with Pip." She thought about telling him about the girl next door but decided it could wait.

"Ah, I see." The muscles in his face relaxed as he folded the paper and placed it aside. "A package arrived for you today. It's on the kitchen table."

Sam hurried over and found a small brown package with her name on it. There was no return address. Maybe it was from Mom and Dad? She inspected it closer. That was odd; it didn't look like their handwriting, and it was posted to the old address. The postal office must have forwarded it here.

She opened it to find an additional lens for her telescope, a book, and a letter addressed to her.

Dear Sam,

Your mother and I are happy to hear you'll be starting school soon. We are so excited for you! As a first day of school gift, we thought you might like this additional lens for your telescope. I've also included a book that helped me in the past when I was going through a difficult time, and hope you find it useful as you continue your journey of discovery. We miss you and Grandpa very much, and hope to visit soon. Please give him a big hug from both of us.

Lots of love,
Dad

Her heart sank. The lettering looked rushed and scribbled, hardly the same handwriting she was used to getting from her father. Like he wrote it as an afterthought. She turned the letter over, hoping to find something more. A detail or clue about how they were doing, where they were going, and why they couldn't visit sooner. How long would it be before she saw them again? She wanted to tell them all about her experiences over the past year, and thank them for the gifts. But there was no return address. No way to contact them.

Her grandfather stood at the doorway a few feet from her, waiting to hear the news. She didn't like it when he hovered sometimes, especially when she just wanted to be left alone with her thoughts. Besides, there wasn't any news to tell him.

"What is it?"

"It's just a letter from Dad," Sam said, placing the note on the table while eyeing the other gifts. "And a book, and a lens for my telescope. No return address or anything."

He frowned. "You know they can't disclose too much information. For safety reasons."

"I know."

"How are they doing?"

"I don't know. They never say." She stood up and handed the letter to him so he could read it for himself. Then she headed upstairs with the new book and telescope lens in her hands, and her mind elsewhere.

* * *

The concave lens slid effortlessly onto the eyepiece of Sam's telescope. The device allowed her to adjust the magnification by 350x, though it proved finicky. She had to adjust it more than a few times to bring the image into clear view.

Like the blurred image in the telescope, she tried bringing her thoughts into focus. They were scattered. Tomorrow would be her first day of school. What would be expected of her? Who would she meet, and would the other kids like her?

She decided to focus her telescope on the moon—something about it compelled her attention.

The lens was more powerful than she first thought. The moon's craters were so close it looked like she could reach out and touch them. She adjusted the settings and re-positioned the telescope to another lunar location, and again, the detail was breathtaking. She was able to capture the ridges of the craters and rocks on the surface. How magnificent!

Nevertheless, her mind wandered.

Would she have any classes with the boy next door? Why did he seem so cold when she first saw him at the window?

She adjusted the telescope once more and jumped as a sudden flash of blue light erupted from one of the moon's craters.

What was that?

She waited to see if it would happen again and focused on the same spot in the moon's crater.

Nothing.

She zoomed in further and waited a few more minutes. She remembered reading in the paper recently that TitusTech was harvesting the moon's resources to make electronics. Was there a connection between the flash of blue light and the TitusTech industrial operations?

Or was she just imagining things? She looked for any structures bearing the TitusTech insignia, but it was still too far to see such details.

Her eyes must have been playing tricks on her.

Frustrated, she focused on the stars instead. There were billions of them. Trillions! Even if she found the Hopewell Star, what could she do? How would it help save Kryg? Where would she even start?

She needed a method of tracking the constellations to learn more about them. Even if she didn't fully understand her purpose yet, she knew she needed to start somewhere.

First, she would check Kryg's location relative to Earth. Then, she would need to determine which star systems were located close by. Each night, she would observe if any new stars in those regions were born. Maybe one of the new stars would carry the answer. Her plan seemed so straightforward, yet it also felt contrived and insufficient. She was desperately grasping at straws.

That was what she needed to do. Otherwise, she wouldn't make any progress.

Thinking about her next steps, she became aware of a strange presence again. She looked away from the telescope. Outside, the moonlight cast an eerie glow. Shadows shifted around her room. She looked through her window at the neighbor's garden and noticed the strange boy again. He was alone, staring up at the full moon, his eyes transfixed on something.

But what?

He turned around to face her, his expression cold.

Sam gasped. Had he seen the strange flash of light too? Impossible! It was too far away, and he wouldn't be able to see it without a telescope.

Had he been watching her?

Startled, she yanked the curtains over the window and jumped into her bed, pulling the blankets up to her chin. She couldn't shake the strange events from her mind.

7

Her first day of public school proved difficult. It was seventh grade, and everyone already had their own groups of friends established. Worse, she shared a number of classes with the odd boy from next door. He wore a black baseball cap and a blue T-shirt with the logo of a band she didn't recognize. His pants were bulky and oversized. He never spoke in class and usually kept his head down, only raising it to look at Sam. Why he kept staring at her like that, why she apparently intrigued him, she hadn't a clue. It made her uncomfortable.

She turned her attention to the girl beside her with purple hair. The color reminded her of the phosphorescent plants in the Mukalak caves on Kryg. The girl had a small diamond nose stud and three piercings on each ear. Sam had her ears pierced last year and didn't like it one bit. She remembered the crusty infection and having to turn them daily. This girl was either super brave or could tolerate pain. Probably both.

The girl suddenly spoke to Sam. "Hey, I'm Kato. That guy over there who keeps looking at you is my twin brother, Kobe."

"Hi, I'm Sam. You...you have a *twin*?" she said in disbelief.

"Yep. He's super smart and likes to read and write a lot, but doesn't like communicating verbally. He doesn't say much or focus on anyone— or any*thing* for that matter. Obviously you've caught his interest in some way. Sorry, he can be super awkward sometimes. I'll talk to him after class."

Sam didn't know what to make of this. "He looks like he's angry with me. I'm not sure why. I don't think I did anything wrong."

A boy with black-rimmed glasses leaned in. "It's because you're the *new* girl. You know, mysterious. Sorry. I'm Simon, by the way."

Sam nodded, extending her hand to meet his. She just wanted to be normal. She wanted to feel accepted. But she felt different, somehow.

Like an outsider.

The constant attention from Kobe this morning wasn't helping. It distracted her, and the other students were starting to notice. How was she supposed to concentrate on her studies?

Kato's smile put her at ease. "It's all good. No worries. He'll probably get over you after a week. He does that sometimes. Like he couldn't stop staring at my hair."

"Well, it's kinda hard to miss," Simon added. "It looks like a unicorn's mane."

Kato rolled her eyes. "Unicorns have rainbow-colored manes, not purple. Anyway, we're going to GameStars after school. It's this local café where you play board games. I was wondering, maybe, if you want to join us?"

"And I'm joining you too, right?" Simon asked. "I mean, you need at least *four* players for JackRabbit."

"Did I mention that not only does Simon like to jump in on conversations, but he also has a knack for inviting himself to our plans?"

Simon pretended to be offended at this comment, placing his hand to his forehead and faking a gasp. He continued defiantly. "You can be on my team, Sam. It's *always* the winning team."

Kato laughed. "Yeah, right!"

Sam laughed too. "Okay, looking forward to it."

As Kato and Simon squabbled about who had the better strategy in their last game, a blond boy who stood half a foot taller than anyone else in the room strode confidently over to their table.

"Oh no. Code red," Simon whispered. "Here comes trouble!"

"What's this I hear about a winning team?"

Kato glanced up at the boy, a sour expression on her face. "Go do something productive, Hunter, like tidying up those bookshelves," she said as she pointed to the back of the room.

"How about a long walk off a short pier," Simon suggested.

Hunter sneered. "What's more productive than giving a little pep talk to my peers?" A tall, muscular boy with greasy black hair flanked him.

"Reality check. We're not your peers," Simon replied.

"Just remember, the only winning team here is me and Vito. You're all losers! You too, *weirdo*," Hunter said, pointing to Sam. Snickering, the boys marched off toward the back of the classroom, eyeing the other students and looking for other potential victims.

"Don't listen to him. He's a total prick," Kato told Sam. "He's just insecure, but thinks otherwise."

Before Sam could respond, a loud clattering at the classroom door commanded everyone's attention. All the students stopped talking and looked over.

A robot as tall as Sam wheeled itself into the room. It was made of shiny metal with piercing red eyes. It moved erratically, shifting on its wheels and scanning the room. Sam recognized the TitusTech insignia, the logo of a crown on its chest.

"Scrappie!" Simon shouted affectionately.

"Scrappie?"

"Yeah. Scraps is our hall monitor," Kato explained. "Some TitusTech junk donated to the schools. It's always breaking down."

The robot wheeled itself over to a frightened student in the front row.

"Badge, please," the robot stated in a neutral tone.

The student fidgeted with his backpack, pulled out a small white card, and held it up. The robot's scanning system emitted red laser beams and its eyes moved left to right as it worked to read the information. At last, the robot said, "Nice to meet you, Googlihe Muiwer."

"It's Gordon Moyer," the student corrected, but the robot wheeled itself forward, already on the move. Students crumpled up pieces of paper and threw them at the robot as it wheeled around the classroom.

Sam's heart raced. The robot's red eyes were threatening and its machinery unpredictable. Its arms swung around as it moved, hitting a couple students as it passed. It stopped in front of Sam, and she noticed lettering on its arm.

"S.C.R.P. What does that stand for?"

"Solving Constant Real-world Problems," the machine responded. Sam considered this for a moment. Why the term *real-world*? As opposed to what, solving *fake-world* problems?

"If you ask me, it's *causing* problems rather than *solving* them," Kato whispered.

"Badge, please."

Sam pulled out the card she'd received in the main office that morning and held it in front of Scrappie's scanner.

"Nice to meet you, Sam-Sana-Samantha San-anderson." It was definitely glitching.

"It's just Sam."

"Go on, Sam. Ask it a question!" Simon said.

"Scrappie, are you...self-aware? Are you conscious?"

"Self-aware-con-compute-com-cannot compute. Cannot

compute." The robot jerked its arms and spun on its axis. Sam backed away so as not to get hit. Smoke poured from one of the robot's arms and a foul smell permeated the air. The students held their sleeves up to their noses. All of a sudden there was a loud popping noise. The robot stopped spinning and its red eyes slowly faded out.

The teacher walked through the door and immediately covered her nose. She wore a gray dress and black blazer, her hair pulled back in a side ponytail. Glasses framed her face. She looked smart and well put-together. She set her briefcase on the table at the front of the classroom, scanning the students' worried faces. "What is going on here?"

"She broke Scrappie!" Hunter shouted, pointing at Sam.

Sam shrunk back and felt the heat rush to her face.

"Scraps was already broken!" Kato quipped.

"I just asked it a question and it sort of malfunctioned," Sam said.

The teacher nodded. "Is everyone okay? Was anyone hurt?"

The students looked around at each other and shook their heads.

"Good. Well then, let's get Scrappie out of here. What a piece of garbage!" she said. "Honestly, I don't know why we even keep him around. He's useless." With that, she wheeled Scrappie into the hall and flagged another teacher to take him away. She returned and opened a window at the back of the room to let in the fresh air. "There. That's better. Welcome to seventh grade, everyone. I'm your teacher, Ms. Lysander. Let's get started, shall we?"

Kato gave Sam a quick high five. "Good job! Scraps has finally been put to rest. Good riddance! We should celebrate tonight."

"May he rest in peace," Simon added.

From Kobe's unwanted attention, to Hunter's unwelcome and accusing remarks, to the upsetting incident with Scrappie, Sam felt uneasy. Now she would be known as the girl who destroyed school property on her first day! What would they think of her? Her face burned as she looked around at the other students who watched her, some frowning. To her surprise, Kobe looked happy, his eyes sparkling as if she'd just done something brilliant. Kato and Simon looked cheerful too, joking with each other throughout the lesson. Despite her attempts to eliminate it, Sam's anxiety clung to her like a leech on bare skin.

Still, she looked forward to joining them that evening at the café.

* * *

Sam arrived at the café around dinnertime. It was so close to her new house, she rode her bike and arrived in less than fifteen minutes. She parked her bike outside and chained it up, resting her helmet on the handlebars.

She opened the door and looked around at the bustling activity. Most of the tables were taken up with eager game players; some were kids, but most were adults. Hundreds of games were stacked against the back wall. She felt out of place with so many adults around. She scooted out of the way as five men dressed in superhero costumes made their way inside. Were they part of a comic convention? She hadn't dressed up in a costume. Was she supposed to?

She checked the time and looked around. Where were Kato, Kobe, and Simon?

"The robot killer has arrived!" Simon teased. He waved her over to their table in the corner. Kato and Kobe were seated with him.

"Congrats again!" Kato said. She gestured for Sam to have a seat beside her.

Sam smiled and sat down. "Thank you…?"

Kobe sat on Kato's other side and maintained his guard. He kept silent, looking shy and a bit uncomfortable. At least he wasn't staring at her anymore, so it helped put her more at ease.

"No one liked Scrappie," Kato said. "Not even Ms. Lysander."

"Wait, I kind of liked Scrappie," Simon admitted. Kato glanced quizzically at him while he continued. "In a sort of curious way. I was on good terms with him, for the most part. He never got my name wrong."

Sam laughed. Earth names were relatively simple. She thought about Kryg and learning how to pronounce Mukalakatakalakum. Would Scrappie have been able to master it as well as she had? Probably not. He couldn't even say her name correctly.

"Just you wait," Simon said. "One day I'll work for TitusTech like my dad and I'll come up with a *way* better prototype."

"Your dad works for TitusTech?" Sam asked.

"Yeah, but he's in IT. Cybersecurity. Boring stuff. I much prefer pushing the boundaries with artificial intelligence. You know, hands on, building robots, AI engineering…that kind of stuff."

"Simon's a whiz with computers," Kato said. "Anything you need, he can do."

Kobe nodded in agreement but didn't say anything. Sam wondered if he was like this with everyone, or just around her. What made him choose to be silent, and how would they play the game if he refused to talk the whole time? Maybe whichever game they were going to play didn't need words. Maybe he could just give a thumbs up or down depending upon the questions.

"I hope you're hungry," the waitress said as she placed a large tray of cupcakes, cookies, and a bowl of popcorn on their table.

"Help yourself," Kato said, passing the plates around.

"Oh, I can pitch in!" Sam said, scrambling to find the twenty-dollar bill her grandfather gave her before she left.

"Don't worry, we've already covered it," Kato said. Before Sam could respond, Kato continued. "Now, let's get started. We have a serious issue. One that needs your vote, Sam. There's this new game I want to try. Kobe found it online, and they have it here. It's a science fiction game, and takes place on another world. It's called Galaxy Diplomats: Starquest."

"Sounds like one of those never-ending games," Simon said. "What about JackRabbit?"

"We played that one the last two times," Kato said, rolling her eyes. "Besides, this one involves more strategy and less chance. Shouldn't we try something new?"

"I'm up for it," Sam replied, turning to Kato. "Tell me more about this game. It sounds interesting."

Kato pulled a box down from the shelving unit beside her and rested it on the table where everyone could view it. The illustration on the front showcased a small, furry blob of a creature with the body of a hedgehog and the face of a koala bear, looking at the viewer with large, pleading eyes. In the background was the outline of a red planet with two moons and a spaceship in the distance.

"Does it have robots?" Simon asked as he studied the illustration, disappointment spreading across his face.

"Actually, yes. It does," Kato said. She leaned over and whispered to Sam, "Maybe. I don't know."

"Let's play and find out!" Sam said.

"Fine. But I'm on Sam's team," Simon said.

"We're all on the same team. Together. It's a collaborative game. We have to make group decisions about what we want to do."

"What? What kind of game is this? Where's the fun in that?"

Sam wanted to get started. "So, what are the rules? What's the objective?" No sense in wasting time philosophizing about what could be. They needed to dive in.

"From what I've read, it's like a Choose Your Own Adventure. Any number of players can play. We each have different skills but are all part of a mining colony. We've gone to another world, Canopa, to make friends with the Carinas. They're the creatures who inhabit the planets in the Carina constellation. Our goal is to make friends with them so they'll allow us to mine their star, Canopus."

A strange feeling tingled down Sam's spine. The theme of the game wasn't exactly traditional, and it sparked memories about her recent journey to Kryg. Was it an uncanny coincidence, or something else?

"Okay, sounds easy enough. Let's do this!" Simon said, shifting back in his chair and grabbing a handful of popcorn. "I mean, how hard could it be?"

It didn't take long for them to choose their characters. Kato decided to play as an interstellar doctor, while Simon chose to be a chemical engineer. Kobe debated between an intelligence analyst with combat skills or a mechanic, and decided on the latter. Sam settled on a linguist with gardening skills. After all, they needed someone with solid communication skills in order to effectively interact with the Carinas, and nutritious food to sustain their long trip in space, right?

Kobe remained silent for the most part, nodding his head and giving a thumbs up or down when asked different questions and when contributing to the decisions.

Simon picked up a card. "Okay. It says, 'On your way to Canopa, your ship needs refueling. If you forge ahead, you might make it to Canopa, but just barely. If you get caught in an asteroid storm, you won't make it. The only alternative is a planet close by called Gorgani. It contains the mineral you need to fuel your ship, but the planet's inhabitants are known to be dangerous and ruthless. As you are approaching the planet, your systems receive a distress signal from the planet Gorgani. Do you: A) forge ahead and try to make it to Canopa with the fuel you have and ignore the distress signal or B) head to Gorgani to see if you can obtain fuel for your ship, and look further into the distress signal?'"

Sam turned to Kato, who looked confused. "They don't really give us any good options here, do they?" Sam asked.

"Yeah. I mean, on the one hand, we could forge ahead and hope for the best," Kato said. "On the other hand, I feel like we're responsible for responding to that distress signal. What do you think?"

"Couldn't we just forge ahead, contact a sister ship to respond to the distress signal, and then ask them to meet us somewhere to provide fuel?" Simon asked. Sam liked that he thought outside the box. If it were real-life circumstances, maybe they could think of other options too. It didn't have to be so black and white.

"That'd be cool," Kato started. "Except, unfortunately, I don't think it's one of the options. And anyways, we're supposed to be *helpful*, right? I mean, that's the name of the game. Galaxy Diplomats. Maybe the test is to approach these Gorgani creatures and make a deal of some sort. Smooth things over, as part of the mission. And if there's a distress signal, if someone's hurt, maybe I could use my awesome interstellar doctor knowledge to help them." She winked.

"Yeah," Sam added. "And maybe I could give the Gorgani some seeds as a thank you gift in exchange for their fuel."

Simon smirked. "Somehow, I don't think it's going to be that easy." He turned to Kobe. "Which is it? A?"

Kobe shook his head and frowned.

"Okay, B it is. We'll go and suffer a slow and terrible fate at the hands of the Gorgani."

As Kato and Simon bickered about the choices and circumstances, Sam's mind wandered to the mission objective. The idea that a star could be mined for power seemed far-fetched, and yet, at the same time, possible. Harnessing it would be tricky. She thought of her mission to find the Hopewell Star. Was it really a star? If it was, could it be mined as well? If so, would its own power dim over time?

All of a sudden it felt stuffy in the room with all of these people. Sam couldn't recall the last time she was in a room with so many strangers. The noise pounded her eardrums as she realized multiple tables had filled up now with groups of people chatting away while playing different games. She needed to get some fresh air.

"Excuse me for a second. Please, continue playing. I'll be back in a few minutes," she said and left quickly through the main entrance. Once outside, she took a deep breath of fresh air and admired the sunset, casting pink and purple streaks across the sky. She took a few steps down the street, enjoying the movement, helping her to relax and recollect her thoughts. She'd been enjoying the game and the company, so why had she suddenly felt on edge?

Was this how Kobe felt around other people? She thought about her own insecurities like wanting to be accepted, not knowing how to act in uncertain social situations, and not knowing exactly what to say. Maybe he was reflecting her own insecurities. Could that be possible?

Maybe she was overthinking it and just needed to let go. As she walked and pondered it more, she watched as a group of adults walked by a homeless man with a sign begging for change. No one was taking notice of him except her. She remembered the twenty-dollar bill in her pocket and headed over. She wasn't going to use it otherwise, so she stuffed the bill into his cup.

"Thank you very much. So generous of you," he said, tipping his hat.

She smiled and started heading back to the café.

"Best of luck on your journey, Miss," he added.

When she returned to the café, it looked like the others were strategizing and debating another scenario. She took a seat. "Sorry, just needed some fresh air," Sam said. "Where are we at, now?"

"Glad you're back, Sam," Kato said. "So, just to bring you up to speed, it turns out the Gorgani sent the distress signal because some of their planet's energy systems were malfunctioning. Luckily, Simon and Kobe were able to help restore it with their chemical and mechanical skills."

Simon and Kobe reached across the table to bump fists with one another in a gesture of self-praise.

"That's good," Sam replied. "Were we able to get the fuel we needed?"

"Yes," Kato replied. "Actually, we used your—uh, your character's linguistic skills. It helped forge alliances and we were able to negotiate a treaty and obtain the fuel for the ship."

"Nice!" Sam said, sheepish that she hadn't been there to participate in her character's actions. Maybe they'd give her another chance the next time they played the game.

Kato continued. "Now we're in the midst of an asteroid storm. Simon was injured, but I was able to patch him up…"

Instead of focusing on the conversation, Sam found herself gazing at some kids her age a few tables down. They were laughing and having a good time. Her eyes rested on one of them in particular. She knew those distinctive features. Blue skin, pointy ears, golden eyes. The boy looked at her and they made a connection.

"Boj?"

It felt so good to see him. She wanted to go over and give him a big hug. What was he doing here?

"Earth to Sam," someone said.

64

Sam snapped back to the present and looked around. Her friends were staring at her.

"Who's Boj?" Simon asked.

"Huh?" She'd been distracted. Her face flushed. "Oh, I thought I knew someone." She looked back at the boy and realized it wasn't Boj, just some kid dressed up with blue face paint and plastic ears. She realized the comic convention was happening that weekend and a lot of people were dressed up in costumes. "I was mistaken. Sorry."

Simon opened his mouth to say something else when Kato's phone buzzed. Everyone went silent.

"Uh…guys? Sorry to cut this short, but I think we lost track of time. Kobe, come on. That was Mom texting. She's going to kill us! We gotta go pick up our sister, Darlene. She's at the ballet studio down the street. Sorry!" Kato got up and placed her phone in her purse. Kobe followed somewhat sluggishly, gulping down one last swig of soda.

"Aw, but it was just getting even better," Simon said. "I think the Gorgani were actually good people. They were just misunderstood."

Sam found it amusing that Simon hadn't trusted the Gorgani at first, and now he did. He also hadn't wanted to play the game at first, and now he was hooked.

"We should pick up where we left off sometime soon," Kato said, looking at Sam. "Glad you could join us."

"Me too. See you tomorrow!"

"See you tomorrow. Have a good night!"

With that, Sam packed her bag. Outside, the air had turned cool and it felt good against her face as she cycled home.

* * *

As the first week went by, Sam felt conflicted about her classes, struggling with some and breezing through others. She already knew most of the material for math and science, so she found the lessons repetitive and boring. French and history were her worst subjects. Having grown up in St. Stephen, most of the people spoke English, and her grandfather didn't know much French. She'd never had to study it in depth until now. People commonly used French here in Moncton. She found herself struggling with the gender aspect of the language. Why would a table be considered feminine and a computer masculine? They didn't have any particular feminine or masculine traits. She had difficulty wrapping her head around the concept. When she thought about it further, even English had rules and exceptions, like words that were spelled the same but had different meanings. And although she had been taught the rule "*i* before *e* except after *c*", she could think of a few examples where that wasn't the case: words like glacier, neighbor, scientist, or species. If only languages were universal, like Krygian. It would make things a whole lot easier, not having to learn all the particular rules of each language. There would be no confusion. However, she also felt the diversity of languages made life interesting and fun, allowing for a lot of freedom. If everything was the same, life would be so boring.

In history class, her mind was always focused on the future and never the past. During class time, she instead found herself thinking about Kryg. How were Boj and Onnisa doing? She missed them, and felt anxious about not making any progress on her mission.

She found refuge in the school's library, the only place where she could focus on her research without interruption. She used part of her lunch hour to study. The library was pretty much dead at that time, except for a handful of students. At least the school's library computers helped. She discovered Kryg's location within the Lyra constellation, approximately 1,200 light-years from Earth. While Lyra's brightest star, Vega, could be seen shining in the night sky, Kryg orbited a smaller star, one much cooler and dimmer than Earth's sun. She decided she would need to study the Lyra constellation in more depth. Nevertheless, it felt like she wasn't making any progress with a task so exceedingly daunting and discouraging.

A feeling of dread slowly crept up her spine. She got up from the library computer to stretch her legs and looked around. Kobe was watching her again, drawing unwanted attention. Hunter and Vito took notice too, and Sam had a wary feeling that they were plotting something.

She packed up her bag, about to leave and head to class when she noticed them approaching Kobe. They tossed garbage at him, called him names, and teased him about his clothes.

"Hey!" She blurted the word forcefully before she could stop herself. Her legs moved forward with a mind of their own into the obvious danger zone. "What are you doing?"

Then her nervous voice kicked in.

Run! Get out, now!

Her terror seemed to magnify in those next split seconds. What had she done?

Kobe grabbed his bag and ran as Hunter and Vito approached Sam. She was immobile, glued to the ground by fear, bound by Hunter's icy glare. What had she gotten herself into?

She didn't flinch, even when Hunter stepped closer and towered over her.

"What's this? The new girl thinks she's all that! Well, I saw your mark in French class today, Sanderson. It's the lowest mark I've ever seen. Five out of twenty? You suck! You should go back to your hick farm where you belong. You don't know any better than the pigs." He and Vito oinked and snickered.

Hunter's voice proved loud enough for other children to hear, along with the librarian. Sam sighed, feeling demeaned and beaten. What was her grandfather going to say if he found out?

"Shh!" said the librarian, reprimanding them both. "Keep your voices down!"

"We're done here," Sam said, returning Hunter's glare. She started to leave, only to realize that Hunter and Vito had followed her out.

Once they were out of earshot of the librarian, Vito made a motion with his hands. He brought two fingers to his eyes and then pointed to Sam, a scowl on his face. "We're watching you, Sanderson." With that, they left and headed to class.

* * *

Sam was unusually groggy that afternoon, as if her mind had been awake for hours the night before and it was just catching up with her now. She didn't feel well rested, and her movements were slow and unsteady from exhaustion.

The hallway bustled with students. Sam walked to her locker, thinking about the events in the library earlier that morning, when her right foot skidded on the ground unintentionally. She tripped forward, falling fast toward the hard linoleum floor. Her books and papers flew in front of her—much to her chagrin, and to Hunter and Vito's satisfaction. Thankfully, Kato and Simon were there, and they helped her pick up her belongings.

Hunter laughed. "Looks like Sanderson needs help with simple tasks. Maybe she needs to go back to the first grade."

"Oh yeah, we forgot, she never passed the first grade because she never went to school," Vito added. They both laughed.

"That's enough!" Kato shot back at them. "Don't you have something better to do, Hunter?"

"Nope," Vito chimed in. "It doesn't get any better than this."

"Don't mind them Sam," Kato whispered. "They're such dimwits."

"Maybe she's like your dumb, mute brother."

That seemed to hit Kato hard. Her face turned bright red and it looked like she was ready to lunge at him. Instead, she maintained control.

"And maybe you need to stop being such a prick," Kato muttered under her breath. She was tearing up.

Sam heard a voice inside her.

What are you waiting for? You're Queen of Kryg! You can do anything!

Without thinking, she ran. She ran fast and hard, straight into Hunter's stomach, her right shoulder slamming against his ribs. She embraced the force and watched him stumble in slow-motion against the wall. He clutched his stomach and cried out. In the chaos, her arms seized up as someone pulled her off of him from behind. One of the teachers held her back and stood between her and Hunter. Sam looked at Kato, who appeared stunned and impressed.

What had she done? Was this how a queen was supposed to behave?

Hunter's sour expression turned to fear, and then anger. He started to get up to retaliate, but the teacher intervened.

"Samantha and Hunter! To the principal's office, now! Violence will not be tolerated!"

Sam looked around, humiliated. Other students had stopped what they were doing to watch. Even Simon and Kato gave her alarmed looks, which fueled her mortification. Was there anyone who hadn't witnessed the incident? Even so, she knew word would spread like wildfire. Panicked and embarrassed, she just wanted to curl up in a ball in the corner. She shouldn't have listened to that stupid voice inside her head. What was she thinking? She sighed, picked up her bag, and dragged her feet toward the office.

* * *

When Sam got home, she found her grandfather seated in the old armchair with his eyebrows creased and a frown on his face. His expression told her he already knew everything that had transpired.

She started to head up the stairs.

"Sam, can I have a word with you, please?"

She let out a sigh. All she wanted to do was lock herself away in her room and focus on her research. The material she learned in school seemed so trite compared to the responsibilities she'd been given by the Krygian people. "What is it, Grandpa?"

"Your teacher called."

Red heat returned to her face. Should she tell him about the fight with Hunter—or the failed grade on her test? What had her teacher told him?

He lowered his glasses. "Is there anything you want to tell me?"

She wondered whether it was best to leave it be or tell him the truth. She figured it couldn't get any worse. She told him everything, blurting it all out in a flurry. She told him about her poor marks in history and French, and about the bullies who picked on her and Kobe. When she finished, she was out of breath and flushed. She waited for the reprimand. Instead, he stood and gave her a big hug.

"Thank you for telling me, Sam," he said. His soothing voice helped calm her nerves. "These things happen, and it's okay to make mistakes. That's how we learn. Hang in there, and I think it will get better. We just need to give it some more time."

"Thanks, Grandpa."

He continued. "We could hire a tutor to help you with the difficult subjects. Lots of kids have tutors. Actually, your teacher said she was impressed with your math and science skills, and thought you might benefit from working on some side projects that interest you."

"Oh yeah?"

"Yes. She said it would be up to you, and you should probably discuss with her further. It may help keep you interested, in case you exceed the regular course material, and she would give you extra marks for it."

Sam was glad to hear some good news after such a terrible day. This made her feel a little bit better, but the issue remained with Hunter and Vito. "And what about the bullies?"

"Both of them sound like rotten apples."

"They are," she laughed. "Big ones, with a million maggots in them both."

"I'm so sorry, Sam. But retaliating with aggression and violence is not the answer. You could have seriously injured that boy."

"I know." Her face fell. "I'm sorry, Grandpa. It won't happen again."

"This is a hard lesson, and it takes time to master, but sometimes you have to learn to turn the other cheek, walk away, and avoid the bullies. One way to avoid them and to keep your mind off of them is to look at getting involved in activities that bring you happiness. Always remember that you are better than those bullies, and they are not worth a single second of your time."

Sam nodded. Nevertheless, she felt troubled. "I try to ignore it, but they're persistent. They get under my skin somehow, and it's hard to overlook."

"I'm glad you told me."

"Is there anything else I can do to stop them?"

Her grandfather frowned, falling silent for a few moments. "We can't change others' behaviors. We can only change our own. A bully will often say something or do something that reflects his or her own weakness."

Sam considered this for a moment. "So, if they're taunting me about my marks, maybe they're worried inside that they're not smart enough or good enough for something or someone?"

Her grandfather smiled gently. "Either way, you shouldn't take it personally."

"Thanks, Grandpa. That really helps a lot." She thought of how Hunter teased Kato. Kato was one of the smartest students she knew. Maybe Hunter felt threatened by her? Or maybe he didn't feel good enough for her? The reasoning her grandfather provided helped cast things in a different light.

He smiled. "You know, your father struggled with bullies at school too. And then he was given a particularly interesting book. An odd assortment of topics, including some life lessons. I'll try to find it, if I can… It seemed to help him, if I recall. Your father liked it very much, and you're a lot like him."

Sam remembered the gift her father had given her. She hadn't even opened the book or cared to read it at the time. Now it was time to read it, and she would start tonight.

She gave her grandfather a hug and headed up to bed. It had been such a tough few weeks in so many ways. Grateful for the weekend now, she was looking forward to having some time to herself.

8

Sam pulled out the book that she'd tucked away in the chest of gifts from her parents. Was it the same one her grandfather had mentioned, that had helped her father deal with the bullying?

The front cover bore the title: *The Mind Traveler's Teachings* by Khema Sunita Mian. Sam's eyes rested on a picture of a monk in an orange robe. He sat cross-legged with his eyes closed, meditating. She opened the book and noticed the creases and coffee stains on its pages. It was old—first printed in the 1800's, and structured in three parts.

The first part focused on quieting the mind through deep, purposeful meditation. It provided instructions for a series of breathing exercises, visual methods, and thought devices for inner reflection.

The second part focused on a series of physical movements and stances. She examined the pictures closely. Each stance corresponded to an animal or creature. She learned it was a form of defensive martial arts. Specifically, kung fu.

The third and shortest part of the book focused on harnessing and applying inner energy through something called Shaolin tai chi. As she studied the pictures more closely, she noticed the monks had peculiar markings on their robes. What did they mean? Was there something special about them? Turning to the next page, her eyes opened wide. The pictures illustrated the monks walking sideways on walls, defying gravity.

How was that even possible? These were just illustrations. They couldn't be real!

Still, the drawings intrigued her. She flipped through the book and found an inscription in a different language on the top right-hand corner of the first page. It looked like Sanskrit, judging by the texts she'd once found while researching a project on Eastern religions. Was the inscription addressed to her father? She wasn't sure if he knew Sanskrit. She wondered what it meant, and whom it was from.

She remembered the letter from her father.

I've also included a book that helped me in the past when I was going through a difficult time, and hope you find it useful as you continue your journey of discovery.

She was surprised her father had also experienced bullying. When she looked at her father, she saw a confident man: well-spoken, intelligent, and kind. It was hard to imagine that he had somehow struggled too.

Grateful for the book, she decided to try out its methods to see what would happen. She read the first instruction:

Be mindful of your breath. It is like a friend who will stay with you wherever you go.

For a few moments, she focused on her breathing—something she found oddly challenging. Her mind wandered to other things, like the way Hunter had humiliated her about her poor grades in front of the other students, the jolt of energy and unusual strength that had sent her flying into him, and the feeling of satisfaction—and remorse—that had come with it.

Shifting her gaze to another part of the room, she noticed the klug glowing bright blue on top of her dresser. It hadn't shone like that before. The sight of it soothed and mesmerized her. She picked it up and held it in her hands. Slightly warm to the touch, it gave her a sense of comfort when she held it. At the same time, she felt an odd, low vibration coming from the device, as if the klug were alive and purring as a cat would if you stroked its fur.

She took deep breaths in from her belly, just as the book instructed, and found that her breathing slowed. Oddly, the klug's glowing seemed to now be in sync with her breathing. After a few minutes, she read the next teaching, and carried out the next few tasks.

With her back straight, sitting cross-legged, she closed her eyes. She took another deep breath from her abdomen and tried quieting her mind. She allowed the thoughts to come and go. She tried to let go, to let her thoughts drift through her. She let her breath out slowly. She tried to focus and become aware of the present moment, but it seemed impossible.

Sam followed the instructions but found it difficult to quiet her mind. Instead, she thought about the look on Kobe's face as Hunter and Vito tormented him. She thought about their terrible remarks, how they intimidated and provoked her, and all the unsettling feelings that swirled inside her from these recent memories.

Focus on breathing, Sam.

She took in a deep breath and focused. In and out. She felt a faint heat emitting from the klug and opened her eyes. As she breathed in and out, she realized the klug now pulsated bright light in tune with her breath. She closed her eyes again as she took in another breath, this time a deeper one that expanded her diaphragm. It felt good to fill her lungs. The thoughts that buzzed around her mind settled and drifted away, further and further, dissipating into the air.

When she opened her eyes again, she gasped. She looked around, startled to find herself no longer in her room, but in a garden. She took another deep breath. The fragrance of flowers and fresh air filled her lungs.

Where am I?

She was seated on a rock shaped like a turtle. To her right stood a large willow tree, its branches long and swaying in the gentle breeze. The garden contained a rose bush and fruit trees, enclosed by four walls.

In the distance, she noticed a figure moving. Dressed in an orange robe similar to the one in the illustrated book, he—or she—wore a mask of a dragon's face. Moving slowly, the figure approached and whispered, "Do not be afraid. You are welcome here. May I ask your name?"

Sam hesitated. "I'm Sam. Who are you? Where am I?" Her heart raced.

"Just breathe," the figure urged. "My name is Aruna. I was born in India, but I live in Toronto. I come here sometimes. We call this place the fifth dimension. I don't know how many dimensions there are in the universe. We're only able to travel to this one so far."

Sam took another deep breath, her uneasiness refusing to subside. "How did I get here? Is this real?"

Aruna fell silent for a moment. "Those are all very good questions. The mind is a powerful thing. Actually, the mind itself has more power than it can even conceive of. So much *untapped* potential. There really is no limit. I too have pondered those very questions more than a few times." She chuckled, then continued in a more somber tone, as if contemplating exceptional and unusual circumstances. "Mind traveling is a very rare ability, Sam, a technique few people have mastered. I didn't think there were any Mind Travelers left in the world. That is, until now. You look so very young. How old are you? Ten?"

Sam was insulted. She always looked younger than her actual age, and felt that adults often treated her differently because of it. "I'm twelve!"

Aruna stood still, looking apprehensive. Sam wanted to ask more about her past, but didn't know where to start or what to say. She allowed a moment to pass, and Aruna continued as if she'd read Sam's thoughts.

"While I was doing my graduate studies in physics—in particular, quantum mechanics—I found a book... *The Mind Traveler's Teachings*. I studied it every day. I became obsessed with it. I found that the more I studied it, the better I could master the techniques. One day, a year or so later, I came across a device much like yours while hiking. That same day, I held the device and practiced the ancient teachings. That's when it transported me here."

"*You* have one too?"

"*Had*," Aruna corrected. "It just disappeared one day. I think it was stolen from me." She paused. "Nevertheless, I still hold the powers it gave me and come here from time to time to...ponder things. And to meet with other Mind Travelers to train. All Mind Travelers come here when they first begin their journeys. It's a training space. But it's been so long since they've been here. I didn't think there were any left..."

Sam shifted uncomfortably. "Who?"

"The other Mind Travelers. There were four that I knew of: Katiya, Lijing, Atticus, and Theo. We used to train together, but I haven't seen them in...well, it's been a few years now." Aruna spoke in a solemn tone, and her voice shifted. "And now...here you are."

"Where did the others go?" Sam asked.

"I'm not really...I fear..." Aruna hesitated for a moment. "There was a time not so long ago when we were being hunted."

"*Hunted?*"

"An organization—they saw us as a threat. We call them the Henchmen. We don't really know who they are or who they work for, but some of us received anonymous threats not to use our powers. Like we were being monitored. They wanted to control us and our abilities. They wanted to limit our freedom. They...well, those that were taken...never came back. We never really knew what happened to them."

"Who was taken?"

"First it was Atticus who received a threat. Then one day, he stopped coming here. When we left the fifth dimension and returned to Earth, we tried to locate him, only to learn he'd gone missing. After that, we decided it was better to hide our identities and not meet outside this space, in case one of us was captured. It's why I wear a mask when I come here now. I want to protect my identity here in case…well, in case the organization managed to track me here. We all started wearing them, to protect our identities. You should wear one too." Aruna shifted on her feet and looked eagerly at the klug that Sam held in her hands. "May I ask you how you came into contact with that device?"

Sam clutched the klug in both hands, her knuckles turning white. Did Aruna want to take it from her? She tried to shift the focus of the conversation. "Why did the other Mind Travelers stop coming here? And how is it that you can still travel here even though you no longer have your device?"

Aruna was silent. Sam concentrated on the dragon mask. Who was behind it? The thought of not knowing whom it might be gnawed at her.

"There is much I don't know. I think we were all scared when we learned people were after us. I think some of them—like Katiya— stopped coming here because she worried about her safety. Theo said he would come back, but…" Her words slipped away into the breeze. "The others achieved far greater skills than myself. Especially Lijing. She talked about traveling to other worlds. Not just in mind, but in her physical form too. Theo wanted to learn this technique and committed himself to the practice. I've been waiting for them both to return but…I keep waiting here, alone."

"How do I get back to my home? To my world?"

Aruna spoke gently and slowly. "Ah, yes. Of course. You should get back to your home, Sam. I hope you will come back to visit again, and perhaps I can teach you more about how to control your abilities. In order to get home, it's easy. Just lift…a finger."

Sam looked down and realized she'd been sitting cross-legged, as if her body was frozen in time. She'd been clutching the klug the whole time, her thumb pressed against the red button. She lifted it slowly, releasing her grasp, and moved her fingers. She found herself suddenly back in her room at home.

Aruna was gone.

Sam looked around, stunned. What had just happened? She looked out her window. It was dark outside, and quiet. She stared at her alarm clock. Quarter past nine! She'd started the book at around seven. Had she been mind traveling this whole time?

She looked at the book, hastily flipping through its pages for some explanation of what had just happened. Who was the mysterious figure who'd suddenly appeared before her eyes? Was she even mentioned in the book? Sam searched the pages desperately for answers, but couldn't find anything about a cloaked figure or unlocking the power to reach another dimension. Were there perhaps some esoteric teachings hidden in the text?

Tired and confused, she decided it was best to get some rest. After all, the long day had taken its toll, and she was incredibly exhausted. Maybe a good night's sleep was all she needed to shake the image of the dragon lady from her mind.

* * *

Kato tapped her brush to the canvas and the colors swirled together almost effortlessly. The act of painting and letting her mind wander calmed her. It took her away from her troubling thoughts and circumstances.

She opened the window and enjoyed a fresh breeze as she took a moment to study her work. She looked down at the photograph of the small fishing boat at sea and held it up to compare.

"Kato!" her mother shouted from downstairs. The sudden yelling broke her concentration.

"Yes, Mom?"

"Can you come down here?"

"Be right there!" Kato let out a sigh. She'd really looked forward to having some time to herself, but things had gotten worse. Kobe was acting out more frequently. She couldn't tell whether it was just a preteen phase or some other issue. He'd become the target of frequent bullying. Subsequently, their mother was more irritable and demanded a lot from her. As a result, Kato had less time for her own hobbies.

Their mother Sandra was fatigued and her movements were slow, mostly due to the effects of the disease. Or maybe it was the crazy situation wearing her down. Her mobility had worsened over the years. First she'd complained of tingling in her legs and trouble balancing. She'd used a cane to help her get around for many years, but the disease had progressed, and she now used a wheelchair most days.

Their father Marlow had lost his job in the fishing industry just last year. He'd been good at his job and loved being out on the ocean each day, but the salmon weren't swimming as much in these waters as they used to, and scientists couldn't determine why. Many locals suspected it had something to do with the technology manufacturing plant located close by. Owned by the billionaire CEO Titus Dyaderos, TitusTech Industries had laboratories spread across the globe and in space, where his company worked toward harvesting the moon's resources. Palladium was a key resource for the manufacturing of electronics and for industrial purposes.

The fish were dying off in large numbers, and as a result, many folks had lost their jobs and moved out of province to find work, including her father. It had been a difficult decision, and an impossible choice to make.

Kato, Kobe, and their sister Darlene couldn't understand at first why their father had left. They'd taken it personally. Their parents explained that they needed the money to feed and support them. Their father would take a job out west where the pay was good. Each month he would transfer the funds to support them. They all prayed that in time, the economy on the East Coast would pick up again, that the fish populations would stabilize, and their father could return home to them and work in the fishing industry where he'd once thrived.

It had been one year since he'd left, and Kato felt a pang of sadness. She missed him a lot. She tried to push the negative emotions aside as she took a step back from the easel, rinsed the dirty brush in a glass of water, and quickly left the room. She would return to the painting tomorrow. It would be a birthday gift for her father.

These days, she made taking care of her mother and siblings a priority.

Kato headed downstairs to find her mother sitting at the table, looking wary, with a large empty pot on the table next to a cutting board. A can of soup stock and a couple cans of beans were the only food items she noticed. They'd picked them up from the food bank last week.

She knew what this meant. They were having stew again. It didn't cost much, if anything, but she figured it would be vegetable stew—they didn't have enough to buy meat this week. They would freeze it to make it last longer.

"Could you go see if there are any more carrots ready to pick from the garden?" her mother asked calmly. "And coriander."

Despite having some financial support from Kato's father, the cost of living was still too high, especially having to feed and clothe them all on top of the cost of medical treatments. Kato knew her mother found it difficult to make ends meet by the way she looked for opportunities to stretch their resources and approach problems in creative ways.

"Yes, Mom. I'm just going to put away my paints, and then I'll do it."

"Thank you."

Her stomach grumbled, but she tried never to complain. It would only make her mother feel guilty.

She wished things had never changed. She hoped her father would return home. She missed when her father would bring back lobster for dinner. Her mother made the best lobster, with her own special recipe. It had been a long time since they'd had that. She wondered if they would ever be able to eat like that again: as a family.

She headed back upstairs, packed up her paints and canvas, and decided to place them in her father's office for now. They wouldn't take up too much space. Besides, it wasn't being used anyway.

She opened the door and took in the familiar surroundings. It was untouched, frozen in time. It looked exactly how she remembered it, before he'd left. The rocks and seashells carefully placed along the windowsill gathered dust, reminding her of their trips to the beach and happier times. Her eyes drifted to the glass bottle containing the replica of his fishing boat, *The Neverland*, resting on the bookshelf. Kobe loved that boat so much. How many times had their father taken them along on his expeditions? She remembered how easily Kobe had picked up all of the skills, and even sailed it a couple of times with minimal intervention from their father.

Her eyes moved farther along the bookshelf, over preserved fish skeletons, photographs, and a few other odds and ends. It didn't look like he had taken anything with him out west. Did that mean he planned to come back? Or did he leave these things intentionally, a final act of discarding those memories, to assume a new identity, a new life?

She hoped it wasn't the latter.

She placed the canvas and paints in the corner of the room and noticed the closet door slightly ajar. She opened it to find stacks of boxes inside.

What were these for?

She searched through one of the boxes and found a giant black binder. She opened it carefully. Inside were what looked like hundreds of journal entries, along with photographs of sea life. She flipped open a page at random and read one of the entries:

June 18, 2019
7:20 a.m. – Charlie and I fish for mackerel. Offshore, about 25 km due north

of the TitusTech plant in Shediac, NB. Calm water conditions. Sunny.

7:32 a.m. – Charlie sees a large wave (8-10 meters?) in the distance, approaching us from the shore. Typical wave direction is toward the shore. Catches us both off guard. What caused it? Where did it come from?

7:34 a.m. – Wave passes beneath us. Lifts the boat 7 ft. approx. Wave continues out toward the ocean.

7:50 a.m. – Hundreds of dead fish rise to the surface around the boat. I don't think it's from natural causes. Never seen anything like this before.

8:30 a.m. – Reported incident to the authorities. They said they'll look into it.

Attached to the journal entry was a photograph of the disturbing scene. Kato gaped in horror at the dead fish surrounding the boat, floating lifelessly in the distance. She couldn't grasp the unusual height of the wave. He was right. It didn't look natural. Had the authorities ever looked into it? She didn't remember him ever telling her about this incident. Why had he left this book here? Did he want her to find it?

She didn't realize her father had kept such detailed accounts of his excursions. It impressed her. If only she could bring him back somehow.

Her thoughts drifted to school. She thought about how Sam had defended her and Kobe on more than one occasion. Kato admired her bravery in the way she stood up to Hunter. It seemed like Sam always turned up at the most difficult times. She sensed a connection to Sam. Was the feeling mutual?

"What are you doing?" Kobe's voice startled her and she jumped back, looking over to find him standing in the doorway.

"Don't scare me like that!" she said as she tucked the book under her arm.

"What is that?"

"This? It's just…some of Dad's things that he left here. I was thinking of reading more of it later, maybe bringing it to school and showing some people, like Sam."

The mention of Sam made him shift his gaze. "What kinds of things?"

"Journals and photos and stuff. It's all in there if you want to take a look." She shut the closet door. She didn't feel like talking or lingering any longer. "You know, it's okay to talk to Sam. It'd probably diffuse the tension. She's not the only one who thinks your staring's a bit creepy." Why was her brother only vocal with her, and no one else? What held him back from speaking in public?

"What? Oh. I didn't even realize I was doing that. Oops."

"Anyway, what are *you* doing here?"

He fiddled with the door handle. "I came to find you. I heard Mom yelling about carrots or something for dinner and I decided to go pick them myself. So, just wanted to let you know it's all taken care of."

She saw a change in her brother. She couldn't quite place it. Normally he wouldn't look after these things. "Thank you, Kobe," she said as she headed toward the door. "I guess I got distracted and lost track of time. I really appreciate it."

"No problem," he replied. He stepped in front of the doorway, blocking her so she couldn't pass. "Kato, I wanted to talk to you about Sam—there's something curious about her. I don't know what it is yet, but it's like she's guarding a secret."

"Why would you say that? She's only been good to you, Kobe. Defending you at school, supporting us."

"I know. I mean… I don't know. I just have this strange feeling. Maybe I'm wrong."

"Whatever." She pushed his arm aside and headed downstairs to get started on the meal. She thought about what he said. Something was distinctive about Sam. Unusual, but Kato liked that about her. She wasn't like the other kids. She thought about things differently, always providing an interesting perspective. If anything, Kato thought she had a positive influence on other people, putting Hunter in his place and not taking any slack from anyone.

She didn't understand what Kobe meant about guarding a secret.

* * *

Hoping she would discover a clue to her mission to find the Hopewell Star, Sam practiced mind traveling in the evenings before bed. The experience lasted around an hour or two on average, and always transported her to the same place: the tranquil garden. She tried to capture the details of the space more vividly. Four walls made of stone surrounded the garden. Exactly eight small cedars lined the east wall, and the same number along the opposite wall. Only one wooden doorway, to the east, existed behind one of the cedars. She could never see what lay beyond the garden, and each time she tried to walk toward the doorway, Aruna stood in her way, blocking it.

"You need to calm your mind, Sam. You cannot go through that door."

"Why not?"

"You're not ready."

"Why? What's on the other side?"

"Focus!" Aruna created a gust with her hands so forceful that it pushed Sam back a few feet and she fell to the ground. "Mind traveling is not easy. It takes practice. Let your mind teach you. Believe in its power. You must learn to stretch your mind outside of what you know. The more you practice, the easier it will become. Diligence. Persistence. Discipline. Openness. Exploration. Again, focus!"

Sam tried stretching her mind to another place. She tried to imagine what lay beyond the other side of the door. It was like a riddle. What could it be? Emptiness? Darkness? Another garden, like the one here? She made guesses at random, but it was no use. The image of Aruna blocked her.

She tried a different approach. She thought about Aruna, *picturing* herself as Aruna, anticipating what her thoughts were, and placing herself in Aruna's mind. She saw a sudden image of a forest. She noticed a klug in the grass beside a tree stump. It glowed blue. She went over to touch it...

The image shifted back to the tranquil garden, only it didn't feel like the present. It felt like the past. Other people were here too—other Mind Travelers. She sensed and understood them as Lijing and Katiya. Sam looked around for the other two... Atticus and Theo. But she felt sad. Tears flowed down her face.

Sam gasped and held her hand up to her cheek. The tears she shed were her own.

Aruna broke the silence.

"You've managed to see my thoughts, my memories, Sam. It's a gift. I know of only one other person who could do that."

"Lijing," Sam guessed.

"Yes. Lijing. I believe she is still alive, and my goal is to find her."

Sam fell quiet for a moment, taking in this newfound skill. "Mind traveling teaches you empathy."

"Yes. It does."

"It felt very real. It's like I was there with everyone. I felt what you were feeling."

Aruna looked ashamed, but Sam wasn't sure why. "Sometimes empathy is a gift...and sometimes it is painful. Learn to control your mind so that you can learn what is important to you, and choose your own path. I must go now. This lesson is over."

With that, Aruna snapped her fingers and vanished from the garden, leaving Sam alone and bewildered, contemplating Aruna's words, and wondering about her own future and the uncertain journey ahead of her.

* * *

As Sam practiced and became more confident in her mind traveling abilities, she started feeling more comfortable at school as well. She focused on her assignments and brought up her marks considerably, which in turn helped to deflate Hunter and Vito's attempts at bullying her. Nevertheless, it seemed Kobe was their main focus now. She found Kato sticking up for him on more than one occasion.

Sam had noticed a change in Kobe recently. He wasn't staring at her as much. Instead, he mostly minded his own business and kept to himself. Had Kato spoken to him about it? She didn't feel it was right to bring it up, so she let it be. In the meantime, she focused on her studies, grateful for Kato's help. Kato had offered to tutor her in French and history, and to meet with her once a week to help get her up to speed on the subjects that were causing her the most difficulty. Her grandfather covered the cost of these sessions, and although Kato at first refused to accept the money, Sam's grandfather had insisted.

"Hey, Sam," Kato said as she took a seat beside her in the library. They were supposed to meet for a French tutoring session today, but it looked like Kato wanted to talk about something else. She set a large, black binder on the table.

"What's that?" Sam asked.

"It's some things from my dad's office," Kato said, her eyes wide. "I just found them recently. He collected all these things over the years." She carefully opened the binder to reveal a bunch of journal entries and photographs. Some of them were disturbing and unnatural. In one photograph, hundreds of fish lay dead on a beach strewn with garbage for miles, most likely a result of human interference and pollution. It reminded Sam of the prophecy.

The future queen will travel to Kryg,
Her spirit as bright as the sun.
Only a girl of pure spirit and heart,
Can reverse all the damage done.

Sam contemplated the words and weight of the last sentence. *Reverse all the damage done.* The Earth's wildlife and oceans were suffering. There was absolutely no question that a lot of damage had been done. Looking at the photographs was a stark reminder of her responsibility to save both Earth and Kryg. The realization that Kato shared the same interest gave her a feeling of strength, of momentum.

"Kato, this is really fascinating!"

They looked through the documents together. In another photograph, some strange purple oil skimmed the surface of the water along the shore. In yet another, a large pink fish with two heads stared back at them. With the information well organized and detailed enough, it provided a lot of insight into the local issues.

"Wow, your dad was really meticulous!" Sam said, noticing that some of the photographs looked old and dated. "Does your dad still go fishing in these areas?"

"No. Actually, he's working out west right now. We never get to see him."

"Oh, sorry to hear."

"It's okay," Kato replied, "I guess."

"I can kinda relate," Sam said, looking up to meet Kato's eyes. "My parents are off on an extended business trip. I never get to see them either. It's hard, sometimes." She let her words trail off as she thought about them again. She hadn't heard from them in so long. "So, why is your dad working out west?"

"It's where the jobs are. He used to be a fisherman, but most of the fish died off so a lot of people lost their jobs here."

Sam wondered why. Was it from pollution alone? Or overfishing? Didn't the government have policies in place to avoid overfishing and depleting the stock? What was causing it?

"Why do you think the fish are dying off?"

"Dunno," Kato said, shifting in her chair. "Probably has something to do with that billionaire who owns the manufacturing plant close to Shediac. He's super rich. Imagine being that rich and having *anything* you want. Can you believe he even owns part of the *moon*? He's harvesting its resources to make electronics, or something."

Sam knew the company, TitusTech Industries. And she knew of Titus. She remembered reading stories about the CEO in the papers, about him not paying sufficient taxes, closing businesses in certain areas, and not paying his workers fair wages.

"I hear he's not a very good person."

"Yeah, I've heard that too. He gets away with things, and it's hard to stop him. I often want to blame him for my father losing his job and having to move away from us."

Sam wondered whether the government had tried to implement sanctions on the company, like upgrading their manufacturing plants so they were less damaging to the environment. If not, why didn't they? Maybe there wasn't enough evidence to make the connection.

Kato continued. "Other times, I want to be like him, having so much money. Not having to worry about anything. Simon's dad works for TitusTech, and his family is pretty well-off. It's not something I can really talk to him about. I mean, I guess the company makes some people richer and some people poorer." She spoke with a tinge of despondency. Or was it desperation? Maybe she and her family were going through tough times financially?

Kato glanced at her phone. "Oh no, I must have lost track of time. Look, I gotta go pick up Darlene from ballet. French tutoring session, can we do a rain date?"

"Yeah, no worries."

"See you soon." Kato picked up her bag and headed toward the door.

The idea of finding a clue as to what was causing these mysterious local environmental incidents gave Sam hope. If they could find out why it was happening, maybe they could find a solution. It would make her mission easier, and Kato seemed like the type of person she could trust. She really hoped they could find the solution, because maybe then Kato's father could come home.

9

At 7:15 a.m., Titus Dyaderos, CEO and founder of TitusTech Industries, paced his balcony overlooking the ocean. He breathed in the salty air and watched the seagulls fly overhead as the clouds grew darker. He always came here by himself when he had a lot on his mind. He enjoyed the remote location and quietude of the town of Shediac, New Brunswick. Once a small fishing village and known as the Lobster Capital of the World, its landscape had changed over the years. Now, it was home to his primary research and development facility, dedicated to human-mind robotics.

The next step in human evolution, his work provided an opportunity to extend one's life indefinitely. With the planet dying, he needed to find a way to preserve humanity's memories, to allow humans to travel off-planet and live forever. The hazardous conditions in space were never favorable nor kind to the human body. Robots posed a practical solution, where artificial limbs proved more durable and could be replaced as needed.

He thought about when they'd started this project and how far they'd come in seven and a half years. Already, the physical prototypes were complete and ready to be unveiled.

Titus let out a sigh as he remembered the date. September 21, to be exact. The anniversary of the car accident. His wife Marie fell into a coma, but he and his daughter Taylor had survived. He tried to repress the anguish that arose when he thought of his wife's fragility. He loved Marie more than anyone. The thought of her not being by his side when he unveiled his latest invention made him lonely and restless. He'd done all of this for her. If he could upload her memories to a new body, he could communicate with her once again.

His research had generated much interest in the scientific and private-sector communities. He already had orders lined up. There were deadlines he had to meet.

He jumped back when he heard a loud knock at the door. His nerves were on edge this morning. He just needed to keep it together long enough to get through his afternoon presentation.

"Come in."

The door opened and Taylor entered. She was dressed in a gray pantsuit with a white scarf around her neck. She looked confident and self-assured, her head held high, eyes beaming. She had her mother's eyes.

This summer, she'd worked an internship in his lab alongside his staff. Her role as a robotic artist required her to develop synthetic faces. It was considered relatively easy work, mostly done with 3D printers. The robotic artists matched pigments and ensured each facial proportion was reflective of the person purchasing it. Titus considered it an important task; one flaw, and the buyer could cancel the order.

"It's ready, Father. Would you like to see it?" She was, of course, referring to the robotic prototypes scheduled for unveiling to the private investors that afternoon.

"Yes, of course."

They made their way downstairs to the laboratories in the basement. They entered the quality assurance chamber where each robot was tested for defects before production. Robots hung along an assembly line on either side of the chamber with partial skin attached to their bodies. At the far side of the chamber, the lead robotic artist, Amber, stood beside three fully-skinned robots, a specification screen resting in her hands.

Titus stepped forward to take a better look. At first glance, all of the robots could pass for humans, but there seemed something irregular about each that didn't quite match their respective buyers. Their features seemed severely distorted in one way or another. The President of the United States's replica looked heavier than usual. To his right, the wealthiest man alive, Gene Kneep, CEO of GeneVortex, looked like he'd aged an additional twenty years. The third robot replica, social media magnate Arnold Goldwinter, looked like he'd started balding, even though in real life he most certainly had not.

"Sir, I'm pleased to present to you the first robot prototype, the President of the United States," Amber said as she flipped through her screen and activated the lighting around the robot. It made his features look worse, sickly even, enhancing his creases and wrinkles and making his skin tone a pale greenish color. "We've taken the specifications and augmented them slightly for more desirability. If you take a look at the specs, you'll see what we've done is—"

More desirability? Titus quickly cut her off. "He's too fat in the face."

"Excuse me, sir?"

"You heard me. His cheeks are puffed. It's like you made him gain an extra twenty pounds. He looks oblivious and hostile. This needs to be fixed at once. We can't unveil him like that! The investors won't buy it."

"I'm sorry, sir. We used—"

"And is that supposed to be Gene?" he asked, cutting her off and glaring at the second prototype. He sighed in exasperation. Then he took a heavy step toward the third prototype and pointed his finger accusingly. "And Arnold? I—I can hardly even recognize him without his hair! How will the investors accept this?" They were less than seven hours from the unveiling. Why hadn't she caught these issues earlier?

Amber looked taken aback. "I'm sorry, sir. We can fix it."

"You'd better get to it."

"Yes. We'll, uh...the machines...we'll order them to print out more hair. We used the 3D printers and the specs we were given, like you asked."

Titus's uncontrollable anger rose up in him. Amber supposedly had years of experience in makeup artistry and had worked in the special effects and robotics industries for years. She should have caught these errors months ago. In fact, he remembered seeing the prototypes briefly a few weeks ago, and they'd looked better than these ones now. What had happened? Even *he* could have done a better job than this!

"I came here two weeks ago, and they looked ready to go." Titus eyed Amber, trying to determine her intentions. "What happened? What've you done? Are you trying to sabotage my work?"

Taylor stepped in, her face flushed. "Father, it's not Amber's fault. She was just doing her job."

"She won't have a job if she keeps making these errors." He turned to Amber, looking her straight in the eyes. "I want it fixed. Now!"

"I'm sorry, sir. No problem. I'll get right on it." She left the quality assurance chamber and headed back to the lab.

"Father, please! I can help her fix it."

"No, you can't. It's entirely Amber's fault. She was the lead on this."

"You can't treat your employees like this!" Taylor pleaded.

He didn't have time for this. He knew she and Amber had become friends while working together, and now his daughter steadfastly defended her despite her poor work.

He needed to teach her a tough but important lesson.

"Taylor, you need to learn something about running a company. Sometimes you need to be heavy-handed, or nothing gets done. In this business, you can never be friends with your staff. They'll start slacking off. You always have to monitor them, and you have to be one step ahead."

"That's not true. Amber put in a lot of work on these robots. She was just going by the specs, like she said."

"My last lesson for today is this: you cannot make excuses for other people, or they'll never learn. We have nothing more to discuss. It's not your fault, honey. These things happen. Anyway, feel free to take the rest of the day off. I have to make a few calls to see if we can delay the presentation, okay? I'll see you later for dinner."

Her face fell. She looked disappointed, but now she'd know for next time. He needed to teach her the difficult lessons if she was to take over the company one day. With that, he left the quality assurance chamber and headed upstairs to his office. He pulled out his phone and dialed his secretary's number, focused on the next steps. He didn't want to look back.

* * *

Aruna waited as the fully-autonomous vehicle came to a slow stop in her driveway. TitusTech had given her the car as a signing bonus. Not everyone received one, but her prominent research position at their Toronto office allowed for it.

As lead scientist at the TitusTech Particle Physics Laboratory, her research focused mainly on quantum mechanics, wormhole theory, and looking at practical applications, such as long-distance interstellar transportation methods like teleportation. She'd studied at MIT. Her PhD in molecular physics and numerous awards had attracted the attention of the company. She'd been working in New York as a university professor when TitusTech approached and recruited her for their new Toronto laboratory.

She walked up the steps to her three-story townhouse in the Distillery District. She'd moved to this neighborhood just last year. Most of the units were small and not really suitable for families, but hers was the exception. It totaled 1,900 square feet and afforded her more than enough space. The new position and higher pay allowed her some more flexibility. She admired the red-brick, low-rise buildings and the cobblestone streets. There were some nearby coffee shops she frequented, and she liked her close proximity to work. It was less than a ten-minute drive to the TitusTech laboratory. When she'd accepted, they granted her the transfer from New York and covered all the relocation costs.

She looked forward to relaxing after a long workday.

A black cat greeted her at the door.

"Hi, Trixie. Did you miss me?"

The cat let out a meow and brushed up against Aruna's leg. Aruna bent down and stroked its fur. "I missed you too. I'm sorry. You're probably starving."

She removed her jacket and scarf and headed to the kitchen, passing the hallway mirror to check herself. She pulled out her hairpin and let her curly auburn hair down, running her hands through it and giving her head a shake. Lab protocol required hairnets and protective gear with careful washing and such. She coveted the time after work to let herself unwind.

A picture of her standing next to the CEO, Titus Dyaderos, hung prominently on the wall in her hallway. They'd been celebrating the new lab opening in Toronto. She remembered the evening well. Titus had gone all out in extravagance, booking an entire five-star restaurant downtown with Le Cordon Bleu chefs, inviting those in the industry, friends, and not to mention foreign dignitaries.

That felt like ages ago.

She didn't see Titus much these days. He lived on the East Coast and focused on running his lab there, dedicated to human-mind robotics. Occasionally, she gave him updates regarding her experiments and research. But it had not gone as well as she'd hoped. The research proved time consuming and, so far, unsuccessful. She wished she still had her wormhole travel device, similar to the one that the girl, Sam, had found. It had gone missing years back, and might have proven helpful for these types of experiments. She still had no clue who'd stolen it.

She opened a can of cat food and scraped it into Trixie's bowl. "Sorry to make you wait. You deserve better."

She opened her fridge, dismayed to find that it contained only the bare necessities: some bread, eggs, apples, and last night's leftover lasagna that she'd ordered from Pamela's Pasta Palace. She'd need to do some grocery shopping tomorrow. Feeling lazy, she grabbed the lasagna and threw it in the microwave.

She took a seat on the couch, flipping through the channels on the TV. Nothing interesting. She placed her meal on the coffee table and thought about mind traveling to see the girl again tonight. She liked Sam, and was quietly intrigued by her. The girl must have had a special strength to show up in the fifth dimension at such a young age. Aruna could tell just by their initial encounters that she held so much potential and ability. She had no doubt that one day, Sam would be able to master the same abilities as Lijing and travel to other worlds.

Aruna opened the drawer of the side table and pulled out a dragon mask, gently tracing her fingers over the sequins. On second thought, maybe it wasn't a good idea. The fifth dimension remained a dangerous place. She felt uneasy going there too often. Even though she hadn't heard from the Henchmen in a while, it was possible they were still monitoring her.

She felt conflicted about a lot of things that had already happened. Each night, the dreams haunted her. How many times had she thought about her actions, about giving Atticus up? Sure, she had been threatened. But she had only given *some* information to the Henchmen. Right? She didn't think they were actually going to kill him. Now, with Theo missing, she carried a heavy weight on her shoulders.

No, she couldn't go back tonight to see the girl. It would be too dangerous for them both. And if the Henchmen found her again, she wouldn't make the same mistake she did with Atticus and Theo. She would keep her encounters with the girl a secret in order to protect her.

Aruna tucked the mask back into the drawer and finished her meal before heading upstairs to run a hot bath.

The warm water soothed her body, releasing tension in her muscles, but no matter how hard she tried, tonight her distracted mind worked in overdrive, constantly reaching for answers and not allowing her to relax. Instead of finding a peaceful refuge, her mind sprinted through an unending maze of uncertainty and lies.

* * *

Titus Dyaderos sat by the fire with a glass of champagne in one hand as he celebrated his newest discovery. He looked down at the detailed drawings the Mind Traveler, Theo, had provided him after hours of constant questioning under duress.

The drawings were of a small spherical device with unusual

hieroglyphic symbols. After inputting the information and drawings into one of his supercomputers, he'd been surprised to learn that the technology—termed a "klug"—was in fact Krygian in origin. Whether the technology would work, Titus couldn't determine at this point. The man alleged it had the power to create wormholes in space, potentially sending people to locations that were light-years away. With it, the possibilities were endless. Titus especially wanted to travel to Kryg's purple moon, Klyne, where he could find the rarest mineral in the universe, perilium. When fused with palladium, it created an energy so powerful it could power a spaceship to travel a hundred times the speed of light through wormholes in space. Titus's labs had tried countless times to recreate the mineral on Earth, but with no success, and the testing had been costly. The experiments were very labor and fuel intensive, not to mention attracted poor media attention from the environmental organizations due to the damage and the fines—hardly a slap on the wrist. For Titus, he saw it as simply the cost of doing business. Other companies and governments were successfully exploring space and studying the possibility of making expeditions light-years away. Titus knew that with the perilium, he could make that possibility a reality. Earth was wracked with overpopulation, pollution, and disease—he needed to find his own planet for insurance purposes, and to continue his business and succession planning.

Theo had explained that someone—a federal agent, he guessed—stole it from him years ago. In its place he'd found a typed note describing it as a dangerous object that needed safeguarding. If it were true that the authorities were after the technology as well, it would be wise to obtain it soon.

If Titus could get his hands on the technology, it would change *everything*.

His other experiments were failing. Amber's recent error with the robots had led to several setbacks: a loss of funding from some of the investors, and a delay in the rollout of the product.

He needed to find the other klugs as soon as possible, and Theo had provided an important clue: a covert Krygian monitoring base in the moon's interior. Theo had stumbled across it while exploring the device's powers. Titus hadn't realized the Krygians were using the moon as a hidden base. There must have been a good explanation, to allow the Krygians to be there at such a close range. He needed to find out their purpose.

He was excited and desperate to find answers. He needed them soon.

Tomorrow morning, he would have his company divert resources to searching for the base's location. If he could dig deep enough to penetrate the moon's surface at the undisclosed site...

What would he find?

* * *

Sam continued to practice mind traveling. On one occasion, she tried picking some flowers in the garden to see what would happen. But if her mind happened to wander away from her breath, she found herself instantly transported back to her room.

During her mind traveling, she made sure to wear a cat mask her mother had made her for Halloween one year using pipe cleaners for the whiskers. Just as Aruna had advised, she didn't want her identity to be known.

Aruna always wore a mask to conceal her identity, but something about her was oddly familiar. It tugged at Sam's thoughts, but she couldn't quite piece it together.

During her practice sessions, as Sam quieted her mind, Aruna would try to draw Sam's attention in different ways. Sometimes she appeared behind Sam and tapped her on the shoulder, causing her to jump up and fall out of her inward focus. Other times, she materialized out of thin air right in front of Sam.

Sam continued to develop her abilities and realized she could float and travel within the garden now, whereas in the beginning she'd always remained seated, never able to move without being distracted from her breath.

Days passed by quickly, and Sam was so focused on her mind traveling that she didn't give much attention to anything else. As she mastered the earlier techniques, she read further in *The Mind Traveler's Teachings*, attempting the second part of the book that dealt with physical training. She practiced in her room, but quickly realized it was too small for proper training when she accidentally slammed her elbow backward through the wall. She'd expected the wall to brace her force, but instead, her strength proved unstoppable, and it resulted in a gaping hole the size of a squash ball that was difficult to hide.

"I'm so sorry, Grandpa. I didn't mean to. I promise not to do it again," she pleaded.

To her surprise, her grandfather wasn't upset. In fact, he chuckled to himself. "It's not the first time this has happened."

He helped her patch up the hole later that day and suggested they build an outdoor training area in the backyard with rubber mats so she could have more space to practice. It didn't take long to construct. Her grandfather had some materials stored away in the garage gathering dust. They agreed they could make better use of them and got to work setting it up. Once completed it was the perfect solution, and not only would provide more space, but also help prevent injuries by cushioning any nasty falls.

Now, with the crisp air, sunshine, and natural setting, she had an extra boost of energy. It was the perfect day to test out the training space. She headed outside with her book and focused on a new technique and form. She studied the illustration in the book and read the teaching carefully. She followed the instructions and tried it herself, but could only hold the position for a short period of time before a sharp pain shot through her legs. She shook them out before trying again.

Pip came running out to the backyard to join her. He looked alarmed and barked in distress as she continued her stance.

"Shush! You'll ruin my concentration!"

Pip opened his mouth wide and yawned, then took a seat on the grass beside her and watched as she attempted the stance again.

On her next try, she held the pose for thirty seconds with subtlety and grace. She closed her eyes to see if she could quietly concentrate with heightened sensitivity at the same time. When she opened them again, Pip bolted across the yard and under a hole he'd dug into the neighbor's backyard.

Where was he going now?

"Pip! Come back!" When did he even have time to dig that hole?

She opened the gate to the neighbor's property and found Pip jumping up on Kobe, trying to lick him. It looked like Kobe had been busy painting the fence. He looked up and smiled.

"Sorry, Kobe. I didn't mean—" She hesitated. "Pip likes you, I guess."

Kobe laughed. It was the first time she'd seen him laugh.

"He's a really friendly dog," he said. His words bounced off his tongue effortlessly. It was the first time he'd spoken to her. His voice had a genuine tone, spirited even. Was this the same boy who'd stared tensely from his window when she'd first moved in?

"Yes, I guess you could say that." Sam half-smiled. She didn't understand his sudden change in behavior. Then again, she'd been too consumed by her training and mind traveling lately to take notice of anyone else. Maybe he'd already been making small changes over time, and she just hadn't noticed until now.

"What were you doing in your yard, earlier?"

"Huh?" She looked up, surprised he was chatting with her. He didn't usually talk to anyone.

"With the kung fu moves. Isn't that what you were doing?"

"Oh, that." Sam's face turned bright red. "It's nothing, really. I've just been practicing some sequences from a book my dad gave me."

"Oh yeah? That's pretty cool!"

She thought more about her recent transformation. Had she changed in the past few weeks because of the book? Had Kobe noticed it too?

"It helps me relax when I'm stressed," Sam said, quieter and more subdued. "I've been having problems at school."

Kobe nodded in what looked like encouragement—she had piqued his interest.

She continued. "I don't really know how it works. I mean, it's kind of mysterious and it grabs my attention. It seems to be working, because I'm finding it's easier to concentrate. I can focus on assignments and get things done faster. I just follow the instructions and usually practice in the evenings. It helps calm my mind. But..." Sam thought about the way Aruna kept blocking her from reaching other stages, as if she wasn't ready for the next step. "I'm kinda stuck on one of the techniques." Sam thought for a moment. "I have an idea!"

"What?"

"Maybe if *you* read the book, it can help you too. I seem to have plateaued with my training, so I'm just going to focus on practicing what I already know, strengthening my skills, and see what happens. But in the meantime, you could try the teachings, if you want, and see if it can help you—I mean, if you want."

Kobe's eyes flickered. He seemed intrigued by this. Would it make him stronger too? Would it help make things easier for him at school?

"Sam?" her grandfather called.

"Oh, that's my grandfather. He's probably wondering where I am. I have to go, but I'll bring the book over later today."

"Okay. See you later."

"See you. Come on, Pip!"

Pip followed her slowly back to the house. He hesitated, looking back at Kobe, who appeared very much in better spirits today.

10

That evening, Sam felt more restless than usual. To make matters worse, she was lonely, and found herself thinking about her parents. How were they doing? She hoped they would visit soon. It had been so long since she last saw them, and she could tell that her grandfather was worried too. He never said it outright—but she knew when she saw the distant and forlorn expression on his face that he'd been thinking the same thing. She tried to focus on something else instead.

She positioned her telescope again on the moon. Viewing its surface up close helped calm her and allowed her mind to wander to her adventure on Kryg. As she thought about her time there and began to miss it again, a strange presence reached out to her, though not on a level she could understand.

Two peculiar things happened: an image of Onnisa flashed in her mind, and a moment later, Onnisa spoke to her.

Make a mental leap and join me on the moon, she pleaded.

Sam froze and her mind grew still, as if in a trance. She saw the vague image of Onnisa, but her words were of the most pronounced and utmost importance. Had Onnisa really tried to reach out to her and spoken to her telepathically? Or was she just tired and confused from all the recent excitement on her travels, and her mind was playing tricks on her?

She blinked a few times, trying to recollect her thoughts but they were drifting now. As Sam refocused her attention on the moon, she noticed a pattern as she looked through the telescope a second time. A definite configuration of lines and shapes appeared on the moon's surface. They looked deliberate, as if someone or something had placed them there to be seen. She realized the shapes took the form of hieroglyphic patterns. She hadn't noticed them before.

All of a sudden, the lines and geometric shapes shone bright blue, the light both soothing and captivating. Sam blinked, and the pattern vanished almost as quickly as it had appeared.

The strangest thing was…

Sam *understood* what the message meant! It was intended for *her*. She was sure of it. As she read the message, Onnisa spoke to her:

Come to the moon. Use the klug as a doorway to enter the hollow. I am waiting.

The message was clear, if somewhat urgent. Sam had felt tired earlier, but the message quickly awakened her senses. She found herself immediately energized and scrambling to get to the klug.

She opened her wooden chest and a moment later the klug rested in her small hands. She took a deep breath and placed her thumb on the red button, wondering for a moment whether she was making the right decision. She shook it as she uttered, "Hollow moon."

The walls of her room spun and she found herself swiftly pulled into a tunnel of spiraling darkness that overtook her senses. Her stomach lurched, and in less than a second, she was pulled out of the tunnel into a small, bright room.

The room had white walls and the floor glowed softly. She placed her hand upon one of the walls—she couldn't determine the texture—and found it felt solid like concrete and cool to the touch. She realized she could breathe in this room, and its temperature felt neither cold nor hot. The atmosphere was controlled in here—but how?

In an instant, one of the walls slid open, and to her amazement she found herself standing in the entryway to what looked like a huge airport.

She'd been to an airport before, on her travels with her grandfather and parents to Disney World in Florida five years ago. They'd sat by the big windows close to the runways, watching the planes take off and land. But here and now, Sam couldn't believe her eyes. This place was massive. Tiered landing pads and runways spread out as far as the eye could see. But where the airport in Orlando had been bustling with people, this one looked abandoned. There wasn't a soul in sight.

On one of the runways rested two disc-shaped spaceships, rusted and falling apart. Pieces of bent metal and debris were strewn about haphazardly. These ships weren't going to be used anytime soon.

An eerie quietness permeated the place, like stopping for gas on the side of the road only to find yourself in a ghost town. It felt strange to be here all by herself. As she took in her surroundings, she sensed something momentous had been lost here. She couldn't quite put her finger on it.

She looked back toward the room she had come from, but the wall had closed, and she wondered where to go.

As if someone had read her thoughts, the floor lit up with hieroglyphic shapes. It formed a pathway to another room, and she followed it.

When she reached the entryway, she noticed a keypad on the right-hand side of the door with a bunch of symbols on it. Her hand quivered as she reached out to touch it, but then immediately retracted her hand and took a step back in surprise as the doorway opened on its own to reveal another room with large windows.

Onnisa sat at a table in front of the windows with a tray of food and a couple of steaming hot drinks, a faint smile on her face. Through the windows behind her loomed the darkness of space and a view of Earth, beautiful but fragile in the expanse.

Sam sighed, happy to see someone familiar.

"Onn—!" she started to call out her name when a loud voice in her mind cut her off.

No! Don't say it! We must only communicate telepathically here, Queen Samantha. Do you understand? It is the only safe method of communication. Other ways can be intercepted or decrypted.

Onnisa's lips didn't move, but Sam heard her words clearly.

Yes, Onnisa. Of course. She was distressed by the sudden need for such discretion and having to bite her tongue. How was she able to speak to Onnisa using this telepathic power? Did it extend to other people as well? Was it all Onnisa's doing? Also, where was Boj? And why hadn't she seen anyone else so far? She had so many questions, and wasn't sure where to start.

As if sensing her unease, Onnisa continued. *I'm sorry to have alarmed you.* She looked fragile and weak, and her movements were slow. Sam wondered how many years she had lived. If Boj was ninety-seven years old and looked Sam's age, she wondered how old Onnisa would be. Maybe one thousand? Was that even possible?

Please, come in and have a seat. Have some food and drink. She gestured to the nicely prepared meal on the table. *We have much to discuss.*

Sam was always amazed and humbled by the hospitality of the Krygian people. She made her way to the table and took a seat across from Onnisa, her eyes still wandering to the window, toward Earth. She felt so distant to everything. It felt strange.

It truly is a miraculous world, Onnisa mused. *And yet, so fragile.*

Sam didn't know what she meant by this, and hoped Onnisa would continue her explanation for this meeting, but she felt in the dark.

Instead, Onnisa remained silent as Sam began eating the food on her plate. It tasted similar to the meal that Boj had prepared for her back on Kryg. Flavorful and spicy, it somehow heightened her senses. She noticed the drink had stopped steaming, but she still blew on the surface before taking a small sip. It tasted like cinnamon and ginger, its consistency smooth and creamy.

It's called kaia. It's similar to something called "chai" on Earth, but it's made with spices only found on Kryg.

It's delicious, thank you. Initially excited about this meeting with Onnisa, Sam was getting increasingly annoyed and impatient. *How is it that you can talk to me in my mind, and vice versa?*

I will explain all of this to you soon.

Sam obliged. She lowered her head sheepishly and wondered if the tone of her questions could also be felt telepathically.

Onnisa began with a brief history. *Part of the moon is hollow, and as you have seen, was abandoned. Created long ago, it served an unknown purpose. Now, it is used by the Krygian Elders to study Earth. The Elders meet here to discuss serious matters, including those pertaining to both Earth and Kryg.*

Sam took all of this in as best she could, but it only led to more questions. *Who were the initial beings who inhabited the moon, and how long ago? Why did they leave? Would they return? Why are the Krygian Elders studying Earth? What are they looking for? And why isn't Boj allowed here too?*

Onnisa continued in a straightforward tone. *Boj is not an Elder, so he cannot join us, unfortunately. But I will introduce you to the other Elders soon. For now, I must show you something.*

She paused and pointed at the window in the direction of Earth. Sam realized Onnisa's finger wasn't pointing at all, but rather touching a clear panel against the glass. In less than a second, Earth magnified into full view. Onnisa pressed again and the magnification intensified. All of a sudden, the screen split and images of different cities came into view.

On one screen, yellow taxis drove every which way, and massive crowds of people walked around Times Square in New York City. On another screen, the Eiffel Tower in Paris appeared, and Sam watched as tourists walked around the structure, snapping photos. On a third screen, the Great Wall of China came into view, with crowds of people walking up its steps, taking their time to stop every so often to catch their breath and take in the view of the surrounding land.

Although Sam had an uneasy feeling about the answer, she asked the question anyway: *Can you monitor every part of Earth?*

Yes.

The wildlife and oceans too?

Two more screens came into focus. One showed coral reefs and fish of magnificent colors swimming through it. The other showed snow-covered mountains and a forest with a red fox darting through the trees to a river to have a drink.

What is it you're studying, exactly?

Everything.

Sam didn't understand. It seemed infinitely complex and difficult to do, but if they truly were studying everything, then for what purpose?

As if sensing Sam's confusion, Onnisa continued. *You must take a closer look.* She quickly tapped the panel again, and the screens divided into several images. These images were disturbing.

On one screen, forest fires raged and smoke billowed above as people shouted to one another, getting into their cars with suitcases and driving away in a panic. On another, a hurricane ripped through a town, blowing roofs off of houses. A frightened father held his daughter tightly in his arms and cried. Sam looked away, hoping to cast the image from her mind, only to return her focus to a different screen, taking in other unsettling images. Massive piles of garbage were strewn along the shore of a deserted beach and were sprawling into the ocean. Birds were trapped in netting and covered in oil, trying to escape. With no one on the beach for miles to help free them or clean them, they would surely die. The Earth was out of balance with the universe.

Sam wanted to close her eyes, but felt compelled to keep them open, to witness what Onnisa was showing her.

Onnisa was silent for a long time, and her eyes filled with tears. Sam couldn't help but feel lost and hopeless.

Why did you bring me here?

I am sorry, Queen Samantha, that you had to witness this. This is one aspect of humanity's greed. Your leaders value many things, but Earth's health is not one of them. Earth is fragile, and so are its inhabitants. You need a leader to heal it. It cannot heal itself on its own, as you have seen. The Earth belongs to you as much as you belong to it. You must follow your path and find your inner strength. Use self-reflection to help you, as this is your greatest strength and your first task. This is your next instruction.

What is it I can do? What are you saying?

Onnisa responded so quietly in Sam's mind that she almost didn't catch it. *Once you find her, she will help you.*

Find her? Who? Who can help me?

But instead of receiving further explanation, a sudden sound jolted them both. A loud, repetitive booming noise shook the ground. Onnisa and Sam got to their feet at once. In less than two seconds, the door slid open. Another Krygian with the same pale blue skin as Onnisa entered, looking fearful and distraught, her eyes wide.

They're here. Titus's men have discovered our location. We must abandon at once. You know the plan.

Onnisa nodded. *Yes, it was only a matter of time.*

The Elder and Onnisa exchanged words in the Krygian language, and Onnisa repeated the words to Sam: *Katu ona vis a hanu daytu. May the light continue to shine bright inside you.* Her expression changed as she looked warily at Sam. *We have no more time. It is not safe here. You must go!*

Desperate for more answers, Sam gasped and stumbled back as the ground spun under her feet. *Wait, I can't leave yet!* Anxious and confused, she realized she had no choice. A feeling of dread rushed over her as her surroundings continued to shift. She couldn't stop or control it. The force that spun the room compelled her to go with it, like a river's current moving a stick downstream.

You must go now, and do not come back here, Onnisa said. She extended her hand toward Sam, and in the moment that their hands touched, a burst of heat and light traveled up Sam's arm toward her heart and chest, filling her body with a deep calm and warmth, like sipping hot tea on a cold day. She couldn't fight the tears traveling down her face as Onnisa became blurred in the moment.

And remember…to look…inside you!

Sam didn't understand what Onnisa meant by these last words. Her thoughts were instantly disrupted and jumbled as the wormhole's strong gravitational force pulled her faster toward its center, forcing Onnisa to let go, and their connection broke. Sam grasped the klug tightly in her hand, transported once again through a wormhole bend and back into her room at home.

She looked around in bewilderment. Had Onnisa escaped in time to avoid the imminent threat?

Onnisa! she called out in her mind.

There was no response.

She only had a moment to catch her breath when she heard a loud knock on her bedroom door.

"Sam?"

She jumped. "Yes, I'm here. What is it, Grandpa?" She quickly hid the klug in her wooden chest and opened the door to see a look of concern on her grandfather's face.

"I've been calling your name. I wasn't sure where you were." He had additional creases on his forehead and his eyes looked more sunken than usual these days, but he always maintained a friendly composure and never yelled at her no matter what happened.

"Sorry, Grandpa. I've just been using the telescope." She glanced over at it. "I guess I was so immersed, I didn't hear you." She flat-out lied, and felt bad about it. But she didn't know what else she could say. "Was there something you needed?"

Her grandfather's expression changed, and for a moment she thought he looked hurt or maybe saddened. "Sam, I…I want you to know that you can always talk to me, if there's anything wrong, for whatever reason. You can always tell me if something is concerning you…"

Sam nodded, but didn't feel like talking now. "Thank you, Grandpa. I know."

He hesitated. "I just wanted to let you know that I'm really proud of you, and I know your mom and dad are too. I know this school year has not been easy. You've managed to pull up your marks and grown so much over the past few months."

"Thanks, Grandpa."

He smiled. "I thought it might be nice to celebrate."

She appreciated what he was trying to do, but didn't feel like rejoicing. Her nerves were on edge. She was tired and distressed from the recent events, but decided to push them aside and make the most of the moment. "Okay. What were you thinking?"

"It's up to you, but I was thinking…how about if we have Kato and some of your friends over for dinner this weekend?" He must have noticed that she'd become closer with Kato over the past couple of months. It reflected her own thoughts exactly.

Sam beamed. "That would be wonderful."

11

For two days, Sam tried making a connection with Onnisa. She wished she could return to the moon to ensure she was okay, but Onnisa had given her specific instructions not to go back. It wasn't safe.

Titus's men had infiltrated their location in the moon's interior. But what would happen now? Was he still a threat to Onnisa and her people? Onnisa had told her to find someone to help her—but who? Aruna? If so, why be so cryptic in her message? And was Onnisa okay, or was she still in danger? Had she returned safely to Kryg?

A million questions raced through Sam's mind—as did the terrible feeling she'd missed something important. She needed to return to Kryg. She *needed* answers.

She tapped her chin. Her friends weren't coming over for another twenty minutes. Time nearly stopped during her wormhole journeys, didn't it? She could return to Kryg and still be home in time for dinner with everyone, couldn't she?

She made her way to her wooden chest and took out the klug, admiring its intricate design and symbols. Her hands clasped around it tightly. She almost had her thumb on the red button when Pip suddenly came barging into her room, barking loudly and catching her off guard.

"What is it this time?"

He whined, then ran over and started barking at the device.

"Oh, this? It's not a toy. You can't have it."

He yapped and jumped up, trying to retrieve it from her hands. She pulled it away just before he could grab it.

Maybe it wasn't a good time for this. She put the device safely away in the chest and shut the heavy lid. Why did Pip make such a huff about it all of a sudden? Maybe he knew something she didn't.

"Is that better?"

He yawned and left the room, clearly focused on something else now.

The doorbell rang and she headed downstairs to find Kato, Kobe, and Simon being greeted warmly by her grandfather. Soon, everyone had a seat at the table and were chatting away and enjoying the food and company.

Kobe remained mostly silent during the meal, but looked up once or twice in acknowledgment during the conversation. Simon, on the other hand, could not stop yapping away.

"My dad overheard rumors that some people are trying to close down the TitusTech lab where he works."

Kato's ears perked up. "What?"

Simon continued. "Yeah. He said people are getting suspicious because of the pollution in the area, and some authorities want to shut it down. But he also heard that some other authorities want to keep it open. It's like there's a hidden conflict going on."

Sam remembered hearing about the environmental issues: the rivers becoming highly toxic, and the negative effects on aquatic life. There had been massive fish deaths in the past. Community residents were highly suspicious that TitusTech Industries had something to do with it, but it proved difficult to establish direct cause due to the secrecy surrounding Titus's labs.

She thought back to the incident with the hundreds of dead fish Kato's father had witnessed. According to his detailed journal entries, it had been close to the TitusTech lab. She wondered whether shutting down the lab would help restore the natural habitat. If so, maybe the fish would thrive again, and Kato and Kobe's dad could return for work. But what would that mean for Simon's dad?

Before Sam could ask more questions, she realized the conversation had already shifted to a discussion about board games, and in particular, Galaxy Diplomats: Starquest.

"Do you ever feel like that game is kind of one-sided?" Simon asked.

"What do you mean?" Kato said.

"Like, it's forcing people to think a certain way. The goal is to make friends with the Carinas so we can mine their star. But, I mean, how do the Carinas really feel about that? It makes you think we're winning if we take advantage of their resources. But are we? What if they would be better off if we just didn't go to their planet in the first place?"

"True," Kato noted. "But then we would lose the game. We wouldn't complete the mission."

"Hmm," Simon mused. "Maybe we should rewrite the rules, or create our own sequel, but from the Carinas' perspectives."

"Now *that* would be cool!" Kato said.

As they continued eating and chatting, Sam wondered how Kobe was making out with *The Mind Traveler's Teachings*, but was too shy to ask. Even if she did bring it up, knowing his non-verbal nature around others, it would probably result in an awkward silence. He probably wouldn't care to respond.

Wouldn't it be amazing if she could communicate with him telepathically, like how she and Onnisa had done? It would make things so much easier! She decided to test her ability in this matter.

Can anyone hear me?

She looked around the table, but everyone was immersed in chewing their food and enjoying the meal.

CAN ANYONE HEAR ME? She thought the words as loudly as she could and directed them at Kobe.

He suddenly looked up from his plate. "I can hear you," he replied, the first words he had ever spoken to her in front of other people. Everyone looked up from their plates. He had finished his meal early.

"What's that, Kobe?" Kato blinked, surprised. She slid him a sideways glance.

He looked sheepish. "Sorry, I thought Sam said something."

Sam felt her face turning red. "No, I didn't say anything."

She heard Kobe's thoughts in her mind.

What is going on? Am I imagining things?

Sam directed the words again at Kobe. *No, you're not. It's okay. Just play along, and I'll explain later.*

He nodded and wiped his face with his napkin. "I guess I just *thought* I heard it. Anyway, I'm finished dinner. Can I please be excused from the table?"

Sam figured this was the most verbal discussion they'd witnessed from him in a long time. Kato and everyone else couldn't find words, and they all just sat there in silence and awe.

"Of course." Sam's grandfather looked delighted with Kobe's good manners.

"Thank you for the meal, Walter, it was really good."

"You're most welcome, Kobe!"

Kobe cleared his plate and left the table, heading to the den to read *The Mind Traveler's Teachings*.

When they finished dinner, Kato and Sam reconvened in Sam's room.

"That's the first time Kobe has spoken publicly in a long time! He really seems to have a connection with you, Sam."

"I don't know. Maybe it's the book that's helping him."

"Maybe. He hasn't put it down since you gave it to him." Kato paused and added, "But it's as if he can read your thoughts, or something."

"That would be strange!" She considered telling Kato about her secret gift, about being able to communicate with other people using her mind, but she wasn't sure if now was the best time to tell her.

The girls both jumped when they heard a loud knock on the door.

"It's Kobe. And Simon. Can we join you?"

"Sure."

They opened the door and closed it behind them. Simon immediately set his eyes on Sam's telescope. "Wow, that's pretty cool. Mind if I try it?"

"Go ahead. Just don't break it."

Kato began chatting with Sam again about the possibility and implications of the TitusTech lab shutting down, but only a matter of seconds passed before they all stopped what they were doing.

Kobe glanced over at them. "Did you hear that?"

They were all silent for a moment, listening.

"What?"

"I don't know—just…listen. It's a low humming noise. I think it's coming from that wooden chest over there."

Sam's eyes grew wide. "I don't hear any…" Her voice trailed off as the noise grew louder. Her heart skipped a beat. It sounded like the klug had been activated. But how? She hadn't touched its red button. She hadn't shaken it nor called out the name of a place. What was happening? She'd wanted to keep the klug a secret, but realized it was probably too late now. She took a deep breath, letting it out slowly.

They all looked to the wooden chest as it began to rock and shake. Seconds later, the chest opened by itself and the klug shot into the air. It whirred louder as it levitated in front of them.

"Sam? What's going on?" Kato got to her feet and took a step backward against the door. "What is that thing?"

"It's…I've never seen it do *that* before!"

The klug floated in front of them, spinning quickly and shining bright blue. A moment later, a hologram of a star system appeared.

"Whoa!" Kobe reached out to touch the stars, his hand waving in and out of the holographic light projected around the room.

Sam immediately identified the star system—the Libra constellation. Was the klug trying to tell her something? Maybe she needed to go there to find the Hopewell Star?

As they watched, something even stranger happened: they found themselves being pulled toward the klug.

"Sam, what's happening?" Kato gasped, trying to hold onto something firm, but it was no use. She leaned back, but the invisible force dragged her feet toward its center.

"I...I don't know! It's like...it's like it's creating a gravitational field, or something!" Sam tried taking a step backward, nervous about the klug's erratic behavior, but it was like being sucked in by a gigantic vacuum.

Simon reached out toward the bed frame, but didn't grasp hold in time. The gravitational force pulled them all toward its center, and a bright flash of light blinded them. A moment later, a wormhole emerged and they fell downward, farther and faster toward the end of the tunnel. Sam felt the familiar air current of the wormhole, the dizzying travel and the tunnel that warped around and twisted every way, causing much disorientation. She heard screaming and shouting, the sound magnified within the wormhole. She tried to focus on her friends, but they were speeding so fast, and the light was so blinding that she couldn't see them any longer.

"Kato?" she called out, the word reverberating around her eardrums and echoing a thousand times inside her skull. She blinked a few times and closed her eyes. When she opened them again, she saw the end of the tunnel up ahead.

Each of them, one by one, emerged from the wormhole. Sam found herself falling and then hitting a hard surface that felt like concrete, and a moment later, tumbling down a sandy hill.

Sam coughed and wiped the sand out of her face and mouth. She looked around. Kobe and Simon were also at the base of the hill, slowly getting to their feet, brushing off the sand. Kato sat on the ground a few feet away, holding her knees, her eyes glazed over and in shock.

"Kato? Are you okay?" Sam asked, crouching down beside her. Kato nodded but continued staring straight ahead. "Come on, Kobe and Simon are just over there." She offered a hand and helped Kato to her feet, then they made their way over to the boys.

It took a moment to get a sense of their surroundings. Somewhat shaken but fully conscious, Sam looked around at the barren landscape that spread for miles. Mostly sandy terrain, there were large purple sand dunes about ten stories high to the north and east, and rocky terrain to the west, peppered with caves. To the south were sparse desert plants; what looked like cacti, only growing at irregular, perpendicular angles. Although it was still daylight, Sam saw two moons in the distance. They were definitely on another planet.

Simon looked up and pointed at the twin moons. "Am I seeing double?"

"Where are we?" Kobe asked.

They all stood silently, taking in their surroundings.

"Beats me," Sam replied.

"Wherever we are, it doesn't look like Earth," Simon said. He grabbed his stomach and heaved up his meal. All of them looked a little pale. Kato went over and patted him on the back.

Sam grasped the klug in her hand, but to her surprise, it didn't react to her touch. She shook it, but it didn't glow like it had in the past. "That's odd."

"What's that?" Kobe asked.

"It's not working like it normally does."

Kato came to her senses and looked over at them both. "Nothing about this situation is normal. Sam, can you please tell us how to get back with that…thing?"

Sam shrugged. "Usually all I do is shake it and say the name of the place I want to go, but it's not working. I'm not sure what happened. It's like it used my mind to activate itself on its own. Maybe something happened to it while we were traveling through that wormhole."

"You mean, you've used it to travel to other planets *before*?"

"I needed to keep it a secret. But now that we're here, I may as well tell you."

"Tell us what?" Simon asked.

Sam proceeded to tell them about her journey to Kryg, and how the Krygians had chosen her as their queen. She told them about the prophecy and her mission to find the Hopewell Star to save both planets. She realized how foolish it sounded, but tried her best to keep her cool. When she finished, she could feel her face burning.

"That's wicked," Simon said. "Almost feels like we're playing Galaxy Diplomats: Starquest, only for realsies."

"So, now what?" Kobe asked. "I mean, if that device got us here, it can bring us back, right?"

"Where did you get it, Sam?" Kato asked.

"My friend Boj, gave it to me. It's a long story," Sam replied. She didn't feel like going into too much detail at the moment. Besides, she wasn't the only one having trouble digesting so much new information and comprehending their strange circumstances. Everyone looked exhausted, and she could feel a heaviness in the air around them, a sense of confusion and uncertainty weighing them down.

Simon sighed and bent to touch the sandy ground. "It's so hot here. I think we'd better start looking for water. We don't want to die of thirst."

Kobe looked around. "Are those trees in the distance?" He pointed to a hill in the west with caves and sparse shrubs near the base. "There should be a water source."

"Good call." Kato dusted herself off and headed in that direction. Simon followed, and Sam and Kobe brought up the rear, exchanging worried glances.

They walked in silence, and after an hour they came to the base of the hill. As Kobe had guessed, a large river flowed nearby, providing a source of water for the nearby shrubs.

Kato was about to place her hand in the cool water when something rustled in the bushes across the river.

"Shh!" Kobe stopped, frozen in place. "Did you hear that?"

"No, I—"

A woman emerged from the other side of the river, dressed all in white, her black hair long and straight. Although short in height, her arms and legs were toned and muscular. She carried a long stick in her hands. When she saw them, her serene expression rapidly changed to one of concern and surprise. "Get back from the river! It's not safe!" she yelled, then hurried back to the bushes.

Kato pointed across the river. "Who is that? How did she get here?"

Sam stared after her, trying to find her through the trees and bushes. "I—I don't know."

"Let's just go back the way we came," Kobe said. "I'm getting a weird vibe about this place." He took one step backward and froze. The same woman who had been across the river a moment ago now stood behind them, with her long stick pointed toward them.

Sam gasped, worried she was about to attack them.

"Get down!" the woman screamed.

They cowered in fear as she placed the stick to her mouth and blew air into the long, hollow structure. A small dart flew from the other end and sped toward the river, striking a large, black, worm-like creature that had emerged from the surface. It twitched and fell back into the river, splashing them.

The woman tucked the stick into her satchel. "Poison, made from the petals of the black rose," she said. "Kills them instantly."

"Wha…what was that…creature?" Sam managed to get the words out, but only barely.

"Black water python. They're dangerous, and it's their feeding time." The woman looked around cautiously. "Is it just the four of you?"

Sam looked at Kato, then Kobe and Simon.

Can we trust her? she asked Kobe silently.

I don't think we have a choice.

"Gliese is a dangerous planet," the woman said. "You won't last a day here on your own. Come, you must be tired. You can rest at my place tonight, and we can talk about how you got here, although I think I already know." She peered down at Sam's pocket, the device bulging out of the side.

They walked in silence for a few minutes, following the woman down a rocky path toward a cave in the distance.

"How did you…you were on one side of the river, and then you just vanished and appeared behind us…" Kato said.

The woman stared at her in a way that made Kato shrink back. After an intense moment, the woman softened her gaze, casting her eyes downward, and said, "It's not important."

"Yes, it is! I want to know that I'm not going totally crazy. All of this feels so surreal—hey!"

The woman grabbed Kato's arm and spun her around—away from a small, prickly bush they'd all failed to notice. "Careful, girl. Some of the plants here are poisonous. Just by touching them the poison can get into your skin."

Swallowing, Kato stared down at the bush and took two more steps back.

"And to answer your question, it's called mind traveling," the woman said. "That is how I got here. And if your friend gives me her device, I'll see if I can fix it later."

Sam put the pieces together and gasped. It was only now that she finally understood the connection. The woman before her was one of the Mind Travelers Aruna had spoken about. The most advanced one, the one who could also travel physically by just using her mind. "You're Lijing, aren't you?"

The woman stopped in her tracks and turned her head slowly toward Sam. "Who are you? How did you find me?"

"I'm Sam. I study mind traveling too. It's how I met Aruna. She told me—"

"You've met Aruna?"

"She's looking for you. She said the others...the Henchmen threatened them. She'll be very happy to know you're alive."

The distant light flickered across Lijing's eyes, and Sam thought she saw a darkness inside.

"Do not trust Aruna. She's one of them. She works for the Henchmen."

"What? That's not what she told me."

"Then she told you a lie."

Confused, Sam tried pushing Lijing further for an explanation. "She said there were others like you who could mind travel. She said you trained together, in the fifth dimension, where the garden is. I've been there too. Katiya, Atticus...Theo—she said you were the strongest of them all, and that Theo tried mastering your techniques. She said she hadn't seen the others in years, and..." She remembered Aruna's reaction when she thought about Theo and Atticus, and the tears they both shed when Sam had traveled into Aruna's mind. "She was sad when she thought about Theo and Atticus... She thought they may have been captured, or worse—"

"Just stop talking." Lijing looked angry now.

"It's just that—"

Sam felt a tug on her arm. She looked back to see Kato, her face red and flustered. She'd stumbled and reached out for support. Kato whispered to her, away from the others. "Sam, I need a break to catch my breath. I'm sorry."

"No, it's okay."

They stopped and looked back at how far they'd come. The steep hill and rocky terrain made it twice as intense.

Sam decided to respect Lijing's wishes for now, despite her burning curiosity. Besides, her friends kept eyeing her with apprehensive glances, making her think it was not the right time to push things any further.

She realized that Kato's hand still clutched her arm. "How are you feeling?" she asked. "I think we're almost there."

Kato took a deep breath, and they continued upward together for a few more meters. Sam squeezed her hand to offer comfort and encouragement, and caught Kobe glancing back at them. His expression changed. He looked upset about something, but Sam wasn't sure what.

When they reached the mouth of the cave, Lijing continued inside as they followed closely behind. The temperature outside dropped significantly as the sun set. Lijing put together some sticks in her fire pit and gestured to Simon. "Hand me that box of matches."

He tossed it at her and she caught it.

"You hungry?"

Everyone's stomachs rumbled. Lijing brought out a pot of water and hung it on a spit over the fire to boil. As they watched and waited, Lijing began to recount her past experiences.

"Theo was stronger than me," she said while dicing vegetables for their meal. "We trained together—separately from the group. We would explore other planets together. First by mind traveling so we could understand our surroundings, and then physically. It's how I got here. At first, we used devices much like yours to travel to different places. But one day, mine went missing. Theo's too. We received threats from anonymous sources, true. We called them the Henchmen, the ones that took them. But we soon realized that it was still possible to mind travel and physically travel without the devices. It's as though over time the devices' powers fused into our minds. We were able to tap into that power, and access it whenever we wanted. You can understand, the possibilities were immense…"

Sam pulled out her klug and examined it. She rubbed her finger over the symbols, but nothing happened. It seemed broken now; it no longer hummed like it used to. Disappointment and intense worry rose up inside her. She realized she wasn't only responsible for herself, but also for Kato, Kobe, and Simon's safe return home.

"Is it broken?" Lijing asked, staring at it in her hands. "How did you get here if it doesn't work?"

"I don't know. It's like it has a mind of its own now. I didn't even touch it. We were all in my room when it started humming and then pulled us into a wormhole. I didn't even say the name of a place. It just took us here. I don't even know why."

"It must have already fused with your mind too, and you were able to unlock its power without any physical intervention," Lijing explained.

"If that is the case, then how did it know to bring me here? Or if my mind is fused with it somehow, then how did *I* know to come here?"

"I sensed that someone was looking for me, and I was looking for someone too. It—or rather, you—must have sensed it too."

"What?"

"Just a moment," Lijing said as she placed some greens and what looked like onions into the large pot. She signaled for Kobe to stir it while she disappeared toward the back of the cave. A moment later, she returned with a small sheet of parchment paper with writing on it. She gave it to Sam. "Not long ago, I had a strange dream about a girl who looked just like you, who was given an immensely important task, one that would have repercussions in our world and beyond. I don't know what that task is or who gave it to you, but it seems essential to the survival of Earth and the human race. It wasn't like my other dreams; I remembered because it seemed so compelling and vivid at the time. After the dream, I had the image of a place in my mind, so I took down the details. I'm not sure if this will help you. I don't really know what to make of it, but perhaps it will provide guidance on your journey."

Sam's eyes grew wide as she took the parchment paper and slowly opened it to reveal two maps of a star system drawn side-by-side.

"I only ask one favor in return."

"What's that?"

"If you find Theo, please tell him I'm safe, and that I'm waiting for him here. Don't discuss the matter with anyone outside of your friends here."

"Of course. I promise." Sam tucked the map inside her pocket. She would view it later to see if it could provide her with a clue.

They ate the soup in silence. The meal, bland but wholesome, offered a decent and welcome respite from their travels. She could tell the others were gaining their energy back too.

After what seemed like the longest time, Sam spoke up again. "What about Aruna?"

The mention of her name upset Lijing. "Do not trust her."

"But she trained me. She taught me how to develop my abilities. Why would she want to hurt me?"

"She's a spy for the Henchmen. Theo found out while mind traveling. He went inside Aruna's mind and overheard her conversation with one of the Henchmen. The person from their organization—we don't have a name—asked Aruna to spy on new Mind Travelers on the organization's behalf and report them. And then…" Lijing seemed to be lost in thought.

Kato spoke quietly. "And then what?"

"And then…Theo went missing shortly thereafter. I've been waiting for him here. It's our meeting place. As for the others, Atticus is dead and no one knows where Katiya is. I've been in hiding here ever since."

"Oh no!" Sam realized the danger and her vulnerability now. "Then the Henchmen know who I am?"

"Most likely."

"What should I do?"

"Aruna doesn't know your last name, so she won't be able to track you back on Earth. Whatever happens, don't go back to the training site, and never speak to Aruna again. That is the only way to protect yourself."

Sam felt a sense of loss. She'd thought Aruna was a good person. She'd trusted her.

Kobe sensed the confusion in Sam. *Why do you trust this stranger? Maybe Aruna is a good person. Maybe Lijing is the one we shouldn't trust. Maybe it's her version of the story that's incorrect.*

Sam coughed. *I don't know anymore. I thought I knew someone, but if that person lied to me, then I don't know how to tell the difference anymore. I even thought this klug was a gift from my parents, but it turns out it wasn't.*

What does it matter if it was a gift or not? You were meant to have it.

But why?

Sam noticed Simon and Kato exchanging confused looks. Simon spoke up. "Are we missing something?"

"Why don't you ask your friend?" Lijing looked directly at Sam. "You should tell them the truth."

"The truth about what?" Kato asked.

Sam and Kobe exchanged glances. "Sorry, Kato. I meant to tell you earlier. That book I shared with your brother…it's given us the power to read each other's minds." Sam sensed Kobe had a predisposition for this power, one that the book only triggered, but she kept that part to herself.

Simon stopped chewing. "No way!"

Kobe smiled awkwardly. "It's true."

"Okay, now I'm really going crazy!" Kato said. "This is like some messed up dream. I'm going to wake up and see you at school tomorrow."

Sam and Kobe didn't say anything in response, just shook their heads.

Sam found herself moving her fingers slowly over the klug, desperately waiting for it to respond. But it didn't. She wondered if Lijing ever ran into this problem with hers. Was the klug truly broken? Why wasn't it responding? Could she trust Lijing to revive it? It seemed she knew a lot about self-sufficiency, living here on this lonely and desolate planet. And she had, after all, saved them from a black water python. Feeling the dilemma, Sam sensed they were running out of options. Trusting Lijing might be the only survivalist thing to do under the current circumstances.

As if anticipating her thoughts, Lijing spoke up. "Now, do you want me to try and fix that device of yours?"

Sam hesitated.

"Sometimes these devices aren't truly broken, they're just entering a new phase. The technology acts differently."

Sam wondered whether the same thing had happened to Lijing, and what she meant about entering a new phase. Lijing definitely knew more about it than she did.

"Yes, please. If you could..." Sam held it out to her, the klug resting gently in her palm.

Lijing took the klug and examined it. "Interesting. It's very similar to the one I had, only...different."

"How so?"

"The hieroglyphics...some of them are more intricate compared to the ones on mine. Also, it's a heavier, denser material." She pulled a paperclip out of her pocket and held it close to the klug. She let go and it traveled in midair and clung to the klug, as if it had magnetic properties. She looked up. "Huh. It's a very strange, very foreign material. It's more like Theo's, only..."

"What is it?"

"Nothing. I'll need some time to work on it."

"Thank you," Sam said. She quietly wondered how long it would take, and if they would ever make it back to Earth. But there was no sense worrying about things outside her control. She pushed the negative thoughts away to make room for hopefully more pleasant ones.

12

As Lijing worked tirelessly examining the klug and testing its structure with her tools, everyone else huddled around the fire to keep warm. Sam pulled out the parchment paper with the star system maps, but no matter how closely she studied it, she couldn't make sense of its details. She tried looking for familiar star patterns—like the big dipper, the great square of Pegasus, and others that she knew of—but with no luck.

"If this is a star system, I've never seen it before. I don't think it's one in our galaxy." She took a moment to compare the two images. They looked exactly the same at first glance. The stars and planets and their placements were identical, except for one glaring detail that stood out now that she reviewed it more closely: one of the stars was *missing* in the second image.

"Can I take a look?" Simon crouched down beside her to get a better view.

Sam turned the paper toward him, then traced her finger around the different objects on the first map. "See, these look like planets here in the first image. The circles are their orbital paths around this star at the center, their sun. But in the second image, the same star has disappeared. And…" She paused, noticing something. "That's weird."

"What?"

"Well, looking at the first image, I'm not sure if it *is* a sun because…" She squinted and brought the paper closer to the light of the fire. Upon closer inspection, she noticed a tiny shaded hexagonal pattern on top of the star, partially covering it. It made the star look darker than the planets circling it. "I'm not sure what that hexagonal pattern represents. It looks like it's covering the star…but *is* it even a star?"

"Maybe it's not a star. It could be something else, maybe," Simon said.

"Maybe there's something else we can't see on the drawings," Kato offered. "Maybe a black hole?"

Everyone fell silent.

"A black hole?" Kobe laughed. "That's the most ridiculous thing I've ever heard. *Nothing* survives a black hole. Not even light. I mean, if it were a black hole, wouldn't it swallow up more of the planets in the vicinity?"

Sam considered it further, exploring Kato's suggestion and its implications. Black holes had a strong gravitational pull, and sure, light and energy would be sucked into one if they got too close. "If it's a black hole, it may explain why the star is no longer showing in the second image," she said. "The star could have collapsed within the black hole, and that would mean...well...if it's the Hopewell Star, that would mean it no longer exists." She hated to think of the consequences, and how Onnisa would take the news if it were true.

"Wait, look!" Kato pointed to the second image. "Look there! There's something else! It looks like there's another planet or something that's not included in the first image, close to where the star was, only it's really small."

Sam peered at the second image, comparing it again to the first. Kato was right. The star was missing in the second image, but in its place, close to where it had been, appeared another, smaller circle.

"Possibly an asteroid, or the remnants of an explosion. You know, two planets colliding, or something?" Simon suggested.

Sam's head spun. She needed a break.

Everyone looked confused and tired. Simon's question dissipated into the air, along with possible answers that floated out of reach as everyone went silent. Sam looked over at Lijing, who continued tinkering with the klug; it didn't seem to respond to the stimuli. It no longer glowed like it once did; its lifeless shell devoid of any movement or glimmer of energy, or hope for that matter.

As if reflecting Sam's thoughts, Kato spoke up, breaking the silence and steering the conversation away from the present issue. "So, I'm curious about what you said earlier, Sam. Can you really read my brother's mind?"

The question caught Sam off guard. "Yes."

Kobe nodded.

"Well, how does it work?"

"I don't really know. It just...happens."

Sam felt awkward, like they were wondering about the extent of her telepathic abilities, and they wanted a better explanation.

"I have an idea," Simon began, a slight grin forming. "Let's see if

Sam can read Kato's mind."

"What?"

"Yeah! I mean, we're just waiting around for now, with nothing better to do. We can test Sam's abilities in the meantime while Lijing is working away. Of course, only if you two are up for it…yeah? It could serve as our entertainment for the evening."

Sam thought about it. "Sure. What do you think, Kato?"

They all perked up. Kato turned to face Sam. "Okay. I'm going to think of an object. You can have two guesses. No clues."

Sam nodded and took a deep breath. She let the air out slowly as she focused on Kato's mind. She imagined herself seeing an image in front of her, but there existed only darkness. She focused her mind on her breath and felt a deep sense of calm. And then…

A shape flickered in front of her, orange and yellow in color. A flame.

"Is it fire?"

"No. One more guess."

The flame in Sam's mind grew larger and transformed into another, more concrete shape. A little girl, with dark eyes and a little flower band around her head, but her facial features were blurred.

Suddenly, the klug whirred back to life and Lijing jumped back.

"Sam, I think it's working now."

Sam snapped out of her trance. Almost at the same time, she heard a thud as the klug dropped to the ground.

Lijing frowned. "Sorry, I was wrong. Don't mind me." She picked up the klug and examined it once more.

Sam took a deep breath and calmed her mind, concentrating again on the shape, the image of the little girl, but stopped when she heard Lijing gasp. Everyone looked toward the klug. Its surface crackled and buzzed, as if it had produced a shock of electricity.

A moment later, the image crystallized: it was a young girl who looked much like Kato and Kobe's younger sister.

"Darlene?" Sam asked.

Kato's eyes grew wide. "Yes."

"Look!" Simon shouted, pointing.

The klug floated up into the air, its light pulsating and radiating outward.

Sam was relieved at the thought of returning home, and she could tell her friends felt the same way. "Thank you, Lijing, for fixing it."

"It wasn't my tools that activated it. It was your mind, just as I thought."

The same gravitational field emerged around them. Everyone gasped as the force became stronger, pulling Sam and her friends closer to its center.

Lijing stepped back, trying to stay outside of the gravitational field's grasp. "Remember your promise about Theo!"

"I will. Thank you for your help, but there's one last thing I need to know." Sam paused, thinking about her training in the fifth dimension. "Aruna always blocked a door in the garden. I want to know...what's on the other side?"

Lijing grinned. "If you can travel into Kato's mind, then you already know the answer. The door is a passageway to Aruna's mind. She's guarding it because she doesn't want you to know the whole truth. Now, go! And good luck to you all!"

The gravitational field pulled them faster now, and Sam felt the same spinning and falling motion as they traveled down the wormhole. What seemed like minutes later, they were back in Sam's room. They all jumped as someone knocked on the door.

"Come in," Sam called.

Kato and Kobe's sister, Darlene, opened the door. "Mom says it's getting late and it's time to come home now."

A moment of silence passed, and everyone looked at each other in amazement. Kato was especially relieved to see Darlene. Sam glanced at her clock. Eight in the evening. Only forty-five minutes had passed since they left her room.

Kato sighed. "Already? Feels like we just got here!"

"I'm just the messenger! If you want to stay longer, you go tell Mom. She's downstairs."

Kato laughed. She went over and gave Darlene a big hug.

"What was that for?"

"Can't a big sister give her little sister a hug once in a while, just because?"

"I guess so." Darlene turned and ran back downstairs, her little feet thumping on the steps.

Kato turned to Sam. "Would it be okay if I stayed over?"

"Yeah, of course. So you're okay with...everything?"

Kato smiled. "I'm good. A bit shaken up, but glad to be home. Seriously, that trip we went on was pretty awesome! And the mind thing…that could be super helpful. You'll have to teach me how to do it."

Sam blushed. "Sure, I can try."

Kobe got up and stretched. "We've got to keep this between ourselves. If anyone else finds out…"

Simon nodded. "You're right. It's dangerous for others to know. Like what Lijing said about the Henchmen. Best to keep this a secret."

"Promise?" Sam asked.

"Promise," her friends replied in unison.

13

Titus looked up from his desk. He thought he heard gentle knocking at the door. "Come in," he commanded.

Dr. Endo Lloyd, lead scientist for the TitusTech Human-Mind Robotics Laboratory, entered the room, his hands shaking. "Sir, I have some bad news."

Titus swiveled around in his chair. "Tell me you found it."

The man cleared his throat. "We found it, sir, the Krygian base in the moon's interior. Just as you suspected."

Titus sighed with relief, relaxing his jaw muscles.

"However, there was a glitch."

"What do you mean, a *glitch*?"

"Sir, they reported to have found underground passageways, and some sort of ancient spaceport, just as your source—Theo—had described. But something disrupted the communication and we couldn't decipher all of it. And then…an explosion occurred."

"An explosion?"

Dr. Lloyd held out a small device the size of a marble, which Titus took and placed on his computer so the images could transfer and upload to a larger screen.

"You can see for yourself."

Titus started the video footage. It began with two men descending with ropes into the massive compound. The camera was unsteady, as if it had been mounted to a helmet, with the image shaking as the person moved. It proved difficult to make out the images clearly in the dark settings at first. The narrow beams of the men's flashlights only carried so far, projecting toward their immediate environment. He made out what looked like tunnels and black cave walls. The footage cut out every few seconds as the men made their way through the tunnels, taking in what they could of their surroundings. When they made it to the bottom of the chasm, one of the men set up a large floodlight, allowing them to see more details of the huge space in front of them.

"Wow! Will you look at that!" he exclaimed. The camera scanned the spaceport, zooming in to catch the details of an abandoned ship. The camera zoomed in closer as it focused on the hieroglyphics along the sides of the tunnels. The audio cut in and out.

As the two men made their way further, the other man shouted, "I think this facility is still in use." Blue lighting lit the tunnels and a white light glowed at one of the tunnel entrances. It seemed to lead to a curved entryway, perhaps to a room.

"Are you seeing this?"

The video cut out as they approached the entryway, then the image reappeared on the screen for an instant. Despite the flicker and delay in video feed, there looked to be other figures in the room, but the footage was blurry. In less than a second, the video went black, but the audio continued, with voices shouting. One of the men yelled, "Abort! *Abort!*" A loud popping noise erupted, and the image on the screen went blank.

"That's all we have, sir. I'm sorry."

"Rewind it," Titus demanded.

Dr. Lloyd rewound the video in slow-motion.

"There. Stop. Go back."

The feed settled on the image of the two blurry figures in the room. One figure seemed to be holding something.

"Can you enhance the image?"

Dr. Lloyd entered a code into the computer and the image became clearer.

"Again," Titus ordered. "Can you zoom in?" The image sharpened and he gasped. It was…a girl. Stunned, his eyes fixated on the device in her hand. A klug? But how?

"Well done, Dr. Lloyd. As you can see here…" He continued with determination and excitement, pointing to the screen. "Another klug has been detected, and it's in this girl's possession. Can you complete facial recognition?"

The doctor complied. The computer ran the algorithm and sorted through its database. After a few moments, another screen popped up, showing the faces of two individuals: a human and a Krygian.

He hadn't seen this particular Krygian before. She looked old, perhaps one of their Elders. Additional information quickly materialized on the screen beside her image.

Name: Onissa
Age: Unknown
Home planet: Kryg
Current location: Unknown

He examined the face of the girl with red hair and freckles. Additional information populated the screen beside her image as well.

Name: Samantha Sanderson
Age: 12
Home planet: Earth
Current Location: 19 Maple River Drive, Moncton, New Brunswick
Current School: Otter Lake Public School
Parents: Dr. Lynne Wilson, Dr. Steve Sanderson

"Hmm," Titus mused. "I didn't realize Agents Sanderson and Wilson had a child, or that she was somehow involved in all of this. Clearly there is a connection between this girl and the Krygian Elder. Dr. Lloyd, from the video feed, it is obvious that this child is in possession of a klug. I would like you and Bjørn to quietly monitor the Sanderson residence. Retrieve the klug and bring it to me. We must study it further. If all else fails, we must find the girl and question her."

"Agreed. But sir—"

"Yes, what is it?"

"Do you still need Theo, or shall we…?"

"No. Actually…yes. He could prove useful in the future. Let's keep him contained for further questioning, if necessary."

"Very good, sir. Will do."

Titus was mindful of the gravity of the situation and the need to plan his next steps carefully. Gathering of information would be necessary in order to confirm his suspicions about the girl.

"Also, contact his colleague—the other Mind Traveler—this week."

"The woman with the dragon mask, sir? Aruna?"

"Yes. I want to know if she has been in contact with any *new* Mind Travelers since we last spoke."

"Yes, sir."

"And Endo, as always, you must ensure that she does not recognize your connection to me or TitusTech Industries."

"Yes, sir. Understood."

When Dr. Lloyd left the room and closed the door gently, Titus studied the image in the database.

"This will be easier than I thought. Sam Sanderson, it's time we pay you a little visit."

* * *

Onnisa did not want to visit the maximum-security prison, Krajakan.

Located on the remote island of Kroog, it held the most dangerous and dodgiest of prisoners. It was the last place she wanted to go.

But she *had* to.

It held the last known Rigellian. The entire Rigellian civilization had gone missing years ago under strange and mysterious circumstances, along with the Hopewell Star. The Rigellians knew most about the twin prophecy of Earth and Kryg. After all, they were the ones who had created the Hopewell Star in the first place. She needed to speak with the Rigellian prisoner, Okruni, and find out whether the prophecy about the girl was true. At the very least, maybe he could provide a clue as to the whereabouts of other Rigellians who could help.

She shuddered at the thought of seeing all the spiteful prisoners whom the Elders had locked away over the years. Like Drutu, from the planet Luyten, with his menacing spiked tentacles and disgusting demeanor, leaving trails of his slime all over his enclosure. Or the Venoba from the Proxima Centauri region, three times the size of any Krygian and one hundred times as strong. The prison's architects and engineers had designed and built a specialized containment system for it.

And, of course, there existed a high probability that she would cross paths with the Krygians Xonat and Xobot, and their accomplices, those others of the Kantak tribe who had been found guilty of killing Mukalakatakalakum. The thought of his death was still fresh in her mind. Seeing them would be a grave reminder of the Krygians' failings to eradicate violence. This marked the first murder by one of their own in nearly a century.

Elder Ajisav had said darkness was coming, but he was wrong. It was already here, and it was spreading.

A prison guard stood inside the entrance. He was a member of the Kantak tribe, with symbols branded into his body. "What business have you here?"

"I wish to visit one of the prisoners. The Rigellian."

"Do you accept the risks?" He was referring to the possibility that the Rigellian would manipulate Onnisa. Rigellians not only had the power of telepathy, but also a way of changing people's thoughts and moods, enticing them to do things they normally wouldn't do.

"I do."

"Sign here." He held a screen up toward her. She pressed her hand upon it. "Block three, cell seventeen. First door on your left leads you there, through the corridor."

She made her way down the damp and darkened corridor of the abysmal prison to block three, where they kept the prisoner containment units. The walls and floor of the prison had an unmistakable acrid scent to them. Cleanliness wasn't their top priority here.

Onnisa shuddered. Lining the walls in front of her, she immediately recognized the graffiti, the words in the Krygian language: ELDERS TELL LIES and NOT MY QUEEN were scribbled in bold black letters. Had the guards written this, or the prisoners? She felt vulnerable, and had second thoughts about coming here. Would she even be able to trust what the Rigellian said? Or maybe the effects of prison had made the Rigellian more cooperative and agreeable? She hoped for the latter.

Up ahead, she saw the familiar containment units. Each section was cordoned off by beams of electric pulses of light and karon, a translucent, robust metal that only existed on Kryg. It could be fashioned for different purposes, its properties sturdy and durable. Gas was regularly emitted into the containment units to keep the prisoners cooperative, relaxed, and non-adversarial. Over time it took its toll, wearing the worst of them down into mindless creatures with vacant eyes and often a loss of memory.

Hopefully the Rigellian still had some of his memories left.

They kept the worst prisoners here, with no chance of rehabilitation into society. Their horrific crimes were numerous. Onnisa had visited the prison only once in her lifetime, years ago, to interview an inmate. She still had nightmares about it.

She passed cells six and seven, which held Xonat and Xobot. They perked up and ran to the edges of the cells to get a closer look as she passed, contempt spreading across their faces. They hadn't been here long enough for the gas to really affect them.

"You won't be successful, Onnisa," Xonat said with a sneer.

"Elder scum!" Xobot yelled. "The human-lover!"

"That girl that's so precious to you, Onnisa…that dirty human is not my queen!" Xonat shouted.

Onnisa remained silent, but the heat rose through her body.

"She's here to see the Rigellian," Xonat continued, a darkness flickering in his eyes. "You'll see soon. The Hopewell Star is dead!" He laughed, a maniacal sound that reverberated against her eardrums. "But go! Go see the Rigellian! Go waste your time!"

Onnisa continued down the corridor, the laughter following her as she made her way to cell seventeen. The Kantak prisoners looked too happy about their dire situation. Did they know something she didn't? Were the Kantak planning something? She feared they were preparing a revolt of some sort. She'd need to discuss with Elder Boku when she saw him next, to see if he had any further clues from his sources.

Okruni sat hunched over, his scaly body thin and his skin lighter from being imprisoned for so long without natural light. Onnisa looked into his large, vacant eyes and heard the familiar humming as she approached him. Rigellians' speech, delivered through a low hum, allowed them to communicate with others telepathically. Hearing Okruni's words put her in a relaxed and trancelike state.

"You've come to see me about the prophecy," he said slowly. "And you've brought me something of value for it."

Rigellians were known for their ability to see and sometimes change future events. They were an extremely advanced society, and had the ability to occasionally change an outcome using just their minds. This proved dangerous to those who didn't know how to block or work with the ability. Onnisa knew how to do both.

"I wish to know more about the Hopewell Star prophecy," Onnisa stated carefully. "And yes, I offer you a gift in exchange." She'd decided to break prison protocol, offering what she had brought in exchange for his knowledge, or what remained of it. There existed a small opening in the containment unit, through which food could be passed to the prisoners. From her pocket she withdrew the gift: a few karamelon berries.

Okruni's eyes grew wide. The berries were a delicacy on Kryg, and the Rigellian probably hadn't had anything like them in years. At least, not in this prison.

Onnisa pressed the button to open the hatch and placed her hand inside, offering them up.

"I have suffered a lot over time, and am remorseful for my actions," Okruni began. "I don't have much time left, Onnisa. You do not need to trick me with berries for the information you seek. I will gladly share what I know." As Okruni took the berries, Onnisa reached for his hand and let the sparks fly between them. Instead of pulling back, Okruni appeared agreeable to share his experiences and knowledge with Onnisa. The images in Onnisa's mind became clearer as Okruni spoke.

"The girl will be successful in saving Kryg, but she will not be successful in saving Earth. She will sacrifice one for the other."

Onnisa held on just a bit longer. "What will happen to Earth?"

"There will be an external force at play, a threat from…another civilization that targets humans, or a human that creates a disease. I see an accident with terrible consequences."

"I did not expect this," Onnisa said, retracting her hand from the Rigellian as he paused to eat the berries.

The information he'd provided was not exact nor fully formed; it remained vague. Perhaps that meant he was mistaken, or the events could be altered if changes were made in time. If the Rigellian's visions proved correct and the Earth could not be saved by the girl, perhaps it still could be saved by someone or something else.

"I know my civilization is still alive," Okruni said. "Please, Onnisa, find them. They can help the girl. I know nothing more. I wish you good fortune in your journey."

"I will do my best, Okruni. Thank you for your time and knowledge. I must leave you now."

Okruni bowed his head in respect. Onnisa acknowledged, then walked swiftly back down the corridor to the main entrance.

Xobot and Xonat watched as Onnisa passed.

"Did you find your answer, Elder?" Xonat asked.

"Maybe it's too late," Xobot added. "Or maybe the Rigellian told her lies!"

"Good riddance to the last Rigellian!" Xonat said. "Good riddance to the prophecy!" They laughed as she quickly exited the corridor.

The guard stood at the main entrance, the screen in his hand. "Sign here."

Onnisa pressed her hand once again to the screen.

The guard shifted on his feet. "Did you find anything else from the Rigellian, compared to the visit earlier today?"

"What do you mean, *earlier*?" Onnisa asked. "I've only come to visit once."

"You weren't the first to visit the Rigellian today. Another Elder came by."

"Who?"

"The one named Boku."

Onnisa was taken aback. She had no recollection of Boku mentioning this visit to her or the other Elders. Typically, they were expected to share this type of information in advance, especially a dangerous visit to the Krajakan prison. Had she known that Boku

127

intended to visit the prison as well, they could have made the trip together. Then again, because Boku was on a covert mission to obtain information from the Kantak people, perhaps this tied in. Maybe Boku deemed discretion necessary in this situation, so as not to share this information with anyone else, not even the other Elders.

But Onnisa sensed something strange about the situation. It did not add up. If Boku were visiting prisoners to gather information for his covert mission, Xonat and Xobot, the two Kantak tribe criminals, would have been the more appropriate choices for interrogation, not the Rigellian. Also, the timing of such rare visits to the same prisoner was odd. What did the Rigellian and Boku discuss? What were Boku's motivations?

Elders were able to grant their own authorization for trips, so there existed no oversight by a higher authority. Boku must have deemed it important to schedule a trip here. Perhaps she was reading too much into the matter.

"Did Boku mention the purpose of his meeting?" Onnisa inquired.

The guard's eyes narrowed. Onnisa noticed an infinity symbol tattooed on his right arm as he slid the screen back into a small compartment. He belonged to the Kantak people, and they weren't always forthcoming with information, especially with other Krygians. "I am not at liberty to say."

Onnisa felt as if she'd uncovered a dark truth. "Thank you. Have a good day," she said as she stepped back and headed swiftly outside to her ship. At least it was still there.

The prison itself had been cold enough, but as she left into the night, she felt a terrible trembling down her spine.

* * *

Sam felt a shiver inside and goosebumps along her arms. A dense fog saturated the air and her mind, but the cave was oddly warm. The heat from bodies. Many of them. Why did she feel so on edge?

She heard muffled voices approaching from the distance. She wasn't expecting visitors. But where was she? It seemed familiar—but how could that be? She'd never been here before, had she?

"Who's there?" her voice boomed. It wasn't her own voice, but that of Mukalakatakalakum. She looked down at her hands, only to realize that in their place were massive claws. She stood up swiftly, feeling power and strength in her body, but an uneasy feeling in the pit of her stomach.

They were coming for her.

Through her sensory night vision, she noticed the natural light emanating from the cave's walls flickering in an unnatural way. The voices were closer now.

"*Mukalakatakalakum mip makabuk!*" the voices chanted. *Mukalakatakalakum must die!*

Her heart pounded as a sudden beam of light pierced into her dwelling. She tried to shield her eyes from the harsh glare, but it blinded and disoriented her. She panicked, unable to make out the figures in the cave. As she tried to claw at them in defense, they struck her with their weapons. She cried out in pain.

The last thing she saw flashed before her eyes and lingered in her mind: the infinity symbol, branded into their flesh.

The dream shifted and Sam found herself back on the moon base where she had met with Onnisa. Only, it looked much different now. The base bustled with activity and otherworldly beings, but there was no sign of Onnisa. She watched as the beings interacted, but they didn't seem to notice her. They didn't look like Krygians. They were tall, slender, and hairless, their skin scaly and lizard-like with elongated and subtle features. Where there could have been ears and a nose, instead were only indents. Their mouths were small compared to human mouths, and didn't seem to move when they interacted with one another. Instead, they emitted a low humming noise. The sound, peaceful and soothing, calmed Sam's nerves. Their large, buggy eyes had hexagonal patterns on them that flickered in the light.

They looked familiar. Mukalakatakalakum had mentioned something about an ancient civilization creating the Hopewell Star. It started with an *r*. The Raglans? No…the Rigellians? He'd said something about a lizard-like race of beings, and recalled images of the creatures as he spoke of them. They looked exactly like the creatures before her.

As she inched closer, it seemed they were all fixated on the screens in front of them. Sam watched as upsetting images displayed across the screens; images of violent interactions between fellow humans and the destruction of habitats.

The Rigellians moved into another space, something that looked like a laboratory of sorts, and she followed them, watching closely. They began working with strange, otherworldly tools and liquids, creating what looked like klugs. In the center of the room glowed a current of energy. One of the Rigellians placed a klug in the center of the energy's current. It seemed to activate the klug, opening up its core. They then placed some glowing white liquid in its center and repeated the process for the remaining five klugs. Next, the Rigellians moved toward the screens again, and Sam followed. She watched intently as sudden images appeared of complex drawing plans, specifications, galaxies, and star systems.

A moment later, Sam noticed a Krygian among the other beings. Why hadn't she noticed him before? He had an odd marking on his forehead, what looked like an infinity symbol, similar to the one she saw on the bodies of the other Krygians earlier in her dream. The ones who had killed Mukalakatakalakum. The Krygian tapped the screen, and each of them took turns signing their names on the plans. They completed the task by drawing another infinity symbol.

They all returned to the laboratory. Sam watched in awe as the current of energy grew stronger, and they placed what looked like a marble at the center. It glowed a fiery yellow and hovered in the room, sending off a wave of heat. Sam felt it flow through her body, and she began to sweat profusely. The beings then operated a machine, and the ball of light traveled through the current and out of the moon base into space. They monitored the screens, and Sam stared in amazement as the ball of light grew steadily larger as it worked its trajectory, moving farther and faster away from the moon base, all the way into what looked like another galaxy. As it sped faster, it expanded in size until it was massive, the size of many planets put together. It looked like their sun, only several times larger.

The star didn't look like any other she'd seen before. It glistened a magnificent, multicolored light. It hadn't formed naturally, but was created by these otherworldly beings…

Had she just witnessed the birth of the Hopewell Star?

Sam woke up in a sweat. The dream hung over her like a weight, and it took her a moment to collect her thoughts. Of course it was just a dream. But if it was, why did it feel so much like a memory? That was impossible! Even so, it was as if she'd been there, witnessing the creation of the klugs and the birth of what she speculated was the Hopewell Star. And before that, while finding her bearings in the cave, it was as if she'd experienced what Mukalakatakalakum had before his murder.

A sadness and unsettling feeling grew in the pit of her stomach. She tried desperately to get back to sleep, but couldn't shake the strange thoughts that permeated her mind. Had the dream lasted longer, would it have provided another clue to the location of the Hopewell Star? She tried to understand the significance of the recurring infinity symbol. What did it mean? Were her dreams trying to tell her some sort of truth? She decided she would keep her mind open in the next few weeks, trying to piece things together. But more importantly, she needed to confide in Kato, Kobe, and Simon. She was at a loss for answers, but maybe her friends could help make sense of it. At least, she hoped so.

* * *

The strange dream sequence stuck with her the next day at school. Things seemed different now, and she had a weird feeling, as if the dream had changed her in some bizarre way. Her memories were precise and comprehensive; she was able to recall entire conversations and experiences with people as she passed them in the hall. Her thoughts and ideas formed rapidly in her mind. She was able to pick up on details she would have otherwise missed, like the way Hunter had mud caked on his shoes, even though it hadn't rained for over a week, suggesting he'd gone hiking or ATVing deep in the forest, or on a trip somewhere close to a body of water. She recalled overhearing a conversation earlier that year between Hunter and Vito. Hunter had mentioned that he goes ATVing with his stepbrother sometimes when he's in town. His stepbrother must have been visiting over the weekend.

Something also seemed different today about Kato. She usually tied her hair back in a braid, but today she wore her hair down, letting her wavy strands frame her face. She looked more relaxed, too; she must've been on top of her homework, so maybe she had some extra time to herself. But it wasn't unusual for Kato to complete her homework early. It must've been something else. Had she heard from her father recently?

"So, my dad gets home tonight. It's kind of a surprise visit," Kato said.

She was right. That's why Kato looked in better spirits.

"That's wonderful news, Kato! How long is he visiting for?"

"Just a week, but it'll be nice to see him. We're going out for dinner tonight to celebrate Darlene's birthday."

"I'm so glad to hear you'll have some time to spend together," Sam said. She thought about her own parents and wondered where they were and how they were doing. How she longed to see them! She had so much to tell them.

It felt strange, processing things so differently, as if she could anticipate the outcome of events. Seemingly unimportant details were quickly imprinted in her mind and accessed instantaneously, as if her mind were an infinite memory sponge, soaking up and analyzing information from every source.

During biology class with Ms. Lysander, Sam found herself knowing what her teacher was going to say before she said it. And more than that, it was as if the entire lesson plan had already been mapped out in Sam's mind and entirely understood. As a result, Sam found that everything Ms. Lysander said was repetitive and tedious.

Were her telepathic abilities becoming stronger? She decided to test her theory. Before Ms. Lysander could ask the class another question, Sam raised her hand.

"Frederick Banting and his assistant, Charles Best, discovered insulin."

Ms. Lysander gave her a quizzical nod. "That's true, Sam. Funny, I was about to ask that question to the class. I guess someone has studied this chapter. Well done!"

Kato and Kobe both shot her a sideways glance, and as she looked around, she noticed a bunch of other students staring at her.

Ms. Lysander continued the lesson. Sam wondered if it had been purely coincidental. She decided to test the theory once more.

She raised her hand, and Ms. Lysander noticed it but kept talking. Sam interrupted, delivering the lesson plan word for word.

"We're going to be learning about single-celled and multi-celled organisms today, and the differences between them," Sam and Ms. Lysander said in unison.

Sam continued. "We're going to look at cell walls and cell membranes, and how certain gases and liquids can pass through them. Now, who can tell me what happens when—?" She stopped in time to watch the blood drain out of Ms. Lysander's face.

"That's enough, Sam! You've disrespected me by interrupting. Unless you're here to deliver the lesson plan, please see me after class."

Sam's face flushed, and she was ashamed about disrupting her teacher. She felt the intensity of the other students' stares on the back of her neck. Ms. Lysander continued, but everyone seemed more interested in Sam's outburst and remained silent for the rest of the lesson. No one felt like answering questions.

When class ended, Sam was so focused on her own mistake and disrespectful behavior that she was taken aback when Ms. Lysander requested that Kobe also stay behind for a few minutes. Kobe looked just as surprised, his eyebrows twisted, his gaze shifting around the room, unsure of what to make of the situation.

When most of the students had left, Sam apologized. "I'm so sorry, Ms. Lysander. It was wrong of me to disrupt you and the class like that. I promise it won't ever happen again."

"It's okay, Sam. Not to worry. I think you've learned your lesson. Just make sure not to read my lesson plans *before* class. Those are my personal notes," she said carefully.

Sam nodded.

"Now, please have a seat. I need to talk to you both."

Kobe glanced at Sam. *Do you know what she wants?*

Sam scrambled to refocus her attention on Ms. Lysander's thoughts, but it didn't work under pressure. *No.*

Do you think we're in trouble?

I'm not sure.

Can she hear our thoughts?

I don't think so.

Do you—

Stop. Listen, she's about to speak.

Kobe tapped his foot against the ground as if he had a permanent twitch.

Ms. Lysander cleared her throat. "To be clear, I've been impressed with your marks—both of you—these past few weeks. And, well…" She sighed, gathering some papers from her briefcase. "I just need to make sure there's no form of…dishonesty going on. Not that there is. But you both, coincidentally, had the same answers on our last test. And so, what I mean is…we just need to do some further testing."

Kobe slid Sam a nervous glance. "We would never cheat, Ms. Lysander!"

"Well, that's good. To be sure, I've prepared a new test for you both to take. It shouldn't take too long, and then you can be on your way."

"I don't understand why we need to take another test…" Kobe said as he rolled his eyes.

Sam responded quickly. "It's fine. We'll do it."

They sat at opposite ends of the room while Ms. Lysander handed out the two math tests. "You'll both have thirty minutes to complete it. If it's any consolation, if you get all of the answers right, I'll give you a bonus five percent on your final grade."

"And if we get any wrong?" Kobe asked.

"Well, not to worry. Okay, you may begin at any time."

Time passed slowly, but soon enough they'd completed their tests. They both handed them in.

"When will we find out the results?" Sam asked.

"I'll try to have these back to you tomorrow. Now, go! Enjoy the rest of the day. It's beautiful outside."

* * *

After school, Sam, Kobe, and Simon met up in a quiet room in the library, away from the other students and teachers. A few minutes later, Kato joined them, carrying a large plate of goodies she'd picked up at the school's bake sale taking place in the gymnasium down the hall.

"Score!" Kobe beamed and reached for a slice of chocolate cake. "Thanks, Sis!"

"Sam, Simon, help yourselves." She pushed the tray toward them, and Sam took a croissant. "So, I think we all need to talk about what happened today in science class."

Sam's face turned red—again. "I couldn't help it, Kato. It was so weird. It was like…it was like I could *hear* Ms. Lysander's thoughts before she delivered the lesson. So…I wanted to test my abilities."

"And you did. A couple of times," Simon giggled.

"You think this is funny?"

"Honestly, that look on Ms. Lysander's face…" Kobe couldn't stop smiling.

Sam smiled slightly, but it quickly dissolved.

"When did this start, Sam? When did you start having these…thoughts?"

She recalled the night before, and her strange dream. She decided to tell them everything, from start to finish, and tried not to leave any insignificant detail out.

When Sam finished, Kato spoke up. "Sam, do you know what this means? That dream—it must have affected your telepathic powers. You're getting stronger." She looked around, making sure no one else was in sight. "We need to keep this on the down low. Today you got a warning because you interrupted class, but tomorrow, who knows? If they find out you helped each other on the test by using your telepathy...you could get expelled."

"I know. I mean, you're right. It's not going to happen again."

"Good. You too, Kobe. We need to make sure we don't raise any more flags with the school's administration."

"Okay," Kobe said. He looked over at Simon, who remained focused on wolfing down his doughnut. "And Simon?"

"Hey—I've been good!" Simon said, chocolate icing smeared across his face and crumbs sprinkled on his shirt. He looked down. "I'm saving those for later."

Sam couldn't help but feel uneasy. The math test they'd taken in Ms. Lysander's office was a tough one, but not impossible. Sam had shared her answers telepathically with Kobe again, because she didn't want to admit that they did it the first time. She and Kobe had wanted to ensure that his mark was consistent with the last test. But now, Sam realized, if they stopped the telepathic communication, Kobe wouldn't score as high, and their cover would be blown. They were now caught in a foolish lie.

But they hadn't been caught. At least, not yet.

* * *

Sam continued to study the parchment paper maps from Lijing. Despite her newfound abilities, she felt somewhat hopeless in regard to her task. Desperate for answers, she felt inclined to approach her science teacher after class to see what she could make of it. Maybe it would help smooth things over, given her recent outburst. Astronomy happened to be one of Ms. Lysander's favorite subjects, so maybe she would enjoy talking about it more.

Ms. Lysander examined the drawings closely, holding the paper up to the light at an angle. "Interesting... Where did you get this, Sam?"

"From, uh...from a friend."

"Hmm." Ms. Lysander took some time studying the shapes. "Well, if I had to guess, it looks most similar to the Cygnus constellation, only...I'm not really sure what this is." She pointed to the large circular object to one side. Smaller hexagonal shapes partially covered it.

"I know. I can't figure that part out either. Only, I thought about it more and wondered...that object isn't in the second image. Do you think it was a star that collapsed inside a black hole?"

Ms. Lysander raised her eyebrows, pushed her glasses higher on her nose, and looked thoughtfully at Sam. "Well, now that you mention it...black holes are certainly one area that continues to puzzle scientists. There's a lot we don't know about them." She stood still and silent for a moment before passing the paper back to Sam. "There's been a lot of activity in the Cygnus region, and a lot of discoveries made with the Kepler mission and mathematical equations. You know, new stars forming, black holes, that sort of thing. So, I guess...well, I guess *anything* is possible. Of course, until it's disproven."

Her response made Sam uneasy. There was so much uncertainty still, and so many questions that had not yet been answered. Nevertheless, she was grateful for her teacher's ideas and feedback. "Thank you, Ms. Lysander."

"Not a problem. Anytime, Sam."

Sam tucked the paper carefully into her bag and was getting ready to leave when Ms. Lysander spoke up. "Oh, and Sam, I meant to discuss your test results, if you have a moment."

Sam's body clenched up like a clam. "Did I make a mistake?"

Ms. Lysander laughed. "No, not at all. Actually, not one. I'm impressed. Some of the material we haven't even covered in this class yet. Did you learn that on your own time?"

Sam wasn't sure how to react, so she just nodded. She wanted to ask about Kobe, but stopped herself since that information was probably private. To her surprise, Ms. Lysander disclosed it.

"And Kobe, well...he did quite well too. You certainly have a positive influence on him."

Sam smiled, not sure what else to say.

"Anyways," Ms. Lysander continued, "I know it's a busy time for you all with your projects. Keep up the good work, and let me know if you need anything else."

Sam let out a sigh, relieved that they seemed to be on good terms again. "Thank you, Ms. Lysander. That means a lot."

14

Over the next two days, Sam noticed a strange smell in the city, like rotting garbage. Other students and residents noticed it too. The local news station picked it up, but no one could figure out the cause, only that the strange and foul odor permeated the entire city.

It put everyone on edge. Both students and teachers were moodier recently, with teachers demanding more homework and students retaliating by complaining or disrupting class.

It wasn't only the odor that made it difficult for Sam to concentrate in class. She was distracted by other odd happenings in the community. For instance, one local news story mentioned that a dog had died recently from toxicity levels after going swimming in a nearby river. In another, a couple of whales had died by beaching themselves along the shores of Shediac. Authorities weren't sure of the cause.

There had been rumors and corporate leaks that locations adjacent to TitusTech properties were experiencing severe environmental disturbances due to the company's actions. It was affecting the fishing and tourism industries too, with many people losing their jobs, just like Kato and Kobe's father.

Sam wanted to get to the bottom of it all, whether these strange occurrences were coincidental or linked to something else.

She found Kato surfing the net on a library computer and looked forward to catching up. She took a seat beside her. "Hey, what're you up to?"

Kato wheeled around and looked at Sam, her eyes intense. "Hey, Sam! Not much. Just got distracted from my studies. Have you noticed weird things happening lately?"

Sam looked at the screen and realized Kato had been reading the same article about the whales. "Um, yeah…like the weird smell, and the dead whales?"

"Yes. And also…" Kato paused as she looked over at the meeting room. The door was closed, with a sign that read DO NOT DISTURB. Visible through the window, Simon labored away at something inside.

"He's shut himself in that room for the past two days! We need to go in and check on him."

Sam nodded and they got up, grabbing their bags and heading to the meeting room. Kato ignored the sign and opened the door. Simon continued working. Books on robotics, circuit boards with wires, and tools were strewn across the table. He had made this room into his own temporary laboratory of sorts.

"Working on a new TitusTech project?" Sam joked.

"Huh? Oh!" Simon looked down at his book. "No. But I'm working on making a new hall monitor. Something that actually works."

"Intriguing," Kato said. "What're you going to name it?"

"Haven't decided yet." Simon looked up from his work, studying Kato's expression. "If it's sparkly, maybe KatoGlitterTech, after your hair, which is really inspiring today."

Sam had also noticed Kato's hair, which was done up in a long braid with silver and pink glittery thread twisted through it.

"Ha ha, very funny. But seriously, how are things? It's like you've disappeared."

Simon hesitated, as if he were weighing the information he was about to tell them against the consequences. "You guys want to hear something bad?"

"What?"

"They shut down the TitusTech lab a couple days ago and sent my dad home from work. He said everyone started having headaches and stuff, so they just sent everyone home."

"Did they say what it was?" Kato asked.

"No. My dad said they probably don't want any bad press, so they've gone radio silent on communications to staff. They just told everyone to take a few days off until further notice. His coworker ended up going to the hospital because he was having respiratory issues."

"Oh no, that's terrible! Is he okay?" Sam asked.

"I don't know. But no one has heard anything more from TitusTech since they closed it down. The thing is…I think I know what caused it." Simon picked up the tablet on the table and brought up a recent article. He passed it to Kato and Sam.

They looked at the images of a beach with the TitusTech lab adjacent to it. Large signs with bold lettering stated SWIM AT YOUR OWN RISK. The beach looked like a wasteland, spread out for miles, and had become a dumping ground for trash.

"Hey, I know that beach!" Kato said. "We used to swim there. There used to be a lot of people, at the time. It was clean and beautiful. Now it's…it's changed a lot."

Sam scanned the article, her eyes resting on a photograph of a pipe with some purple metallic liquid oozing into a body of water. A close-up image of the purple liquid allowed her to make out the details more clearly. Oily and thick, the liquid didn't mix well with the water, and floated at the surface.

According to the story, Titus wanted to recreate an element that didn't exist naturally on Earth. It was called perilium, a substance with incredible power to advance space flight. The story claimed that initially Titus had first discovered trace amounts of perilium on a piece of asteroid while his technicians were mining minerals on the moon. It had been a chance encounter, but the substance was highly unstable and there was not enough to make any practical use of it. Titus had then tried to recreate perilium in his lab, with failed results. They'd used particle accelerators to smash atoms together in high-energy collisions, hoping to create the element, but most of this was pure chance, and the odds were slim. They couldn't get the complex quantum makeup of the substance quite right, and the radioactive by-products had been leaching into the ocean, poisoning the ocean life and causing the odor.

Sam thought about the dead whales and dog. Things were starting to add up, and not in a good way.

"My parents were on a mission," Sam said, "and my friend Boj mentioned that they'd used perilium from Kryg's moon to repower their ship. If Titus is after the same fuel, do you think he could be trying to reach Kryg as well, so he can gain access to this substance in larger quantities?"

"I don't know," Simon said. "But one thing's for sure."

"What's that?" Kato asked.

Simon placed his hands on his cheeks, fear and dread spreading across his face. "It's only going to get worse."

"Why do you say that?" Sam asked.

"Well, my dad said the workers aren't treated well at all," Simon explained as he stuck his hands in his pockets and paced around the room. "He started complaining about all this stuff happening at work, and we had *no idea* it was happening."

"Like what?" Kato asked.

"That Titus is a terrible employer. He puts pressure on employees to not take breaks, delays pay for some people, or docks pay if they're like ten minutes late. He hasn't given some employees raises in years."

"Wow," Kato said, disgusted.

"I know. But it's not just that," Simon continued. "Now, with the work environment and health issues, and things getting worse, my dad said he and some of his coworkers are going to start a revolt. You know, rise up. Like refusing work, and striking when the time's right. They're hoping to make it difficult for TitusTech to run its operations so the company will be forced to make changes."

Sam thought about the consequences. It seemed like a good approach, at least, to try and change things. Simon was right about things getting worse. It seemed like everyone was feeling the negative effects, not just the workers. "I'll help you in any way I can," she offered.

"Me too," Kato added. "And Kobe's not here, but I'm pretty sure I can speak for him."

"Thanks. Just don't tell anyone else for now. It's supposed to be a secret."

"You have our word," Sam responded.

They needed a plan. They needed to stop TitusTech.

* * *

That evening, Sam found it difficult to sleep. She kept thinking about dogs dying in rivers and people fainting in labs, and of herself drowning in a pool of toxic purple liquid. The information and images from earlier that day were disturbing enough, but something else gnawed at the back of her mind.

Ms. Lysander's insights about the star maps.

She'd mentioned the possible black hole, but also the new stars, the ones forming in the Cygnus region. That couldn't be a coincidence. And Lijing's maps? Could they really lead her to the Hopewell Star? If they did, it still didn't explain the hexagonal patterns around the star. What were they? She needed to find out. She needed to mind travel there.

Then she remembered Lijing's warning about Aruna. If Aruna really was a spy for Titus, traveling there would put her in danger.

It didn't matter. She *had* to confront Aruna. She had to learn the truth. And to do that, she needed to return to the garden and see what Aruna was hiding.

The klug let out a faint humming noise. She held it in her hand, running her index finger over its smooth surface, the metal cool to the touch. As she examined it, she felt a small bump that she hadn't noticed before. She looked at it closely. There was definitely a small protrusion in its workmanship.

She pressed it.

To her astonishment, it opened up to reveal a hollow core. Initially, she thought the klug was powered from the inside by an energy source of some sort. But in front of her, all she saw was emptiness. It reminded her of the hollow part of the moon. This inner compartment measured no more than three inches in diameter, small enough to carry a message, perhaps. She drifted off to sleep, thoughts of the last few days swirling around in her mind, taking her to a forbidding and unsettling place.

* * *

Aruna pulled back the curtains of her three-story walk-up apartment in Toronto, revealing a dark, tree-lined street. Rain blurred the shapes of the trees, obscuring their details, making them look like shadowy figures. Across the street, music blasted from another apartment unit, and she watched drunken people making out on the steps. Probably some kids having a party. She considered calling in a noise complaint if it got any louder.

She peered from her window at the mostly empty street and noticed a black SUV parked by the curb. Panic rose up in her chest as she looked farther down toward the entrance to her apartment.

The two men had returned.

"Oh no," she whispered, her throat dry. Dread coursed through her veins. She couldn't tell them the truth. She didn't want to put the girl in danger.

She'd tried a few times in the past to leave town, to change her identity. She thought this would stop the men from finding her, but they always showed up sooner or later. Somehow, they always managed to find her, and they always brought with them a special device—one that blocked her mind so that her power to mind travel was rendered useless. She hadn't heard from them in years, and thought they were no longer looking.

She knew why they were here. They showed up for one thing only. And if she didn't tell them the truth…

She didn't want to think about the consequences.

The doorbell rang, the high-pitched sound piercing at her temples.

She thought about calling the police. It wouldn't matter—the police couldn't help her. These men defied the authorities. They'd threatened her before with their device—draining her powers and easily coercing her with their guns. Besides, she didn't know their names or who they worked for.

She heard a loud knock on her door. Her hand trembled as she reached for the knob, then stopped herself. "Who is it? What do you want?"

A man with a deep voice spoke up. "Open the door, or we'll open it for you."

"I'll call the police," she replied, her voice shaking.

The other man delivered his words in a menacing tone. "I wouldn't do that, if I were you."

She stumbled back as something rattled against her door. She realized, to her horror, that they were using a lockpick. She stood shaking as the door swung open.

A large, burly man stepped inside.

She tried to mind travel to escape, but a second, hairless man with dark, piercing eyes and a tattoo of an eel on his arm held the device close to her. It was a pyramid-shaped object, and froze her in her place, light emanating from its core.

Her breathing slowed.

"Have you met any other Mind Travelers recently?"

Aruna hesitated. "None. You know that. Not in the last few years." She needed to protect the girl. It was the least she could do. She still felt guilty after giving up Theo under duress. She wanted to ask about him, but stopped herself.

"Don't lie to us!" the first man grumbled.

"I'm not! I'm telling you the truth!" she protested, her voice cracking.

The pyramid-shaped device started flashing, smoke emanating from it as if it were a hot coal. The man with the eel-shaped tattoo cried out in pain as it scarred his hand. He dropped the device.

"What's happening?" demanded the burly man.

"I don't know. It's never done that before!" The bald man took off his sweatshirt and used it to pick up the smoking device. As he did so, an access card fell out of his pocket. He picked it up with his other hand as fast as he could, but it was too late.

Aruna's eyes opened wide as she saw the familiar insignia on the card. The man worked for TitusTech Industries. *Dr. Endo Lloyd*, it read. Was it possible that Titus was behind all of this? The kidnappings of the Mind Travelers, and the murder of Atticus?

"You work for TitusTech too?" she asked incredulously.

The two men shot each other anxious looks but remained silent. They quickly headed toward the door. Now that she knew at least one of the men's identities, it wouldn't be difficult to track him down later.

"If we find out you're lying, we'll be back," the first man muttered under his breath. They left in such a hurry that they didn't bother to shut the door behind them.

Aruna took a breath and sank down to the floor, her head spinning. She tried to keep it together, but her head pounded. She'd trusted Titus. She'd spent so much time on her work in the lab. What was going on?

She heard the two men yelling at each other from a distance now. Then she heard an engine rev and tires squealing as the SUV sped off, leaving Aruna shaking, trying to make sense of it all, and wondering about the fate of the girl.

She had to warn Sam. She needed to tell her the truth about her past. If she could help the girl strengthen her powers without TitusTech knowing—maybe *she* would be able to stop them.

* * *

Dr. Endo Lloyd and Bjørn monitored the Sanderson residence just as Titus had asked, quietly and periodically so as not to draw attention. Using a drone the size of a fly which they operated remotely, they were able to collect useful information including the habits of the girl and her grandfather over the past few weeks.

The girl typically left the house between 8:10 a.m. and 8:20 a.m. to walk to school. Her grandfather mostly stayed in the house during the day, but left the residence at 11:15 a.m. and at 3 p.m. to take their dog for a walk, usually to the nearby park, a good fifteen-minute walk away. The grandfather usually returned to the house between 3:30 p.m. and 3:45 p.m., and the girl returned around 4:10 p.m.

With their tools and cover ready, today was the day to put their plan into action and launch the extraction.

At 11:20 a.m., with the girl at school and her grandfather and the dog out on a walk, it gave them the perfect window of time to enter the house and locate the klug, but they needed to move quickly so as not to attract any unwanted attention from prying neighbors. They made sure to have a cover story ready in case they were questioned.

Bjørn pulled into the Sanderson driveway with a white van marked "B. C. Milton & Sons Electric Ltd." He lowered the window and pulled the drone out of its case, opening a tiny screen and pressing some buttons to activate it. A moment later, it hummed and left through the window on its way to the park where the grandfather had taken the dog.

Endo sat in the passenger seat and fiddled with the pyramid-shaped object TitusTech had developed. Among other capabilities, it had unique properties that allowed them to locate alien technologies made of non-Earth metals and minerals, such as perilium.

"Everything okay?" Bjørn asked. "What are you doing?"

Endo glanced up quickly. "Just getting ready." He lifted a switch and the pyramid beamed with green light. He stuffed it into the pocket of his one-piece suit with a B. C. Milton & Sons Electric Ltd. logo emblazoned on the front and placed a small comms device inside his right ear.

When he'd taken his first job with TitusTech Industries, he felt eager to please his boss, no matter what the cost. He'd been fascinated by the projects and ready to learn and discover new inventions. Over time, Titus had asked him to do things—questionable things. Endo had shown restraint initially, but the way Titus described it to him made him feel important, that only he could obtain the required outcome. And so, he complied in the name of science.

"Well, we don't have all day!"

Endo looked up, feeling the pressure now. He knew the power of klugs and what they could do, and the importance of securing them in order to test them. They had secured a klug recently from one of the other Mind Travelers, Katiya, but she'd gone missing shortly after, and they were unable to question her further. They had completed preliminary experiments on her klug, but the technology was quite sophisticated, and they weren't able to activate it. After doing vigorous, aggressive experiments on the klug, it had exploded, and so they'd ended up melting the technology down and conducting experiments on the trace amounts of perilium that remained. Those experiments had also proven futile, to Titus's dismay.

Endo had become so used to Titus's requests that today was no different. He didn't need Bjørn to remind him a second time of the urgency. He shuddered at the thought of things going sour with the plan.

"Right. Let's get to it, then." He exited the van and carried his toolbox down the pathway toward the side door of the house. He took out his lockpick, and in less than a minute made his way inside.

How easy.

He headed toward the staircase leading up to the second floor. He figured the klug would be somewhere in the girl's bedroom. He pulled out the pyramid-shaped device. As he made his way upstairs and down the corridor, it emitted a brighter light. Getting closer to its source, he stopped in the hallway just outside a bedroom. The device glowed stronger, this time sending out a faint buzzing noise that it hadn't before.

He entered the room and immediately noticed the strange plant on the bureau in the corner. It looked alive, but encased in an unusual container that glistened in the light.

Focus.

He took a step into the left-hand side of the room, embarking on his search for the klug. He passed the windowsill and a telescope in the corner, continuing along. As he passed a wooden chest at the foot of the bed, the device grew even brighter. It seemed to respond more powerfully to this particular klug. It probably contained more perilium. Titus would be ecstatic. This could mean the final solution they were looking for.

He opened the chest, and sure enough, inside he found the klug resting among other odds and ends.

Voila.

He picked it up, briefly feeling the weight in his hand, and stuck it into his toolbox.

"Radio one. What's your status?"

Endo stumbled back at the sudden ringing in his ears from the comms, some of his tools falling out of his case and scattering across the floor.

"I have eyes on the resident. He is leaving the park and will be here in fifteen minutes."

"Radio two, copy," Endo replied. "The prize is secured. Currently on the second floor, making my way to the exit." He scrambled to pick up the tools, nuts, and bolts that had fallen, packing them back into his toolbox. He headed downstairs and left the way he'd come, locking the side door and heading toward the van. Relieved to see Bjørn had already started the engine, he pulled open the door and slid inside, placing the toolbox at his feet.

A moment later, they drove off down the street.

Endo felt a faint smile forming on his face. He couldn't wait to show Titus, who would be so very pleased.

* * *

On her way home from school, Sam noticed Hunter walking with one of his friends a few meters ahead of her. She figured he must be going to his friend's house. They kept looking back at her, whispering things to each other and laughing. Together, they started chanting a rhyme loud enough that she could hear every word.

"Sam and her fam,
They lived on a farm,
Talked to the animals,
And slept in a barn.

"Sam, the simple girl,
She never takes a shower,
She smells like a horse,
And she always looks sour!"

The boys laughed and looked back at Sam, mocking sour expressions to witness her reaction. She kept a calm face and did not let it disturb her. Disappointed in her response, they repeated the verses louder this time, walking slower so she would catch up to them and hear their every word.

You are projecting your weaknesses. You try to bring me down due to your own shortcomings.

"Hey, did you hear that?" Hunter asked his friend.

"What?"

"Sam, did you say something?" he asked.

"Nope," she replied. "You must be hearing things."

He started walking backward, eyeing her.

You suck, Hunter! she screamed in her mind.

Hunter gasped and held his hands up to his temples.

"Dude, what's wrong with you?" his friend asked.

"Let's go!" Hunter shouted, running away. "She's a witch!"

Repeat these words in your head: I will no longer hurt even a fly. I will help people who are suffering. I will be kind, gracious, and supportive.

Hunter's expression changed. His running slowed and he no longer looked fearful, but amazed. He looked back at Sam and nodded, then turned to his friend a few paces ahead. "Hey! Wait up!"

Sam thought she heard his thoughts, even though they were distant now.

I'm sorry, Sam, he said, as he and his friend continued running.

* * *

By the time Sam arrived home from school, the rain poured down in heavy sheets, flooding parts of the street. She took off her soaked shoes and placed them on the mat close to the heater. She took off her socks and put on some comfy slippers.

"Grandpa?" she called, but there was no answer. She went upstairs and found him fast asleep in his room. She decided not to disturb him.

Instead, she headed to her room and thought about the nasty words Hunter had said. How could someone be so cruel? She thought about the look on Hunter's face when she told him off, and the look on his friend's face when he started running as fast as he could. She chuckled to herself and wondered whether he would repeat what she'd told him, and if he would change. Would he still bother Kobe? If so, she would stick by Kobe's side to deter the bullying.

At the thought of Kobe, she wanted to mind travel again. More than a couple of weeks had passed since she'd last seen Aruna, and she desperately needed answers. She felt closer to finding the solution, and if she could find it…maybe it would help her find the Hopewell Star.

Her thoughts drifted to Onnisa and Boj. She missed them, and worried about their safety since she hadn't heard from them in ages. She wondered whether she should visit them again, and if so, when was the right time.

She started going through the belongings in her chest. A strange feeling tingled up her spine. Where was the klug? It wasn't in the chest. She took everything out and checked each item one by one. She searched twice, just to be sure.

It wasn't here.

No!

She started pulling out her drawers and rummaging through her clothes, a sense of uncontrollable panic rising up in her.

Something wasn't right. She needed to warn Onnisa and Boj.

The klug had been stolen.

15

Titus held the klug in the palm of his hand, examining it closely, trying to contain his excitement. It was heavier than expected. He gazed at its intricate design and hieroglyphic inscriptions. The alien technology looked ancient, but the lab would be able to date it. He would send it later this morning for analysis and reverse engineering. He wanted to ensure he had a copy, an exact replica he could use in case the Krygians came looking for it.

It was only a matter of time before they found out.

* * *

Sam was busy packing her bag with a couple of books from her locker when Kato met up with her. They made their way down the hall toward history class. They still had about ten minutes until class started, and most of the students hadn't arrived yet, so the hallways were pretty much empty except for a few stragglers.

Although anxious from the revelation that the klug was missing, Sam tried to keep focused on her schoolwork. But despite her best efforts to deflate her fears, an unsettling feeling remained in the pit of her stomach.

Kato's constant questioning made matters worse.

"You haven't been acting yourself these days, Sam," she said. "You're so quiet. Is everything okay?"

"No, not really," Sam replied, speaking in a quieter tone. "The klug is missing."

"Oh?"

"Yeah. Either that or it's been stolen."

"Oh no. Do you remember where you put it last?"

Sam thought hard. "I'm pretty sure I put it back in the chest in my bedroom. That's where I always keep it. But when I looked there a few days ago, it was gone."

Kato paused. "Hmm. Who would know about it? And who do you

think would want to take it?"

"Not many people knew about it. Just you, Kobe, Simon, Aruna, and Lijing. Well, Onnisa too, and Boj…" And maybe other Krygians who had ulterior motives. How many of them knew about it?

Sam thought back to her earlier discussions with Aruna. She'd said the Mind Travelers were hunted, and Aruna's klug had gone missing. Sam recalled Aruna's warning about the fifth dimension, and how it could be monitored by the Henchmen. Maybe that was how the Henchmen found out about the klugs in the first place. And if that were the case, maybe the Henchmen had taken her klug as well. There were any number of possibilities!

Sam let out a heavy sigh. "I really don't know."

They were both silent for a few moments, taking in the gravity of the situation. Kato nodded, but didn't press it further.

They passed Hunter and Vito in the hall. The two boys did a double take when they saw Sam and immediately turned and walked briskly in the other direction.

"Hunter hasn't been bothering you much these days. It's like he's trying to avoid you at all costs. Did you say something to him?"

Sam laughed. "Oh, I don't know. Probably."

* * *

Later that afternoon, Sam and Kato arrived at the library and found Simon in the quiet room, rummaging through the books and papers spread out on the table. He had a bunch of circuit boards and realistic robotic flies lined up in front of him. It looked like he was about to test them out.

"Hey guys, what's up?" he asked as they entered.

Kato shut the door behind them. "We need to talk."

"About what?"

"About Sam's safety," Kato replied.

"Wait, what?" Sam asked, turning to Kato.

"Simon and I were talking about what you said, with your klug getting stolen…and think you could use some extra protection."

"Like, as a safety precaution," Simon added.

"Oh…I don't know if that's really necessary," Sam replied.

Sensing Sam's hesitancy, Kato continued. "If the klug was stolen, whoever took it could come back. They could take something else, too."

Sam thought about this. What else would they want to take? They'd had their chance, but they didn't take any other valuables the first time. But then she thought about her otherworldly gifts: the crown that the Krygians had given her, and the kylie flower from Boj. Okay, so it was possible they could come back. Whoever *they* were.

"So, I've been thinking," Simon started. "I've been working on my own project and want you to be the first to test it out."

Sam was about to ask what it was when she looked down at the flies strewn across the table. "Let me guess…"

Simon opened his right hand. A robotic fly rested in his palm. It looked almost real. He placed it on the table, then picked up a tablet with a display screen and started inputting data. "I call it Fred," he said as he waved his other hand around the fly, then set the tablet down so they could view the image. "It's a Flybot. It's extra eyes and ears. You can place it on your windowsill for safety purposes. If there's another break-in, it will detect movement from its motion sensors and start recording."

Immediately, the image of Simon's waving hand appeared on the screen, along with the audio; the Flybot had recorded his actions.

"And what if I want some privacy?" Sam asked.

Kato stepped in. "Just place a blanket over it when you're not using it."

Sam picked up the Flybot and examined it closely. It had a hairy body, just like the real ones. "Does it actually fly?"

Simon cleared his throat. "No, but I'm working on another model that does. Eventually, I'll recommend it to replace Scrappie as the new hall monitor."

Kato stifled a laugh. "Won't the students try to swat it?"

"Maybe. But with the motion sensors, it would just move out of the way." He gave Sam a box and she placed the Flybot inside carefully.

"Fine. Thank you both. You're like my adopted helicopter parents," Sam said as they headed to class. "I guess I could try it out."

* * *

Titus leaned forward in his chair in front of the fire, considering his next move in the chess match. Across from him sat the robot replica of his wife, Marie.

"It's your turn," she reminded him coolly. Her impatient tone caught him off guard. His real wife wouldn't speak to him like that. Marie's speech patterns had been transferred along with her memories to the best of his AI team's abilities. It was a temporary measure, until his real wife woke up from her coma. He'd missed her presence, and at least now he could talk to something like her. It brought him some temporary comfort, but it could never replace his wife. The robot had been one of the first prototypes at the lab. There were still some kinks in the coding to work out, but it was coming along. Nevertheless, he wondered what he would do with the replica once the real Marie woke up. He was careful not to tell the robot too much.

"I know!" he snapped, then immediately caught himself. "Sorry Marie, I just need some more time."

"Of course," she replied.

The room became so eerily quiet that he heard the mechanical movement of her eyelids opening and shutting and her head tilting from side to side as she waited for him to make the next move. He found it difficult to concentrate, and held up his mug. "Could I have some more coffee, please?"

If it had been his real wife, she would have picked up on these details, like recognizing that his coffee cup was empty and offering to refill it without him having to ask.

"Yes, darling," she replied. He gasped as she grabbed the cup from his hands rather forcefully and headed to the table at the back of the room to refill it.

Titus felt particularly on edge today. Progress moved slowly on multiple fronts, but especially with the perilium project. They had tried and failed numerous times to recreate the substance in its purest form. The experiments were wreaking havoc on the local environment, the lab had to be shut down for a few days, and the staff had been sent home so they could resolve the toxic spill and fumigate the building. Alas, they were nowhere closer to attaining their goal than when they first started years ago.

He didn't care about the environmental impacts. He was obsessed with his goal of space travel deep into the universe, along with fame and money and being written into history books. His desperate attempts to recreate perilium remained his top priority because it would allow him to advance space flight. It could fuel his ships and take him to galaxies light-years away in a fraction of the time. At first, they'd tried to concentrate different base metals and minerals together, but with no luck. Then they'd hired top chemical and engineering scientists who used secret, specialized processes to try to develop this new source of power for spacecraft. He'd attempted to transform earthly materials into cherished, otherworldly prized possessions; a farcical, desperate scheme.

Acquiring klugs and reverse engineering them so they could travel to other galaxies where perilium was found was the only alternative. The project wasn't excelling fast enough, either. It didn't help that they weren't getting any more information from Theo. They had already tried and failed to reverse engineer Katiya's klug. Since then, they'd learned from their mistakes and spent time and resources upgrading their systems with the latest technology to try again. Now that they had a new klug to work with, Titus was hopeful. From preliminary experiments, this klug seemed to behave differently than the others; it contained a higher concentration of perilium, suggesting more power and capabilities. But nevertheless, an unsettling feeling crept up his spine.

Marie returned with the steaming hot coffee and placed the mug in front of him.

"Thank you." He took a sip.

"Get it yourself next time!" she yelled.

He was so startled that he coughed up his coffee onto his shirt. He jumped at a loud knock on his door, spilling the rest of the coffee all over the table. He pulled his handkerchief from his pocket and wiped up the ugly mess.

"It's Dr. Lloyd, sir."

Despite his nerves, Titus had been expecting him. He looked forward to Dr. Lloyd's status update on the reverse engineering of the klug. He cleared his throat. "Yes, come in."

The robot followed Titus's gaze. "Hello, Dr. Lloyd," she said in a neutral tone. "Can I offer you some coffee? My husband spilled most of it, but I can make some more."

Dr. Lloyd entered the room like a child approaching the end of a diving board, arms crossed and eyes wide in alarm. His black eyes bore into Titus's, and Titus felt his jaw tighten and snap.

"No, thank you," Dr. Lloyd said. "Sir, I have some bad news."

Titus frowned and turned to the robot. "Marie, please leave the room and close the door."

She hesitated, an almost defiant expression on her face. A moment later, she left.

He waited until she'd shut the door before continuing. He turned to Dr. Lloyd. "Get on with it."

"The klug, sir. It's encrypted." He spoke so calmly and casually that Titus wanted to stand up and slap him.

"What do you mean, *the klug is encrypted?*" Titus bellowed. His lead scientist shakily took a step back. Stunned that his expert staff and cutting-edge technology could not decode it, Titus challenged him further. "Surely our new supercomputer systems can unscramble it? Isn't that what I paid you to work on for the last two years?"

"I'm sorry sir, but the technology is very complex. I've never seen anything like it. It's not like the other klugs. This one seems to have an unusual biometric authentication system fused with the technology, and it won't allow tampering. It also means we cannot reverse engineer a replica. We would need the original physiological marker to do so."

Titus fumed, his face turning the color of a ripe beet. "Get me the girl!"

"Sir?"

"You heard me! As soon as possible!" He whipped the chessboard across his desk and looked directly into his subordinate's eyes. "*Why are you still here?*"

"Right, sir," Dr. Lloyd responded, hastily reaching for the door. "Yes, we'll go get her. Right away, sir."

* * *

Sam was peering through her telescope when her phone chimed. It was a text from Kato.

Hey! My mom's taking us to St. Andrews for a couple of days to visit my aunt and uncle, so I won't be around, in case you're wondering.

Sounds fun! Sam texted. *Hope you have a good time!*

Thanks. Make sure to keep Simon's Flybot on. I don't want anything bad happening to you.

Sam sighed. Geez, why was everyone so worried about her safety?

Sure thing, she replied. *See you when you get back.*

She turned off her cell and looked at the Flybot on top of her dresser. She stood and threw a shirt over it for privacy, then got ready for bed.

She had trouble getting to sleep with the events of the day continuing to play back in her mind. When she finally fell asleep, her mind wandered to another place. She thought back to the map Lijing gave her, tucked away inside the klug. She could still recall all of its intricate details.

She found herself fixated on the main star in the first image—the large circle with the strange hexagonal pattern concentrated within and around it, and wondered whether it truly was the location of the Hopewell Star. It didn't really explain the surrounding hexagons, though. Were they planets, or something else? And why were they missing in the second diagram? She studied its location and relative distance from the other stars in the system.

Without warning, the dream shifted. She found herself traveling through a wormhole toward its location. As she exited the wormhole, she emerged into a sparsely furnished room, inside of a spaceship. The room looked empty except for some discarded blocks the size of refrigerators placed in the corner. Sam wasn't sure what they were used for. Beyond the blocks were large tinted windows in front of her. An observation deck, perhaps. She gazed out into space and noticed other spaceships flying in the vicinity.

She walked over to take a better look.

Out of the large windows, a bright light emanated from the planet ahead. It looked like the light emerged from the core of the planet, through cracks in its surrounding structure. But how could that be? She thought about the Earth's core. Even though it could reach temperatures as hot as the sun's surface, the core never emanated so brightly as to be visible from the surface. This was unlike anything she'd ever seen before.

As the spaceship traveled closer, she realized she wasn't looking at a planet, but at a star. However, it wasn't a typical star; bursts of multicolored light bubbled and radiated outward from it. It reminded her of something Mukalakatakalakum had told her, something about the light inside her and how it shined all the colors of the rainbow. And…how he thought the Hopewell Star might look or behave the same way. But could it really be?

As the ship drew closer, she felt something else: a tingling sensation in her body, like the star was alive and reaching out to her. She felt the heat, like sunlight shining against her face, only more powerful. The heat radiated within her body, enlightening her.

Then she heard it. A faint voice. The voice of the star.

Help me, it whispered. It wasn't just one voice, but a collection of voices, including Mukalakatakalakum's and her parents', all pleading with her. Were her parents here as well, held captive?

The ship approached the star, giving Sam a better view. Surrounding the star were hundreds if not thousands of spaceships, some synchronizing their flight paths. It looked like they were building something around the star, some sort of hexagonal shell, on a massive scale. The hexagonal megastructures acted like platforms, each containing ships and technologies, and what looked like mass solar charging stations that converted energy from the sun into fuel, like massive solar batteries that then transferred back to the ships.

Some of the spaceships projected blue lasers containing a material that solidified as it approached the surface of the hexagonal structures. The beam increased the area and connected it with other structures. Once it solidified, it turned black, dampening the light of the star. It looked like they were harnessing the Hopewell Star's energy, and at the same time, building a wall around it, shielding its light and making it look like a planet.

Sam lost her balance for a split second as the spaceship jolted and flew toward the star. She crouched down and placed her hands against the window to steady herself. If this was a dream, it was the most vivid she'd ever had.

The spaceship hovered a few feet from a hexagonal megastructure and then touched down. Her face glued to the window, Sam gasped at the horrific scene unfolding in front of her eyes.

She recognized the familiar lizard-like features of the Rigellians, the ones from her dream. Although they were dressed in protective gear, Sam saw their elongated faces and large, dark eyes through their helmets. They were the ones building the shell, and they looked exhausted. A group of Krygians with markings on their bodies lashed at the Rigellians with brightly-colored sticks, forcing them to work against their will.

One of the Rigellians hesitated as he worked on repairing a connecting bridge between two hexagonal megastructures. A few moments later, he collapsed. Sam watched as he turned to face her, anguish in his eyes.

She heard a low hum in her ears, just like the voices of the star.

Help me.

She wanted to help him, but couldn't.

One of the Krygians zapped him with a gun and threw his lifeless body down a crack in the structure, where it was pulled into the star's fiery core. She gasped as other Rigellians were forced to extract a substance from the star, connecting power lines to the charging stations on the platforms and waiting for the energy to transfer to the ships. They were harvesting the star for fuel and using it to power their ships. The ships took off and all headed in the same direction. There was a small planet in the distance, and they were heading toward it.

Why were they doing this? And why didn't the Elders know about it?

She heard someone approaching and quickly ducked into a small, dark room to hide.

"…and Onnisa does not suspect this?"

"No. None of the Elders do."

"Good. Boku, you have proved your loyalty to us. You will be granted a space on our new planet."

"The Kantak tribe has always been kind to me. When will the planet be ready for habitation?"

"As you can see, we are nearing the final stage of development. The solar envelope structure around the star is eighty-five percent complete and on schedule. The construction of the artificial planet is ninety-five percent complete. We continue to test the durability of both structures, as we want to ensure continued and sustainable habitability and power generation. I would estimate not more than a month until completion of the planet."

Sam thought back to the star system maps Lijing had given her. Now she understood what they meant! In the first diagram, the hexagonal patterns around the star were the megastructures during construction. In the second diagram, the circle was the new planet they were creating. The star didn't show because the megastructures enclosed it, hiding it from view.

"What shall I tell the Elders, if they ask? I worry they may suspect something soon. They are no longer trusting of me. I can only deter them for so long."

"Keep to the story we discussed and switch the focus to the girl. They will continue to have blind hope in her. Soon, she will no longer present a threat."

Sam muffled a gasp.

Boku and the Kantak stopped talking and approached the room she was hiding in.

Please, no. Oh no. I need to get out of here. I need to get back to Earth!

She closed her eyes, and a moment later a wormhole opened and she found herself traveling, speeding through its core and back to her room at home.

She sat up in bed and pinched herself. Had she been dreaming?

Or had she mind traveled?

Either way, she needed to warn Onnisa.

* * *

There was a gentle tapping at her door. Sam rubbed her eyes. Her brain was foggy like she hadn't slept in weeks. She could've used some more rest. Rain drizzled down her windowsill, and she looked at her clock. Seven. Too early to think.

"Sam, are you awake?"

Now she was, but not exactly bright-eyed and bushy-tailed.

"Yes, come in."

The door creaked open. Her grandfather poked his head inside, wearing a golfing shirt and shorts.

"Are you planning a trip?" she asked, perking up.

"Yes. Well, I'm thinking of heading to Fredericton for a game of golf with some friends in town," he said, practicing his imaginary golf swing.

Located only a couple of hours drive from Moncton along the Saint John River, Fredericton offered a short, pleasant getaway. He and his friends usually made at least one golfing trip there each year.

"The weather is supposed to be beautiful later today. Do you think you'll be all right here on your own for the day?"

Of course she'd be okay on her own. She could take care of herself. Plus, it would be nice having some time to herself to figure things out. She was old enough that she could stay home by herself. She could hold down the fort. Besides, she didn't want to get in the way of his plans.

"Yep, no problem."

He paused and looked around her room, searching for something, then stopped when he saw her phone resting on her side table, plugged in and charging. "Call me if anything comes up. I'll be home in time for dinner, but if I'm a little late, I left some money on the kitchen counter to order in. There's food in the fridge if you want to make a sandwich."

"Thank you, Grandpa. Yeah, that's fine. No problem."

"Okay, see you in a bit." He closed the door gently behind him.

Sam took a moment to gather her thoughts. She considered calling

Kato and Kobe to hang out, but remembered they were in St. Andrews this weekend.

She had the whole day to herself.

Rain poured outside her window. Although gray and dreary outside, she liked the gentle sound of the rain drops against her window. She opened it a crack to let in the fresh, moist air. She let her mind wander to the events of last night. The wormhole journey and the experience in the spaceship felt too real to be a dream. The voices of the star were real.

The *threat* was real.

She thought back to what Aruna had said. It was possible to mind travel without the klug, she knew that for a fact. She only knew one person who could do that—Lijing. But if Lijing could do it, could Sam have mastered these powers too? If so, was all she'd witnessed last night true? Were those Krygians really using the Rigellians to build a new, artificial planet, and harnessing the Hopewell Star's energy to build it?

Something else didn't seem to fit into the picture. Why did Lijing still not trust Aruna? What was Aruna hiding?

Sam decided it was imperative to return to the garden. She had to confront Aruna and find out the truth. She needed to enter the space Aruna guarded.

She took a deep breath and took a seat in the middle of her floor to ground herself. She crossed her legs, letting her arms and hands rest gently upon them. She let out her breath slowly, steadily, and closed her eyes. She relaxed her mind, her thoughts drifting as she focused on the garden and its familiar details.

To her surprise, despite not having the klug in front of her, it worked. She could access the device's powers remotely with her mind. As she opened her eyes, she found herself once again in the peaceful garden, surrounded by large walls on all sides and no decent views beyond them.

She waited a few moments, taking in her surroundings. Nothing much had changed within the garden.

Or had it?

The turtle-shaped rock remained in the center, the one she usually found herself seated on when she first arrived. To her right, the willow tree's branches swayed gently in the breeze. The cherry tree stood in the northeast corner and the pear tree in the opposite corner, just like they always had. Rose bushes with their many thorns lined the south wall, and the north wall bore hydrangeas. Cedars occupied the west and east walls. There used to be an outline of an entrance along the east wall. But where was the door now?

It wasn't just the door…

Something else was different now. She could feel it. But what was it?

The cedars were much taller than she remembered, and they blocked her view of the doorway.

"Hello?" Sam called. She looked around for Aruna, hoping for answers, expecting a response. Where was she?

"I'm here to find out the truth," Sam said defiantly. Yet, her words felt like they were bouncing off the stone walls.

She quietly ventured through the cedars to where the entrance stood hidden behind them. "I'm opening the door," she exclaimed, stumbling as she inched closer. She looked around and waited. There was no sign of Aruna. This was the first time she'd ever been completely alone in the garden.

She pushed gently against the door; it opened effortlessly to another garden sanctuary. She hesitated. Would she be allowed to go further?

No one tried to stop her this time.

She continued through the doorway and found herself in a smaller garden with four walls. With only some grassy patches and a few creeping vines, the space looked quite bare compared to the lush garden she'd exited moments before. A circular stone fountain at its center caught her eye. It was about ten feet in diameter, and clearly not a typical fountain. The water, at closer gaze, traveled up through a glass ball in its center and cascaded down its circumference so slowly there were hardly any ripples on the surface of the pool. It didn't look very deep, and the water sparkled at the surface.

She made her way slowly toward the fountain and looked down at her reflection in the water, surprised to see someone else's face staring back at her.

Aruna.

She remembered the unmistakable almond-shaped eyes, curly auburn hair, and suntanned skin from her parents' class photo she'd seen in their scrapbook at home. She'd never met Aruna in person, but her voice had sounded familiar. She must have overheard it during one of the conference calls her parents had with other people in the scientific community. It took a moment for Sam to piece it together, but now she understood the connection.

Aruna's lips moved in the reflection, trying to speak to her, but Sam couldn't understand what she was saying. It looked like she was trying to tell her something important.

Sam gazed at the water, almost as if in a meditative trance. The clear water beckoned her. The reflecting pool acted as a mirror; smooth, calming. It created a stillness in her mind. Sam focused on the reflection and allowed her mind and thoughts to expand and merge with the water. After a few moments, it transported her to a small living room with white walls. Aruna stood there, along with two men in dark jackets, their backs turned to Sam. They didn't seem to notice her. Who were they? Sam peered up at their faces. One stood at least six feet tall with a curly brown beard and a strong, muscular stature. The other, a bald man with a thin build, had pale skin and a tattoo of an eel on his right arm. Sam listened in on their conversation.

"How many are there?" the large man demanded, his voice gruff.

"I don't know." Aruna stood trembling in the corner, her eyes darting around the room in search of something to fend off her intruders. "Just the ones I told you about. Please, why do you need to know this?"

"We need to know exactly how many, and their names."

"Where's…where's Atticus? Did you kill him?" she cried.

"We just need the names of the others, and then we'll leave you to do your job."

"I can't do this anymore," she whispered, crouching and hugging her knees, shaking uncontrollably.

"The new one…is his name Theo?" asked the bald man.

Aruna gasped, and Sam heard her thoughts.

How do they know?

"Turns out Atticus was useful before his…accident," the other man said.

Aruna nodded meekly.

"So it *is* Theo. Do you know where he is now?"

"I don't—"

"Don't lie to us!" The massive, intimidating man pulled a gun from his pocket and held it up to her face while the bald one held up a small, otherworldly device, a pyramid-shaped stone with dazzling green light emanating from it. Aruna seemed more affected by the device than the gun, shrinking back from it.

"If there are any other Mind Travelers, you need to tell us."

Tears streamed down her face. "That's all I know. We don't share our last names with each other."

"Then that is your next task. Find him. Find Theo…or you'll be next."

The two men left, leaving Aruna huddled in the corner, holding her face in her hands.

Sam lifted her gaze from the water. The fountain—it had to be a collection of Aruna's memories! If that was true, then Lijing was right. Aruna was working for the Henchmen. She'd given Theo up—but she'd been threatened and gave in under duress. Yet, she'd put Theo in danger all the same.

Then Sam had another thought—a more chilling one: if Aruna had given her up like she had the others, she would be in danger as well.

She gazed at the surface of the water. It seemed like Aruna was trying to tell her something else. Sam refocused her mind on the water.

This time, it transported her to a forest. Aruna hiked along a dirt path. Sam walked beside her, but Aruna didn't seem to take any notice of her. Instead, she kept looking down at her watch.

As Aruna stopped and hesitated, Sam caught a glimpse of her watch and the date on the display. This memory had formed quite recently. It had happened only three days ago.

Aruna made her way down some wooden steps along the hiking trail, when the same two men approached her from below, both wearing suits and blocking the path.

Aruna stopped. "Leave me alone!"

"Have you seen this girl?" the man with the eel tattoo asked, stepping forward and holding up a picture of Sam.

Sam suddenly felt shaken. Somehow, the Henchmen had made the connection. Worse, they were actively looking for her. She studied Aruna's reaction carefully, but she didn't flinch.

"Never seen her before."

The two men looked at one another, then back to Aruna. "You sure? You don't sound so sure."

Sam watched in horror as the man with the eel tattoo took out the device again and held it up to Aruna's face.

"I don't know who she is. I can't help you," Aruna lied.

Had Aruna lied to protect her? It was as if she didn't care about the consequences—even if it meant her own death.

"Let us know if you come across her." The man placed the photo in Aruna's hand, and Sam recognized the small, familiar TitusTech insignia emblazoned on his cufflink. She shivered.

Aruna folded up the photograph, her hands shaking.

Sam lifted her gaze from the water once again, returning her focus to the fountain and the surrounding garden. Aruna was probably still in danger, along with herself.

She was about to leave the garden when she saw a mask floating in the fountain. It was Aruna's dragon mask, but where was Aruna now? She never came to the fifth dimension without her mask.

Sam picked it up and examined it closely. It was wooden, and covered in a series of multicolored sequins. She held it to the light and admired its beautiful craftsmanship. Slowly, she turned it over to reveal a message on the inside:

LEAVE NOW. YOU ARE IN DANGER.

Sam suddenly felt very vulnerable. She snapped her fingers to return to her room at home.

But it was too late.

16

Sam opened her eyes as thick hands grabbed her around her waist from behind and scooped her off the floor. She screamed, loud and shrill. Then she remembered her grandfather was gone. Probably no one could hear her.

Across from her stood the man with the eel tattoo; the same man who had worn a suit with the TitusTech logo on the cufflink. He was getting ready to cover her mouth with duct tape.

The Flybot on her dresser was still covered, and Simon wouldn't be able to catch them on camera. But maybe if he listened in, he would get the hint and call for help. At least, she hoped.

"They work for TitusTech!" she screamed.

Her feet and hands still worked, and she dug her elbow hard into the side of the man holding her. She heard a muffled moan and kicked blindly behind her, reaching nothing but air.

"Nice try!" The man's distinctive gruff voice echoed inside her brain. She tried whipping her head away, then biting the man's finger, but couldn't stop them from covering her mouth with the sticky tape.

The man with the eel tattoo slipped a canvas bag over her head. She tried to scream again, but the tape over her mouth stifled it. She looked around, but all she could see was darkness now. She felt tight restraints—thick rope—wrapping around her wrists, and her stomach lurched as she found herself being lifted.

She heard the creak of doors opening. She felt a solid surface beneath her as she landed hard on her right side, scraping her knee along the floor. The engine of a vehicle roared to life, and she felt the unsteady movement as it reversed and then sped forward.

"*Help!*" she screamed, her voice muffled under the thick fabric. Her heart raced. Where were they taking her?

Kobe? Can you hear me?

No response. She tried again, this time louder.

KOBE? CAN YOU HEAR ME?

Silence. It was as though her telepathic powers were somehow blocked inside the vehicle. A dampening stillness grew inside her, like the mysterious, expansive dark energy of space: foreboding, uncertain.

I need to be strong. I need to hold on.

They drove for what seemed like hours. Then, without warning, the vehicle came to a juddering halt. Someone grabbed her arms and legs and carried her forcefully into a building. She kicked and screamed, but to no avail.

"Here we are," the man with the gruff voice said as he tightened the ropes around her wrists. They took her inside and locked her in a room. They removed the canvas bag and tape. She took a breath. The air smelled putrid.

"The boss will be here soon," he added, a sneer permanently glued to his face. "He's prepared a meal for you." With that, the man shut the thick steel door behind him with a loud thud.

"Where—where am I?" Sam's voice was faint and weak. Then her fear and anger set in. "Let me out!" She kicked heavily at the door. No response. She shivered as she took stock of her surroundings. The small, windowless room was cold, the lighting dim. Water stains lined the walls and ceiling. She tried pounding the door again, but it was no use.

She took a seat on the dirty floor, feeling deflated. She looked over to her right. A metal can half full of leftover corn with a thick layer of mold on top was a few inches away. She reached over and held it between her knees. She started running the ropes on her wrists over the sharp rim. The twine began to break apart slowly. A few more minutes and they would be loose.

She tried reaching out telepathically.

I need to get out of here! Onnisa, can you hear me?

There was only silence. She tried again, but still nothing. She couldn't lose hope. Not now. She took a deep breath and concentrated hard, focusing her thoughts and using the best of her ability, like she did when mind traveling. She desperately attempted to make a connection with the only other person she knew who could hear her thoughts.

Kobe, can you hear me?

Nothing. She was about to give up when she heard the faintest response.

"They can't hear you."

The words were so soft she almost didn't hear them. It was a man's voice, one she didn't recognize.

"What?" She stumbled back and looked around, wondering where the sound had come from. She'd thought she was the only person here.

In a dark corner of the room was a sickly thin man with pale skin. He sat on the stone floor, his eyes sunken. His expression was emotionless, despondent. It looked like he'd been kept in this room a very long time.

"I've tried already," he whispered while looking straight ahead, as if he were thinking about something else and not fully present.

Sam slowly made her way over to him. He looked like he needed medical attention; his body was so thin and malnourished, an outline of a skeleton. "What is your name? What have they...done to you?"

His eyes were wide and he looked nervous around her, like he didn't trust anyone, not even a twelve-year-old girl. He didn't respond for the longest time, just sat and stared up at her with a worrisome expression.

She started to turn back toward the door when she heard it in her mind.

Theo.

She gasped. Was this really Theo—the man Aruna had spoken of, and who Lijing was waiting for? Or was she just hearing things in her mind?

Theo? I'm Sam. Can you hear me?

Yes.

She turned to face him. *I need to tell you something. Lijing is safe. She's waiting for you on Gliese. My friends and I visited her there. She'll be so relieved to find out you're alive.*

Tears rolled down Theo's face.

Sam continued. *You need to hold on. I'm going to get us out of here and then you can see her. I'm going to find a way to—*

It's no use. We cannot leave. He has the building secured. Telepathy doesn't work beyond this compound. We cannot get out.

What? What do you mean? Who is "he"?

Titus.

The name echoed inside her skull. *Titus.* Of course. Titus was behind it all. The two men were the ones who'd captured Theo. And the two men who'd stolen her klug worked for Titus.

A chill ran down her spine.

What have they done to you? How long have you been here?

He didn't answer the first question. All he could manage were a couple of words.

Three years.

Sam's eyes bulged in sudden, awful awareness of their present circumstances. She took a deep breath and tried to push the negative thoughts aside. But this time, the thoughts were deep and foreboding. If they had taken Theo, one of the strongest of all the Mind Travelers, and if it was true that he'd been here three years...surely she would eventually suffer the same fate. Who knew how long he had left?

She didn't have much time. She needed to find out exactly what was going on and how to escape. Surviving, escaping, saving Theo...these were her sole priorities.

The door clicked and opened, casting light into the dark room. Now that the canvas bag was removed, Sam could finally make out the features of her captor. The large man who had taken her now stood in the doorway, crouching to avoid his head hitting the top of the doorframe. His massive arms were the size of tree trunks, his eyebrows twisted in a knot. He pointed to Sam, his voice a low growl. "You. Come with me."

Sam wondered what he would do if she said no.

Sensing her hesitation, he added, "The boss wants to meet you. He's prepared dinner."

"What about Theo? He needs medical attention. He doesn't look—"

"No. The boss was specific. He asked for you."

Sam glanced at Theo. *Don't worry. I will get us out. Just please hold on as long as possible.*

She followed the large man down the corridor toward an elevator. The white walls reminded her of a hospital. She tried to take in as many details about her surroundings as possible, but it proved difficult. Given that there were no windows to the outside, she wondered if they were in the basement of a bunker.

They passed a couple of rooms with observation windows. Sam glanced inside as they passed and noticed a number of scientists working on developing what looked like humanoid robots. Some of the robots looked eerily familiar, like she had seen their faces before.

But where?

It took her a moment to recognize the faces, her mind still groggy and spinning from the recent events. Then she gasped in horror. The lab was replicating prominent and wealthy people in positions of power. She could have sworn she saw a replica of the President of the United States on a conveyer belt, being outfitted with additional robotic enhancements: steel limbs, advanced circuitry, synthetic skin. Beside him, a familiar synthetic face hung from one of the robotic arms on the conveyor belt. It was the face of the wealthiest man alive, Gene Kneep, CEO of GeneVortex.

But why? What was the purpose of these robots?

They arrived at the elevator and Sam took a breath as they waited for the doors to open. They entered, and the guard pushed *G* for the ground floor.

So they *had* been in the basement.

The elevator ascended, and a few moments later the doors opened again. The guard led Sam down another corridor and into a large room. She gazed in astonishment at the extravagant decorations throughout the space: beautiful place settings, a crystal chandelier, and rare, glistening wooden floors. Since trees were considered an endangered species, wood had been banned in many places and made illegal in building construction. Not that Titus had any trouble getting away with it.

Sam tried to take in every detail she could. There were large glass windows, but the lace curtains were drawn slightly. Still, she could make out some details of the scenery—a wooded area in the distance and a large grass lawn, but nothing more.

As she scanned the room, her eyes soon darted to a man seated in a chair by the fireplace.

"Sir, she's here," the guard said.

The man by the fire immediately got up and approached them, a welcoming and pleasant expression on his face. He wore a gray suit that looked expensive, and his black hair was combed to one side. Sam immediately recognized his face, which was plastered on every packaged product he sold. On the packaging, however, he looked stately, young. In real life, his hair had started to fade to a peppered gray color, complemented by large dark circles under his eyes.

His lips curled upward slightly and he extended his hand in greeting. His skin remained tight when he spoke, like his face had been frozen in time. His expression didn't change.

"Welcome, Sam. My name is Titus. Titus Dyaderos."

Sam hesitated, surprised by his even tone and friendly temperament. His voice sounded normal—thoughtful, even. Nevertheless, she refused to acknowledge his seemingly cordial gesture, instead recognizing it for what it truly was: a fake attempt to gain her trust. She saw right through his trickery.

He cleared his throat and continued, sensing her reservations. "Sorry to alarm you, Sam, but it was for your own good. I keep the interior of this laboratory secret and secure from the general public. Lots of my inventions are not yet ready to be unveiled. I can't have people knowing exactly what's going on here, now can I?"

She wondered if he was also referring to the way Theo had been tortured.

He continued. "Every day, I'm the target of threats—people wanting to steal my ideas and technologies. Now, I apologize for the way you were taken. I wanted to show you the lab, of course, but I couldn't just have you walk on site and risk you revealing our secrets. You understand?"

Sam hadn't the slightest clue what he was going on about, but decided to go along with his musings for the time being. At least long enough to get her head together and think of a plan to escape.

She shrugged. She hoped Titus would take her reaction as a confirmation of her seemingly gullible nature, expected of a young and naive girl.

"So, would you care to join me for dinner? You must be starving!"

"How do you know who I am?" she asked, skepticism in her voice.

"Oh, right. I thought you might ask. Well, I know your parents, Sam. I worked with them before. The highly regarded scientists, Dr. Lynne Wilson and Dr. Steve Sanderson." He pulled a chair out from the table.

A wave of panic ran through her. The room started to spin.

Titus lowered his hand and gestured to the chair. "Please, sit. I apologize if my staff kept you in the dark. I sometimes worry about security on the premises."

"*You* worry about security?" she blurted in disbelief. She'd just been taken forcefully from her home!

He cleared his throat. "I guess there's no time to waste—we should get down to business. But first, I've had my staff prepare a meal for us. We can discuss everything over dinner. You must have so many questions."

Something didn't feel right. Sam didn't trust him. She needed to find a way to escape as soon as possible.

"When can I go home?"

Titus's jaw tightened. The question seemed to irritate him. "As soon as you give me some answers. That's all I want, just to ask you some questions. Then I'll send you home."

His response seemed odd; too simple and contrived. He was probably lying and wanted something else…but what?

Reluctantly, she took a seat. In front of them on the table rested a big roast turkey, mashed potatoes and gravy, and a platter of carrots and cranberry sauce, all neatly arranged and waiting to be eaten. It seemed like a lot of food for only two people, and she didn't feel particularly hungry at the moment. In fact, she'd lost her appetite completely.

Theo, can you still hear me?

"Ah, are you speaking to your friends now?" Titus asked as a sneer spread across his face.

Sam gasped.

"I wasn't one hundred percent certain that the Krygians would have given you the power of telepathy, but since you've arrived, that theory is confirmed. Thankfully, your mind reading doesn't work on me," he replied, pointing to a spot behind his ear. "I have a neural implant to prevent you from hearing what I'm thinking. But even so, I decided I needed to take…precautions. This building is equipped with state-of-the-art sensory devices that track your telepathic conversations with others and intercept them if needed."

Sam wasn't sure if she was more shocked about his connection with the Krygians or the fact that he took these precautions.

"For instance, your telepathic conversation with Theo proved very helpful. Now we can locate Lijing and bring her to the lab as well. Thank you for your help with that."

Sam suddenly felt disgusted with herself. She should have been more careful. But how could she have known? She felt the weight of the guilt pulling her downward. Now Lijing was in danger, and all because of her.

Titus's words raced through her mind. She needed to know more about his connection to her parents. None of it made sense.

"How do you know my parents? How do you know about the Krygians?"

Titus smiled. "Please, have some food and we can begin. It's difficult to discuss important matters on an empty stomach, is it not?"

She peered down at her plate but refused to eat for fear of poisoning. She didn't trust him.

Titus sensed her hesitation, but nevertheless dug into the turkey.

"Your parents and I go way back," he began, taking a large bite, gravy dripping down his chin. He quickly patted it away with his napkin. "We all went to school together, but after we graduated they ended up working for the government and academia, whereas I chose to work in the private sector and start my own company."

She wondered what Titus was getting at, and the strange coincidence that he knew her parents. Did he know where they were now? She hadn't heard from them in ages. She remembered the details of the last letter she'd received from her father. The characters had been scribbled quickly, like he was in a hurry to write it. Upon second thought, was it even her father's handwriting? What was going on? She demanded to find answers, to find out the truth! Were they in danger? And did Titus have something to do with it?

"So what?" she responded, impatience in her tone as her temper grew. "You built a company and sacrificed everything for it, including poisoning the planet with all of your pollution and waste!"

"No, you're wrong," he snapped, helping himself to some stuffing. "Think about it, Sam. If it was that bad, the government would send me to jail. They could rewrite the legislation and their policies, but they haven't implemented such harsh penalties. Instead, I go by the rules they have set forth, and I pay my dues. I continue because it helps everyone in the long run."

"Your *fines*, you mean. Not dues," she corrected him. "It doesn't help anyone in the long run but you."

He looked taken aback by Sam's audacity. "Ah, but you are young, Sam. There's so much you don't know about things."

"Oh yeah? Tell me something I don't know," she said, challenging him.

He chuckled. "You're so much like my daughter." He cleared his throat and reached for his glass, taking a quick sip of wine. "She's older than you are, but you're almost as headstrong as she is—stubborn, sometimes."

"Does she realize what a monster you are?" Sam fumed. "You're robbing her and everyone else of our futures on Earth, the way you pollute the environment for your personal profit. She and everyone else are inheriting the bad air and spoiled soil and food. It will be an ugly world by the time she reaches your age."

Her words had angered him and his eyebrow twitched. She hoped this would help her get closer to the truth—if she could only break him in some way.

To her surprise, Titus relaxed his jaw muscles and his eyes became softer, as if something had calmed his mind. He became still and unwavering. His lips curled upward slightly, like he'd been enlightened about some deep, dark secret. "You know, she won't need Earth once she reaches my age." His voice was both serene and apathetic. He took another sip of his wine. "Didn't you notice the research and development lab earlier? What we're building here?"

Sam thought back to the robots she'd seen through the observation window. She had a sick feeling in the pit of her stomach as Titus continued.

"Soon, humans will become immortal. Soon, we won't need air or water or our environment to survive. Body parts are replaceable. The mind can be uploaded. AI really is advancing at lightning pace. I already have completed orders."

Sam couldn't believe what she was hearing. Was it true? Was Titus really building a fleet of superhumans? Robots that would eventually replace their human forms?

"No. The Krygians will find out and stop you."

Titus's face contorted, his eyes glaring at the mention of the name. "The *Krygians*? Let me ask you something: why would the Krygians give a klug to a *child*? A child shouldn't be in possession of such a dangerous weapon!"

She realized now that it was Titus who had stolen it. "It doesn't matter the reason—they gave it to me, not you. It was a gift. It's not yours, so it's best if you give it back before we have a problem."

He almost choked on his food. He cleared his throat and tried to maintain his composure. "Or what?"

Sam didn't answer.

"The only reason I can think of that they would give a device like that to a child is that they're using you, Sam."

"What?"

"That's right. The Krygians are using you to serve a larger purpose. Maybe it's to help rekindle their sun so they can use it to create fuel to power their spaceships. The Krygian people may seem accommodating, but they're a manipulative bunch. They use telepathy to get what they want at all costs."

"You're lying!" she retorted, though she wasn't so sure anymore.

"No. Think about it. They convinced your parents to give you the klug. Why? Why could they not use it themselves? Your parents and the Krygians put you in inherent danger. Why? Because your parents owed the Krygians a debt, and they manipulated your parents to have you pay it."

What was he talking about? Was everything she'd been told a lie? Where were her parents, and why hadn't they visited her? Were the Krygians holding them hostage until she delivered the Hopewell Star to them? No, that wasn't possible!

"I don't believe it," she said, her voice quavering.

"Let's find out. Shall we?" He wiped his face with his napkin and tossed it onto his plate. "I think dinner is finished, now. I hope you enjoyed your last meal. You really should have eaten."

* * *

Sam's mind raced. She needed to escape.

Titus's men took her to another room and bound her in a chair. They brought in the klug, resting it on a table.

Titus motioned for his staff to leave the room with a flick of his hand. "I'll take it from here."

Sam twisted and turned, trying to upend the restraints, but it was no use. She would probably die here after Titus got what he wanted. The situation felt utterly hopeless; her thoughts turned to despair. She wished she could somehow turn back time and avoid this whole mess…

And then she heard something. The soft voice sounded small inside her, but she definitely heard it.

Calm your mind. Trust in your abilities. There is a way to get out of here. You can do it. You are stronger than you know. You can defeat Titus.

She wondered where the words were coming from. Were they her own? It was a female voice, but older. An older version of herself. But how was that possible? She looked over at Titus. Was he able to intercept this telepathy too?

She concentrated. To her surprise, Titus seemed more focused on the device than the mysterious voice speaking to her, sounding louder now. Maybe he couldn't hear it?

"This doesn't have to be painful, Sam," Titus began, laying out some tools on the counter. "I just need you to show me how to unlock the klug. Can you do that?"

"You're giving me a choice?" she asked incredulously. She needed to buy some time to figure out what to do next.

You can escape. You have the power inside you.

Titus's hand pounded down on the metal counter, the sound reverberating around the room. "Well, we don't have all day!"

"I won't help you," she stated calmly, glancing up into his unsteady eyes. "It only works if you do good for others. That's how its power works," she lied. The truth was that no one else could use it since she first touched the klug with her bare hands. The technology had fused with her body and mind. It was a part of her—inseparable. "And really, I don't see you doing any good for others."

He scoffed. "What do you mean?"

"Well, you need to do some sort of good deed for someone else. Like helping Theo. He's really sick. Or removing my restraints, for example. I don't really need them."

Titus shook his head. "Silly girl. Don't you understand? I'm helping humanity escape from this doomed planet. A war is coming."

"What do you mean, a war?" she asked.

His eyes flickered. "As you know, we're not the only ones in the galaxy. There are other beings that will try to eradicate us. The klug is the key to humans traveling farther than ever before. And we need to, in order for our species to survive. The klug would allow humans to travel to Kryg to extract perilium from their moon, for example. It would allow us to locate a small, but powerful star that is believed to have massive amounts of energy that can be harnessed for fuel. Some say its unique properties can be used to create new planets, and even extend life."

Was he talking about the Hopewell Star? How did he know about it? Either way, she would never let him find it.

He continued. "And with perilium, or even this star's substance, well, that would allow us to travel light-years on a regular basis. It would allow humans to locate and occupy other habitable planets. We're doomed if we stay on Earth. It's what I've been working on since I opened my labs. The only plan B is to upload human memories into robots. That way, we become more resilient. We can live indefinitely and acquire knowledge rapidly. Robot parts are replaceable, but humans are not. We are, in the galaxy, considered a very weak species."

It took a moment to process everything Titus had said. If it were true, then it confirmed that Titus had been conducting experiments on perilium, trying to recreate the substance without success. He wanted to find the substance at any cost, even if it meant wreaking havoc on the environment. That's why he'd searched for and stolen her klug—to travel by wormhole to other galaxies and obtain the material from host sources. But what did he mean, a war was coming? Was it really true that humanity was in danger?

"I don't understand. You said a war is coming. What do you mean? How do you know that, and who's after us?"

Titus paused as one of his guards entered the room. He provided Titus with a tablet and whispered something to him, unintelligible to Sam. Titus spoke up. "There's really no time to explain." He tightened the restraints and Sam squirmed, trying to keep calm. His eyebrows furrowed as he concentrated harder. "We'll just have to do this another way." He approached her with the same tablet and held it in front of her. "Looks like at least *someone* cares about you."

She watched the image on the screen come into focus. Her grandfather stood on a golf course, dialing her number into his phone and trying to get a hold of her. In the background, his friends practiced their golf swings, all oblivious to the fact that Titus was monitoring them. Seeing her grandfather now and being unable to respond sent chills down Sam's spine. Had they been watching him the whole time?

"You know, I could send Bjørn to bring him in for questioning too." He gestured to his guard. "I could find a place for him. Maybe where we keep Theo. Ah…yes. The more the merrier. And then, maybe I could use these tools to get what I want, if that's easier for you."

Sam felt the blood drain from her limbs, replaced by a coldness inside her. She felt sick, knowing now that she'd put her grandfather in danger too.

Titus gestured to the tools laid out on the table. Needles and wrenches and ominous multicolored liquids were neatly placed on the surface.

"You won't touch him!" she cried, her voice dry.

"Would you prefer that we took one of your friends instead? Maybe the one that likes making robots. What's his name…Simon? I believe his father works for me. Maybe he would be more useful."

Sam fumed, rage brewing inside her. "You wouldn't."

"Oh, Sam. I thought you were starting to know me better," he laughed. "Indeed, I would. But for now, maybe your grandfather should have the pleasure of meeting me first. We'll get what we need to use the klug, one way or another."

Titus started to leave when Sam spoke up, feeling the heat of anger in her face. "You can try." She felt Titus was getting desperate.

He lost his patience. "The war has already started, Sam. Haven't you wondered why you haven't heard back from your parents yet? Why their mission keeps getting mysteriously extended when it was only supposed to last three months?"

A feeling of dread washed over Sam like a tsunami. She started shaking. How did he know about the details of her parents' mission? What was he saying?

"They've been taken. By the beings you thought were your friends."

No! It wasn't possible!

"The Krygians. They're holding your parents captive, and there's not much time to find them. They're probably dead by now."

None of it made sense. It couldn't be true! Onnisa and Boj—they'd never allow that to happen.

"*No!* You're lying!"

Titus didn't flinch. His eyes were cold. "Keep her in the restraints for now," he told Bjørn, who now stood at the doorway. "Just in case we need her later."

"Yes, boss."

Titus left the room, shutting the door behind him, and leaving Sam feeling worse and more alone than ever. Then, in less than an instant, disbelief crept in, and she came back to her senses. He had to be messing with her. It couldn't be true. Her heart skipped a beat as she remembered what he was going to do. She needed to stop Titus from taking her grandfather and Simon.

She took a deep breath and concentrated on mind traveling. She wasn't going to let her surroundings stop her. If she could travel to another dimension remotely without holding her klug, she could do it again.

The klug rested on the table in front of her, just a few meters away, but her hands were bound tightly. She shifted her gaze to Bjørn, who took a seat on a nearby chair. She closed her eyes and began concentrating on his thoughts.

The girl ain't going nowhere. I have some time to kill. He reached into his pocket and pulled out his phone. Sam realized he was texting his girlfriend. With Bjørn distracted, she had the perfect opportunity to escape.

She concentrated on the light source inside of her, the same light source Mukalakatakalakum had described. She thought about the light filling her body with a gentle warmth, traveling from her head all the way down to the tips of her toes. She focused deeper and concentrated on its power—*her power*. Its intensity grew stronger than before, and the light radiated outward. She could feel the light, the energy, expanding, emanating into the hallways and filling up the building. The light became so bright and forceful, everyone had to shield their eyes...

* * *

A massive explosion rocked the atmosphere, sending shock waves throughout the building. Fires erupted instantaneously in the electrical equipment, sending glass and metal spraying outward. The fire spread within the building.

The initial blast of the explosion caught Titus off guard, and he stumbled back, trying to avoid the flames that burst forth from a nearby electrical outlet, the fire rippling across the floor. He stared in astonishment at the frantic scene unfolding in front of him. His staff were thrown about forcefully, some losing consciousness. A couple of laboratory assistants scrambled for cover under a table, worried that another explosion would ensue. He watched as they joined others running down the hall, some tripping over broken glass, scrambling to evacuate the building.

But it was too late.

The alarm went off and the sprinkler system activated. Titus watched in horror as the water drenched the flames along with his precious equipment, rendering it completely useless and unsalvageable.

He ran toward the room where Bjørn guarded Sam, but a large, bloody gash on his leg from the explosion hampered his speed. He limped and wavered down the corridor. He stood in a daze when he reached the entryway. The door had been blown out from the inside. The walls of the room were charred. There was no sign of the girl or the klug.

"*No!*"

Bjørn limped toward him. Titus noticed a large shard of glass in his arm. By the way he approached, dragging his leg, it looked like he'd broken his foot.

"Sir, it's the girl...she's gone!"

* * *

The tide was out. Kato and Kobe walked along the ocean floor in St.

Andrews, stopping every so often to check out what the sea had left along the shore that day. They were staying at their aunt and uncle's place for a few days.

Kato bent down and checked out some coral attached to a rock at low tide, admiring its intricate design. She shifted her gaze farther down. "Hey! I think I got one."

Kobe looked up. He'd been actively scavenging the beach floor for sand dollars and starfish, with no luck as of yet.

Kato picked up the sand dollar and held it up.

"Nicely done," Kobe said.

She tucked it safely in her pocket. When she looked at her brother again, his expression changed. His eyes grew wide.

"What's wrong?"

"I—I don't know. I tried to make a connection with Sam, but it's not working. The telepathy isn't working."

"Maybe it just doesn't work anymore," Kato said. "Like, maybe it was only meant to last—"

"No. It's not that. It's like…like I have a weird feeling something is wrong."

"I'm sure it's okay. I'll try texting her."

Sam? Are you there?

No response. She dialed Sam's number. It rang seven times and went to voice mail.

"Hey, it's Kato. Can you please call me when you get this?" She hung up.

"Maybe I'll ask Simon to check the Flybot. See if he's seen anything unusual," Kobe said.

"Yeah. Good idea."

* * *

Simon's phone buzzed.

"Hey Kobe, what's up?" Simon asked, pressing pause on the most intense moment of his video game and putting down the controller.

"Simon, I think something's wrong with Sam." Kobe's words were rapid and his voice manic. "She's not answering our messages. Can you please check on the Flybot?"

Simon leapt from the couch. "Yep, will do." He ran up the stairs two at a time toward his room. Sure enough, the Flybot was flashing red, indicating activity. He opened up his computer program to check on the video feed. Sam had placed something over the Flybot, so the image was blurry.

"Just a moment." Simon pressed a button to activate the audio feed and waited, listening.

The blood drained from his face and his mouth went dry.

"Simon, are you still there? What's up? Did you see anything?" Kobe asked.

"It's TitusTech…" Simon started, his voice barely a whisper. "They've taken Sam!"

"Oh no!" Kobe said. "What are we going to do?"

"We need to stop them," Simon said. "And I can think of only one place they would take her…the TitusTech lab in Shediac."

There was a pause on the other end of the line, then Kato's voice interrupted in the background. "Let me…speak to him. Hand it over…what? Now." Her voice grew louder. "Simon, we're nowhere near Shediac. What if we don't get there in time?"

"You're not close, but I am. It's a half hour away. I have an idea, hold on. I'll call you back in a minute." Simon hung up and grabbed one of his Flybots, sticking it in a bag. He grabbed some paper and a pen and began writing.

Dear Mom and Dad,

Please don't hate me. I need to help a friend. I'll be home later.

Love, Simon.

Simon's mom had gone out to lunch with a friend that day and taken her friend's car, and his father was away on a business trip. The keys to his mom's autonomous car rested on the coffee table. Without thinking, he grabbed them and made his way outside. He opened the car door, climbed into the front seat, and began calibrating the GPS navigation system. Searching through the list of TitusTech addresses, he finally pulled up the address to the laboratory in Shediac.

"Bingo."

He selected the address and hit the start button. The car roared to life and reversed down the driveway in fully-autonomous mode.

He knew his mom would be livid when she got home, and he didn't want to think about her reaction. He'd probably be grounded indefinitely, but it was for the best. He needed to help Sam.

He dialed Kobe's number. "Hey, I'm on my way to the lab. I, uh…borrowed my mom's car."

"Okay, how did—oh. I forgot it's autonomous. Okay. Let us know when you get there. In the meantime, I'll try making a connection again. I'll let you know if I hear anything."

"Copy that. Keep in touch. Over and out." Simon hung up and started calibrating his Flybot. This one could actually fly, and would be able to get close enough to the building to see what was happening inside.

The seconds ticked by like minutes and time seemed to stretch on slowly. Simon kept checking his phone to see if any texts came in from Kato or Kobe. Nothing. And no texts or calls from his parents yet, so he still had time.

Finally, after what felt like eternity, the car came to a slow stop in a visitor parking lot outside of the TitusTech laboratory. A security guard stood at the main gate up ahead, at least a hundred feet away from the main building. At this distance, he wouldn't be able to get a good view of the lab.

Simon opened his backpack and took out the Flybot and operation screen, rolling down his window enough to allow the Flybot to escape.

"Okay, Flybot, do your thing." He used the screen to activate the Flybot's wings, and it started buzzing. He studied the guard up ahead. Even though he was pretty far from the main entrance, he didn't want the guard suspecting anything unusual.

"Hmm. Let's try stealth mode." He pressed a few buttons on the screen. The Flybot immediately changed its color from a solid black tone to a silver mirror, reflecting its surroundings and effectively camouflaging itself.

"Brilliant!" He could no longer see the Flybot directly in front of him. However, it still showed up as a red dot on his screen, along with the video feed around it, motion capturing its 360-degree view of its surroundings in separate images. He pressed a few more buttons to remove the audio buzzing sound, and a moment later the buzzing ceased. "One last step…" He keyed in the locational info to control its flight path, and watched as the Flybot flew toward the lab, capturing video as it quickly zoomed through the air.

Simon dialed Kato's number this time. He wanted to tell her the good news, that he'd made it to the lab and that the Flybot worked.

"Hey, it's Simon."

"Simon! Have you seen anything? Are you there at the lab?"

"Yeah. Just got here now. The Flybot's working." He glanced down at the screen, and the images came into view. "It's...oh, wait! Oh...oh no!"

Simon slowed the Flybot so that it hovered in midair. Images of smoke and the burning building came up on the screen in front of him.

It was too late.

He saw some police cordoning off part of the property in the area behind the lab. It looked like there were dead bodies lying on the ground.

"Simon? Are you okay? What's wrong?" Kato's voice sounded distant on the other end.

He took an unsteady breath. "I'm sorry, Kato. It's..." He sighed and continued, his voice barely a whisper. "We're too late."

17

Titus's jaw dropped. "What do you mean—*gone?* She was here a few minutes ago! How could you let her get away?"

"I, uh, sorry—"

"Find her!" Titus bellowed.

"Yes, sir!"

Titus could feel his anger erupting like a volcano ready to explode. Years of hard work, countless hours of trial and error, expensive and irreplaceable equipment…all gone in an instant.

Because of her.

Now, he wouldn't be able to use Sam's capabilities to reverse engineer the klug and crack the sequence. He wouldn't be able to obtain the perilium or star samples. Everything was lost. He had failed, because of her.

Rage erupted inside as he witnessed the disastrous effects of the blast taking their toll. He brought his sleeve up to his mouth to keep the smoke away from his face. He needed to evacuate the building. With the lab equipment demolished and the fire spreading, there wasn't a lot of time. He felt the searing pain of the gash in his leg wearing him down. He tried putting pressure on the wound, the blood oozing between his fingers. He felt dizzy and faint. He steadied himself against the wall, and with the other hand he pulled at his tie, twisting it off. He wrapped it over his leg to control the bleeding. Then a thought occurred to him.

She was going to find Theo.

Titus made his way slowly to the stairwell, limping and coughing out the smoke that invaded his lungs. His head spun. He held onto the railing as he descended the steps one by one in a feverish rage, with the sole fixation of stopping her.

* * *

Sam opened her eyes and blinked a couple of times. She was alive. Miraculously, she'd survived the explosion, but it wasn't over yet. She needed to find Theo and escape. She stood up and brushed herself off, surprised that she was no longer restrained in that room with Bjørn. She must have activated the klug and mind traveled. But where was she now, and where was the klug?

She looked around and noticed an emergency floor plan bolted to the wall. She ran to it, trying to figure out her location in this maze-like building. She checked her bearings and realized she was still on the main floor. She needed to get down to the basement where Theo was located.

Screams sounded down the hallway, then a man's voice, shouting. It was Titus.

Sam ducked into the stairwell and raced down the stairs. She entered a hallway and ran toward Theo's room. As she got closer, she noticed the door slightly ajar. There was a chance they could escape if he'd survived the blast.

What had caused it? She couldn't remember the moment before the blast. It had happened all too quickly. She only remembered a feeling of heat and warmth inside her, coupled with anger, fear, and electricity. Had she caused it?

Her heart fluttered with the hope that Theo was still alive. She was almost there, just a few meters away when she heard a familiar loud, ugly voice.

"Stop right there, or I'll shoot!"

Sam slowed to a halt and turned around.

Titus had a gun aimed at her head, shaking it frantically.

A moment later, she heard a familiar noise. It was faint at first, but the whirring of the klug grew louder as it approached, a gentle, soothing sound to her ears. It zipped down the hallway and levitated in front of her. Then she heard footsteps approach from a distance. She looked over to see Theo walking toward her slowly, trying to steady himself. Being locked up for so long had weakened him over time, but she was glad to see him now, alert and able to walk. They didn't have a lot of time. She raised her hand slightly to warn him to stop, as she realized he wasn't yet in Titus's line of sight. But it was too late. He took another step into the main hallway, and his eyes widened in shock as if he'd seen a ghost.

Sam saw everything, every millisecond, in slow-motion. The klug shone brighter and brighter, altering the surroundings of the room into a whirling, spinning wheel. A force field of shimmering light radiated from its core, with Sam at its center.

Titus clasped his gun tightly and pulled the trigger, just as Theo dived in front of Sam, trying to block the bullet's trajectory and its intended target.

As time seemed to slow down, Sam saw the bullet approach—only to ricochet off the klug's force field, breaking apart and falling to the ground. The klug's force field became larger and stronger, expanding toward Theo and Titus, pulling them toward it. When it reached Titus, his gun flew to the other end of the room, as if the klug's force had caused its repulsion like two ends of a magnet. The room spun faster, and in an instant the three were consumed within the klug's gravitational field, falling down the wormhole.

It seemed different than before—exhilarating. This time, Sam knew what to expect.

The wormhole journey wasn't as disorienting. She knew exactly when the hole would twist and turn, and she anticipated the falling and twirling patterns, preparing herself mentally and accordingly. There were no surprises this time. She looked back to see Titus lurching from side to side, holding his stomach, his face looking pale and sickly, in absolute fright. Theo's eyes were closed, looking nonresponsive.

Please, Theo. You can make it. Just hold on a bit longer.

The familiar flashes of light and sparks up ahead meant they were close to reaching the end of the tunnel. In three seconds, they found themselves lying in a grassy field near Kassa Lake. Sam saw Onnisa, Boj, and the other Krygians looking down at them with apprehension.

Why had the klug brought them back to Kryg? Had she deliberately mind traveled here? She glanced over at Theo, lying lifeless on the ground a few feet away. She then looked at Titus, sputtering and trying to get up but having difficulty as he held his leg to steady himself. His face red with fury, he looked determined, about to lunge at her.

Before Sam could react or catch her breath, Onnisa stepped toward Titus, placing her hand on his shoulder. A sudden shock of electric current burst forth, throwing Titus backward. He lay on the ground, trembling and speechless. A moment later, a few large, muscular Krygians dressed in black approached and surrounded Titus with glowing blue bands in their hands. They quickly placed them around Titus's wrists and bound him tightly so he couldn't move.

"Titus Dyaderos, you will be tried for your transgressions," Onnisa exclaimed, turning to one of the guards. "Take him to a holding cell."

Sam finally found words. "It's really good to see you, Onnisa," she said faintly. She suddenly felt weak and light-headed. She wanted to say more, but found it difficult. All she wanted to do was sleep. She touched her face and shrank back at the sight of blood on her hands. Her arms were scratched and bruised.

"And you, Queen Samantha. But you must rest. Let them take you to the infirmary."

One of the guards approached. He lifted her effortlessly, and everyone made a pathway for them to proceed.

"Wait! Theo needs help too. Please. He's my friend. Can you heal him?" She pointed to the spot where he lay on the ground.

Onnisa nodded. Then everything went black.

* * *

Sam wasn't sure how much time had passed when she woke up. Something that looked like seaweed had been placed on her arms. She felt soft bandages on her face as well. She went to prop herself up, but her arms trembled when she tried to put pressure on them. She looked down at her legs. They were probably the same, like soft jelly.

"How are you feeling?"

The familiar voice made her smile. "Boj! Thank you for taking care of me. I'm feeling a little weak, but better."

"Good to hear. I made some herbs for you to accelerate the healing process. Keep the bandages on," Boj ordered as he caught her touching them. He placed a small bowl by her bedside. "Here, drink."

She drank it slowly. It tasted like chicken soup, only heartier, and with what looked like vegetables in it. Instantly she felt more energized.

"Don't sit up too fast. Take your time. We still have until sundown, which will be in a few hours. That's when they're going to announce the list of Titus's wrongdoings in front of the Elders. They will provide evidence. He will have a chance to respond. After that, they will determine his fate."

Sam wanted to ask Boj how they knew so much about Titus, but stopped herself. The Krygians had monitored humans from their moon base for who knew how long. She suddenly felt naive, considering how much she didn't know.

Something else nagged at her. "How is Theo doing? Is he going to be okay?"

The question made Boj fidget. His eyes darted around the room and he shook his right hand a couple of times at his side before answering. She'd never seen him look so apprehensive.

"He will be okay, but it's going to take some time. We're working to restore his health." He looked at her bowl of unfinished soup. "Drink up."

Boj left the room, giving Sam some privacy to rest and collect her thoughts. She finished her last drop of soup and set the bowl aside. She heard footsteps outside the door, then two voices speaking softly to one another in another language. A moment later, the door opened and Onnisa made her way inside.

"I came to check on you." She placed her hand on Sam's face and pulled the bandage off ever so delicately to check the progress of the advanced-healing salve. "Good, just as I expected." She removed the bandage and checked the others, taking them off one by one.

Sam looked down at her arms and legs where the bandages had been. The bruises were gone. The places where she had been bleeding had already healed, and she could only make out a few faint scratches, but nothing more. She put her hand to her face where the bandage had been. It felt smooth to the touch, like silk.

"Thank you, Onnisa." Still a little groggy and weak, Sam nevertheless thought about her mission to save Earth and Kryg. She felt the weight resting on her conscience. "Onnisa, I've failed you. I'm sorry."

"What do you mean?"

"The Earth, it's…it's dying. I didn't stop Titus in time. There's so much damage…I wasn't able to reverse it…"

"Shh. That is not true, Queen Samantha."

Sam winced at the mention of her title. She didn't feel like she deserved it. She felt like an imposter, and a failure.

Onnisa continued, as if sensing her reservations. "You have done so much for so many. You have changed your planet's fate. You have helped take down Titus, and in doing so, you have saved your planet and many more planets in the future that Titus would have compromised. He will be brought to justice in due time. You will see. The environment of Earth will soon be restored."

Sam wondered how Onnisa could be so certain about this. Her thoughts became jumbled and she couldn't get the words out quickly enough. "There's something else I need to tell—"

Onnisa looked up with a faint smile. "Shh. You must rest, Queen

Samantha. You have not fully healed. I must go now and prepare for the hearing that will take place in a few hours. I will see you soon."

* * *

Dusk fell on the planet Kryg. All of the Krygians congregated at Kassa Lake where a small bonfire had been lit. Their purple moon shone brightly in the starry sky.

Sam stood beside Boj and watched intently as the guards brought Titus onto a small stage in front of the panel of Elders. Onnisa strode to the front of the stage, nodding to the others as she passed.

Sam wanted desperately to tell Onnisa everything. She had tried earlier, but Onnisa had cut her off. She had so much to tell her about mind traveling to the Hopewell Star, the voices she'd heard, the Rigellians who had been taken hostage and were working as slaves to the Krygians, and the strange discussion she overheard with someone named Boku. After the trial, her priority was to find Onnisa and tell her the truth, and as quickly as possible.

"We call to the hearing Titus Dyaderos," Onnisa began. She looked directly at Titus, who sat bound in a chair looking horribly nervous. "You are being tried for your transgressions against humanity, the Earth, and its inhabitants, and for your crimes against the planet Kryg."

"Please, this is a misunderstanding," Titus pleaded. "We can negotiate terms. All I wanted was a sample of perilium from your moon. Can't we discuss this? Please!"

"What will happen to him?" Sam asked. "I mean, if they find him guilty?"

Boj whispered to Sam. "If they find him guilty, I imagine the Elders will banish him to serve the rest of his sentence in our prison. He would never be allowed to return to Earth, even if the leaders of Earth demanded it—we do not yet have an extradition treaty in place, and I understand his crimes are quite significant."

"Hmm." Sam thought about Boj's words for a moment. "I didn't realize Earth leaders knew so much about the Krygians, or that we even had laws between our two planets."

"Only a few Earth leaders know about us. They keep it a secret from the general public to avoid panic."

"Why would they panic?" Sam asked. "I mean, you're all quite friendly. I don't see a reason why you'd have to keep it a secret. I feel like there'd be more value in sharing knowledge between our civilizations. And there's certainly value in more people knowing we aren't alone."

Boj sighed and paused for a moment. "I agree with you, but it's not really up to me. I mean, there will be a time when that happens, when more people know of us, but I'm not sure when. I think it will be soon, because after all, you're here, and that is part of the prophecy. As you know, Earth has been at risk, and we really do need more people from Earth to help make things right. We have a lot of technology we can share, but the Elders say humans need to prove that they are ready and worthy of it before we guide them further. Otherwise, bad things could happen. People could take our technology and use it for other purposes, if you know what I mean. Like what Titus did with the klugs. He sacrificed a lot of species and resources in pursuit of that technology, and he did so in a dangerous and wasteful manner. All because he wanted to get something for his own personal gain. That doesn't align with our values."

"I see." Sam switched her focus and thought about Titus's predicament now. "In a way, he's lucky. I mean, if I had to be banished somewhere, Kryg would be my first choice. I could think of worse worlds to be banished on." She thought of Gliese with its black water pythons and its forbidding and dreary landscape. She thought about Lijing, and wondered how she was doing.

Onnisa ignored Titus's pleas. "I now request the list be read and heard, and the evidence be provided."

There were whispers among the Krygians, and everyone went silent. A moment later, another Elder stood and brought a device to Onnisa. She opened it, and a hologram appeared in front of them. The words on the hologram were written in Krygian, but Onnisa translated it as she read.

She first listed Titus's crimes against humanity. The words and images projected in front of them all brought back recent difficult memories for Sam. "Item one: kidnapping, forcible confinement of a minor, assault, torture, and attempted murder."

Sam shuddered to think about how Titus had treated Theo and herself, and wondered how many others had been affected. As Onnisa read each line, a secondary hologram appeared. It shone in front of the audience, displaying photo evidence of Titus and his company carrying out each infraction.

Sam watched in silence, glad to have Boj next to her for support. She stuck her hands into her pockets, gently running her fingers over the familiar smooth form of the klug. After this was over, she needed to talk to Onnisa as soon as possible. She needed to show her the map to the Hopewell Star that Lijing had given her, which she kept in the klug's interior compartment. She needed to tell her about how she'd mind traveled to the Hopewell Star, and what she'd witnessed there.

Onnisa continued. "Item two: theft of Krygian technology and intentional interference with Krygian-Human relations, causing conflict…"

It wasn't long before Onnisa moved on to list Titus's crimes against nature and the environment. "Item twenty-six: illegal dumping of waste products into rivers and aquifers. One thousand, seven hundred and eighty-seven infractions."

Everyone watched intently, and the crowd seemed to grow restless over the course of the evening as Onnisa continued translating the very long list. "Item fifty-three: toxic water contamination and resulting destruction of an ecosystem, related deaths and extinction of species and wildlife. One thousand three hundred and ninety-six infractions. Over three billion casualties, including fish, birds, turtles, plants, and other wildlife. Item fifty-four: greenhouse gas emissions. Eighty-seven billion metric tons of carbon dioxide emitted."

A projection of Titus's laboratory—or what *had* been his laboratory—along with images of his robots, came into clear view. "Item fifty-five," Onnisa continued, "planning to secretly replace the world's leadership with lifelike robots to serve nefarious purposes."

After what seemed like an hour, the anticipation was replaced by feelings of relief as the last transgression was read aloud. Everyone had been standing for a long time, and they looked exhausted as the night crept closer. Sam was eager for the closure of the hearing and the final decision.

The Elders took a moment to discuss matters among themselves, then Onnisa spoke up again. "Titus Dyaderos, you have been found guilty. You will be banished to Kryg and made to serve the rest of your years in prison. What do you have to say for yourself regarding your offences?"

Titus cleared his throat. "I'm not the only one who committed those crimes on Earth, so why are you only banishing me? It isn't fair. I don't deserve it. I want to go back to Earth."

There were sudden restless murmurs in the crowd.

Onnisa continued. "Titus Dyaderos requests an exception. Only our queen can grant such a request for a human to return to Earth. I now call upon Queen Samantha Sanderson to decide the fate of Titus Dyaderos."

Sam thought about what might happen if he returned to Earth. If everything had been destroyed in the fire, the evidence would be gone too. Titus would claim it was an accident. She and Theo would be made to testify at a hearing. Without any evidence, there was a chance he would get away scot-free. She couldn't let that happen. She needed to honor the Krygians' wishes and the results of the proceeding.

She made her way to the stage and tried to think about what she would say with all of her thoughts racing through her mind. She decided to address him the same way the Elders had. The words formed slowly, but she knew what she wanted to say.

"Titus Dyaderos, your crimes are numerous and unforgiveable. You have done more harm to Earth and its inhabitants than good. If I send you back, you will surely continue your terrible ways. I recommend your banishment to Kryg—it's probably more of a privilege, rather than a punishment. As such, I must agree with the Krygian Elders and respect their decision. There will be no exceptions."

The Krygians cheered, and she took another breath. "I would like to take this opportunity to thank the Krygians for their hospitality, for this due process, and for saving my life." She suddenly remembered the words Onnisa had spoken to her when she'd visited her on the moon base. She looked out at the scores of Krygians watching her intently, and acknowledged them by addressing the crowd with her clearest, most confident voice. "*Katu ona vis a hanu daytu.* May the light continue to shine bright inside you."

A moment of silence fell upon the crowd, and the Krygians looked moved. They repeated these words to Sam and she quietly made her way off the stage, her heart still pounding, but feeling triumphant. Titus protested as the guards took him away, but none of that mattered now.

She marveled at the irony of how Titus had wanted to visit Kryg in order to take a sample from their moon. Now that he'd been banished here, each time he looked up at the night sky, the glowing purple moon would be a reminder of what he had never accomplished on Earth.

"Well done, Sam," Boj said as they made their way to the huts near Kassa Lake.

"Thank you, Boj, but my mission is not over." Her hand brushed against the klug inside her pocket. The device felt smooth and cool against her fingers. "I must see Onnisa as soon as possible."

* * *

Sam walked along an unassuming grassy trail that led away from the other huts. She ventured down the pathway to Onnisa's hut, bordered by large vertical stones that jutted out of the ground. Phosphorescent plants lit the trail, making it easy to see where she was going.

It seemed Onnisa had been expecting her, because the door opened before Sam had a chance to knock.

"Greetings, Queen Samantha." Onnisa gestured her inside.

As Sam entered, she noticed the familiar fragrant scent of cooking herbs, possibly the same ones Boj had given her while he helped her heal. Theo was sleeping in the corner of the room, bandages wrapped around his body. Onnisa carefully tended to his wounds.

"Will he be okay?"

"Yes. He will get better. But he needs to rest before he can get stronger."

Sam remembered how dire the circumstances were at Titus's lab. Those difficult memories would always remain with her. Although Theo looked somewhat better now that he had progressed in his healing, she couldn't erase the image of his look of fear and hopelessness when she'd first met him.

"Onnisa, there is something I need to ask you."

Onnisa nodded and stirred the herbs as they cooked.

"When Titus kidnapped me…I mean, he said some pretty terrible things." Sam exhaled a heavy sigh. "I wasn't sure how he knew so much about…well, about you, and my parents."

Onnisa looked up but remained silent, allowing Sam to continue.

"I wasn't sure if what he told me was true, or if they were all lies."

Sam felt awkward saying this to Onnisa. She wanted to believe Titus had lied to her about everything, but part of her worried that some of it might have been true. Was it best to question Onnisa about it? She wanted to. She trusted Onnisa, and the uncertainty of not knowing would no doubt continue to nag at her if she didn't.

"Can you tell me more about the klugs? Lijing told me there's more than one. Is that true? Can you tell me what purpose they serve?"

Onnisa stood silently for a while. "Yes, there are more than one. They are given to different…*gifted* people, to serve a higher purpose. I cannot tell you that purpose."

"Why not?"

Onnisa looked wary and avoided the question. "I can only tell you that the Krygian Elders were given the task of dispatching the klugs. Since Titus's imprisonment and the explosion at his lab, of all the ones that were still intact, most have since been returned to their rightful owners."

Sam thought about Onnisa's words. *If you and the Elders were monitoring Earth from your moon base, wouldn't you know that the klugs were going missing? Why didn't you intervene sooner?*

Onnisa's words flowed into her mind softly. *Queen Samantha, we are not meant to intervene in human affairs. It is not our way. Only when the fate of the planet is in danger are we required to intercede.*

Did my parents ever owe a debt to you? Is that why I was given the klug?

No. They've never owed us any debts. That is not why you were given the device.

Are they… Sam couldn't even think the words. She was too nervous about the potential answer. Still, she needed to ask the difficult questions, even though she couldn't bear the thought of the worst news.

"Titus said my parents are being held captive. By your people. Is that true?"

No. That would never happen.

Sam let out a deep sigh. She didn't realize she'd been holding her breath so long. Titus had probably said it to get to her. So why did she still feel on edge? Then she remembered.

"Onnisa, when I was in Titus's lab, when I was tied up and thought I was going to die…I heard a voice. Inside me. And I…I was just wondering who—"

You know who it was. It was your own voice. You listened to your voice.

"I thought maybe it was. But…why? How?"

Onnisa continued. *We are not always attuned to our inner voices. Sometimes we only listen to the voice that questions things and casts self-doubt. But you listened to your true voice, the one you needed to hear the most to help you at the time. Your voice is powerful, and you have much to offer. Be patient with yourself, trust your inner voice, and you'll find that your voice, your intentions, your ideas, and your dreams may travel far, and will spark a light in others while serving as a guiding light for yourself at the darkest of times. After all, if you do not trust in your own voice, who will?*

Sam let the weight of Onnisa's words sink in. She remembered the voice speaking to her at the time. At first, she wasn't sure of its origin. She always seemed to listen to what other people said about her, but she never really stopped to listen to what her own voice had to say. She didn't realize her voice could be so powerful or positive, or give her support when she needed it most. Now it made sense.

She was about to ask Onnisa more questions but stopped herself when she felt something buzzing beside her. She took the klug out of her pocket and watched in awe as it began to float in front of them, opening up to reveal the map inside.

"Sorry, I meant to give this to you earlier, Onnisa. I think it's a map to the Hopewell Star, located in the Cygnus region. At first I feared the star had collapsed inside a black hole," she said, pointing to the main star in the first image, and then pointing to the second image, where the same star looked like it had vanished. "But I don't think it's a black hole." She held out the map for Onnisa to take, and noticed Onnisa's eyes now glowed a bright golden color as she studied it closely.

Thank you for this. The Elders will need to review it, but I believe this will help us further…

Onnisa's thoughts trailed off, and Sam wondered about how exactly the Hopewell Star powered Kryg with it being so far away. She was about to tell Onnisa more about her observations when her thoughts were interrupted.

What do you think the Hopewell Star is?

Confused by the question, Sam thought hard, her mind racing. She ventured a wild guess. *A star contains lots of energy. It's a power source, is it not?*

Yes. And what do you think it powers?

Your sun?

Precisely. But also so much more. The Hopewell Star is made up of concentrated life energy that permeates the cosmos. It also powers your klug. This life energy is also inside you. It is inside me. It is inside all humans, Krygians, and other creatures. We are made of this stardust. You were able to tap into its energy when you were suffering in darkness, and you used its power to create the explosion at Titus's lab.

Sam suddenly felt bad after hearing these words. If Onnisa was telling the truth, she was responsible for the deaths at Titus's lab. She hadn't wanted to hurt anyone. She'd just desperately wanted to get out.

I don't understand how I tapped into its power like that, and I don't understand how one small star can affect so much, even across galaxies.

It affects everything. We are all interconnected, Sam. What happens on your planet has ripple effects across galaxies. What your scientists might refer to as the butterfly effect, but on a much larger scale.

But if the Hopewell Star powers so many things and people, then where does it get its power from?

We have studied this to some extent, but soon we will be able to study it in more depth with the location you've provided. Our understanding is that there is an exchange of energy in the universe. The Hopewell Star's energy is extracted from the universe's beings. It is a life source, powered by the will and good deeds of the universe's beings. When you do good things to help those that need it most—the vulnerable, the weary—it awakens their inner energy, and they are able to help others too. This light source inside everyone grows stronger by helping others, and as it grows, so too will the Hopewell Star grow in size, and our sun will become brighter on Kryg as a result. Over time, it will extend the life of our sun.

Sam considered the implications. *If doing good helps bring light to Kryg's sun through an exchange of energy, then doing bad deeds would cause it to dim over time. But I can't control others' actions, only my own.*

Yes, only your own. But…you can influence others in a positive way, too. You can lead. You can inspire. You can continue to reach out, to help others find their own light inside them, Onnisa explained.

Sam realized now why the words the Krygians spoke to one another—*may the light continue to shine bright inside you*—meant so much to them. It was what gave them hope and essentially life, because without it, their sun would dim over time. It was also a reminder of their duty to inspire and help others grow.

Onnisa continued. *As you know, Earth is suffering. It is very fragile and unique. You must work with others to keep it healthy, in order for it to survive in the long term. This is your next task.*

Sam thought about this for a moment. She didn't particularly feel like a leader, or someone who inspired. She didn't know how to influence others. And yet, looking back at all of the things that had changed over the past year, she wondered. She had grown closer to Kato, Kobe, and Simon. Kobe had become more comfortable talking to people. Hunter no longer bullied others. She had saved Theo. She had banished a grown, wicked criminal to a Krygian prison.

She wanted to tell Onnisa about how she had mind traveled to the Hopewell Star and witnessed a group of Krygians harnessing its energy and building a new planet, and of the strange conversation between Boku and the other Krygian, but she lost her train of thought when she heard someone stirring. Theo was awake and reaching for his bandages. She decided she would tell Onnisa later.

Sam leaned down beside him. "Don't be afraid, Theo. You're going to be okay. This is Onnisa, a Krygian Elder. She's helping to heal you. You are on the planet Kryg, and once you get better, we can head back to Earth. Just try to rest and relax as much as possible."

He nodded. When he saw Onnisa, he didn't look fearful, but rather, fascinated.

"Thank you for saving my life," he whispered to Sam, and then went back to sleep.

18

As Theo slept and recovered, and as Onnisa tidied up her tools and medicines, Sam felt a heaviness in her heart and mind. Telling Onnisa the truth about what she witnessed would likely upset her. But nevertheless, she knew it was important—essential, even—to help the Krygians and humanity unite to save their planets. As such, she couldn't wait any longer.

Onnisa seemed to sense Sam's concerns. *You have a heavy heart, Queen Samantha. What is the matter?*

Sam sighed and took in a deep breath. *Onnisa, I fear something terrible has happened. The Hopewell Star...I mind traveled there, and I think...I think your people are harnessing its energy. They are using it to create a new planet.*

Onnisa stopped what she was doing and held out her hand. Sparks flew as Sam recalled each memory in detail, including the conversation between Boku and the other Krygian. Onnisa's expression changed, and trepidation flickered in her eyes. By the end of the exchange, Onnisa was physically shaking.

Onnisa, are you okay? Sam reached out to steady her. *What can I do to help?*

Onnisa's eyes glazed over in a daze. She uttered three words: *Tell no one.*

Sam nodded. *Of course, Onnisa.* She trusted Onnisa and would honor her wish. She suspected that leaking this information to the wrong people would have disastrous consequences, and she didn't want that. She felt better after telling her, like a heavy weight had been lifted. She suddenly sensed something had changed inside of her too. Whether it was a premonition or something else, it was as though she could see that things would resolve eventually. She even felt an unusual sense of happiness, despite the circumstances.

She reached out just in time to steady Onnisa, whose demeanor had shifted.

Onnisa's eyes widened as they met Sam's. *This...will change everything.*

* * *

Onnisa called a private meeting with Elder Sika. She trusted her the most of all the Elders. She needed to tell the others, but did not want to cause panic among them until they had figured out a plan together. If Queen Samantha's observations were correct, the Kantak tribe had been secretly building a megastructure around the Hopewell Star to harness its energy, and working on constructing an artificial planet in close proximity. The star would eventually become enclosed and inaccessible if they did not put an end to it in time.

The negative effects of the dimming star were already being felt by the Krygians. Illnesses were spreading, there was a reduction in plant potency, and plant species were going extinct. Moreover, the Kantak people had captured the Rigellians and were forcing them to work on harnessing the star's energy to build an artificial planet. Their queen also worried about a potential threat to her parents. Onnisa would need to quickly determine if this threat was real and act accordingly.

Sika looked equally disturbed by the allegations. "The Kantak tribe's actions are rippling across the galaxy. Their greed is increasing and darkness is spreading. First, with the murder of Mukalakatakalakum, and now this. And Boku is part of it. Why didn't he disclose this information to us? That was his role and primary responsibility to the Elders."

"Precisely. He failed us, Sika. Instead of working with the Elders to protect all Krygians, he has been compromised. He is now solely working for the Kantak."

"And worse."

"Yes, and worse. Instead of preserving Kryg, they are creating a new one, previously without our knowledge, and it won't be open to all Krygians, only the Kantak."

"The Hopewell Star's power belongs to everyone, not just a select few. It must not be closed off, ever."

"Agreed. That is our code. And the Kantak have broken it."

"Why did we not see the signs earlier, Onnisa?"

Onnisa had always suspected something, but it was the girl—their queen—who had brought the truth to light. She had provided the missing link in this.

"While we were so concerned about how humans were treating their Earth and humanity's crimes, we did not focus on what was happening here, and the crimes of our own people."

"Surly not all of the Kantak are involved…"

"No, but we need to seek out those responsible and bring them to justice."

"The badges they wear on their bodies…the infinity symbol…"

"Yes, the infinity symbol. Have they forgotten the true, original significance of that symbol? It is meant to uphold the oath to protect both planets for eternity, and honoring the power of the Hopewell Star."

"They have only shown us dishonor. They do not abide by our code."

"The code of what it truly means to be Krygian. Have the Kantak forgotten? We are an older civilization, and therefore have a duty to protect our younger siblings, the Earthlings. Instead of protecting them, the Kantak have robbed them of a future. Of our future, also."

"This will mean war, Onnisa."

"Yes, it will."

"We will need a plan. We will need resources and ships to intercept and dismantle it."

"And we will need to continue as if nothing is amiss. We cannot risk the girl in all of this."

"Agreed. Only when we are ready, and the plan is set in motion…"

"Yes, Sika. Only then will we act."

* * *

After sharing the news with Onnisa, Sam felt a significant burden lifted from her. Even though she didn't know exactly what would happen next, or what Onnisa would do with the information, things carried on as usual, with one exception: Onnisa was absent for longer periods of time.

Nevertheless, Sam was grateful to have at least a few extra days to spend on Kryg and catch up with Boj while Theo recovered. She enjoyed the lower level of gravity on the planet, and the way the kylie flowers floated, adding beauty to the landscape. Theo made a lot of progress, and on the second night, all three of them were entertained by the kassa insects that lit up the lake at night with different colors and shapes, sending messages to their audience.

It was easy to lose track of time on Kryg, where it seemed to stretch on forever. Sam was especially thankful for not having to go back to Earth right away, knowing that when she and Theo returned in less than a week, not much time would have passed on Earth. Still, she missed Kato, Kobe, and Simon. How were they doing, and were they okay? There had been so much going on. So much had happened in such a short period of time, she hadn't even had time to process a lot of it. She thought about them often, and looked forward to seeing them again soon.

* * *

It took three days, but Theo's healing progressed well, and he was now in much better spirits. Sam realized he must have sent a message to Lijing, because she showed up rather quickly to see him. They spent most of their time together, and they looked happier than Sam could remember.

Now, they were free. They would never have to live in hiding again. They would never have to worry about the Henchmen. They could live in peace together.

Lijing mentioned to Sam one day, "Honestly, I was getting sick of Gliese. It was a difficult planet to live on. Besides the black water pythons, there were these sky hawks the size of buses that were so unpredictable. There weren't many good options for food, either. After you left, I decided I needed to hold on. But the days were so long. Earth wasn't safe, not with Titus's men looking for me. When I got the message from Theo, I came here as soon as I could, and now everything's changed. All of what's in the past is over. We can finally go home and live in peace. We're free now."

Theo looked at Lijing with a smile, the color returning to his face. They were enjoying a meal on a grassy area overlooking Kassa Lake. "How about we stay here?" he suggested as he offered her more to eat. "What's the rush to go back to Earth? This place is paradise, really."

Lijing looked at Sam. "Would the Krygians make another couple of exceptions, for us to stay?"

Sam pondered the possibility. Although humans were typically banned from living on Kryg, they had already made one exception for Titus. Perhaps they could make another couple of exceptions. She decided she would run it by Onnisa. "Well, I'll have to ask for their permission, but I don't see why not. It seems times have changed."

They continued to enjoy their meal together, sharing stories and catching up. After they finished and began getting ready for a hike, Lijing spoke up.

"So, what's next for you, Sam?"

Sam thought about the tasks Onnisa had given her. She thought about having to go back to Earth and how she would need to help change things for the better. She would continue to help others and look for opportunities to protect the Earth. It would be a difficult task, but one she felt she could do with the help of others. She felt confident and determined.

"I have a few things to work on when I go back to Earth."

* * *

It wasn't long before Sam had to say her goodbyes. She was sad to leave, but when she saw how happy the Krygians were and the cheerfulness that emanated from Theo and Lijing, she felt comforted and more confident this time.

The klug hummed, and she soon found herself traveling through the wormhole. As she neared her destination, something felt off. Time sped up, and she braced for a hard landing on the forest floor. She hit branches and bushes and fell forward, scraping herself. She looked over and saw a building burning in the distance, the remnants of the explosion at Titus's lab. There were police on the scene, setting up barricades and sealing off the area. In the distance, she heard someone call out. She blinked, and what felt like minutes later, someone approached her.

Then everything went black.

* * *

Sam woke up in the hospital. Confused and a little groggy, she looked around and noticed her grandfather seated by the window. Numerous flowers and cards lined her windowsill.

"Grandpa?" she said, quietly assessing the state of her body. She slowly stretched her legs and fluttered her fingers, making sure they were still in working order. She tried piecing together the recent events, her mind still focused on her crash landing through the wormhole. Did her grandfather and the paramedics believe she had been hurt in the explosion? That would be an easier lie to tell. "What happened? How long was I out for?"

Her grandfather woke out of his reverie with a jolt. She immediately felt foolish for waking him so suddenly.

"Sam!" He got up from his seat and leaned down to kiss her

forehead. "I'm glad you're awake. I was…everyone was so worried about you. How are you feeling?"

She thought for a moment. She didn't feel much pain, just a bit stiff. "I'm okay."

Suddenly, the memories of being kidnapped, being taken to Titus's lab, and the explosion flooded her mind, and for a moment, she couldn't express the words fast enough. She found herself drifting into that painful experience, the images playing like a movie in front of her eyes.

"Sam? Are you okay? *Nurse!*"

"Grandpa," she sputtered, tears rolling down her cheeks. She couldn't stop them now. "Titus and his men kidnapped me! They took me to some building and I was worried I wouldn't escape!"

"Shh, it's okay. You're safe now," her grandfather reassured her as he gently squeezed her hand. His eyebrows creased. "Your friends told me what happened. I'm so sorry, Sam. I…I can't even imagine what you went through."

Sam wondered how much her friends had told him, and if they'd given him an altered version of the story to disguise what really happened. "It's okay, Grandpa," Sam said.

"No, it's not. I should have been more vigilant. After all, you are the daughter of some very well-known scientists, and I believe that's what made you the target of the kidnapping. I should have been more careful about your safety. I'm sorry. I'm just glad you're okay and you're here now. And, well…you won't be bothered by Titus anymore. He died a couple of weeks ago."

"What?"

"Yes. There was some sort of accident on his property—a fire and an explosion. The damage was so horrific, they never recovered his body. When paramedics arrived at the scene, they found you in the woods close by. I'm just glad you're okay," he said, handing her a couple of tissues. "The police have launched an investigation. When you're feeling better, they want to talk to you, but don't feel rushed. You went through a lot. Just focus on getting better for now." He looked out the window at the sky and added, "I'm just glad you're safe now."

"Grandpa," Sam continued, piecing his version of the story together. "I'm glad you're here. I missed you." She gave him a hug. She wanted to tell him about what had really happened, but stopped herself. Instead, she thought it would be better to keep silent. "Are Mom and Dad still alive?"

Her grandfather looked at her quizzically, his lips forming a puzzled grin. "Of course they are. Why wouldn't they be? In fact, I just spoke to them recently. They said they'll be coming to visit in a couple of weeks and want to take you on a trip as a way of celebrating you completing your first year at public school and pulling up your marks." Immediately his eyes went blank and his mouth dropped open. He looked sheepish. "Ah, I wasn't supposed to tell you—it was going to be a surprise," he confessed, and then winked. "Just make sure you *act* surprised when you see them, okay?"

Sam laughed, feeling relieved. "Okay."

"They, uh…actually, that reminds me. They were supposed to arrive here sooner, but they…well, I think there was something they had to take care of first." He passed her a folded letter. "Anyway, you can read it yourself."

She quickly unfolded letter, reading its contents:

Dear Sam,

We look forward to seeing you very soon, and we apologize for the delay. There was one last task we had to complete. During our mission, we responded to a distress signal, and so we are a little delayed. But we can assure you that all is well now. All we have to say is that it's best to value and encourage one another's strengths, and supporting our friends and allies is most important and necessary in difficult times. Be well. We look forward to seeing you soon.

Lots of love,
Mom and Dad

P.S. Onnisa and Boj send their warm regards.

Sam didn't have to read the letter twice to understand its meaning. They didn't say it explicitly, but she understood the significance of their alliance with the Krygians, and realized her parents had been called upon to assist the Krygians in impeding the Kantak threat and defending their way of life, even if it meant battling an opposing force. They'd responded to a distress signal, and since they referred to Onnisa and Boj, they must have seen them recently. Her parents must have gone to help dismantle the megastructure around the Hopewell Star, to help the Krygians regain its light.

Sam thought about the reference to friendships in the letter. If it was true, the human alliance with the Krygians was stronger than ever, and it gave her hope that if Earth needed help in the future, the Krygians might step up and help protect it too.

She looked over at her grandfather and smiled, folding the letter and handing it back to him for safekeeping. They both turned toward the door. Sam's friends were on the other side, their excitement and eagerness growing. Sam could hear them whispering.

"She's awake!"

"I think your friends are here to see you," her grandfather said, making his way toward the door. "I'll go so you can all catch up."

"Thank you, Grandpa. See you soon."

Kato, Kobe, and Simon all piled into her room at once. They'd brought gifts and flowers.

"It's so good that you're back, Sam!" Kato exclaimed, taking a seat beside her bed. "We were really worried about you." She gave Sam a hug and placed a gift bag on the side table. "Just some treats we picked up for you—when you're feeling better."

"Thank you. It's really good to see you all."

They spent the next hour catching up. Sam gave them the details about what had happened. She was overwhelmed but grateful that her friends were here now. They listened and nodded, intrigued but patient and understanding. Relieved to be able to trust her friends with the information, it felt like a weight had been lifted from her chest. Afterward, Simon and Kobe left to go to the coffee shop downstairs, leaving Kato and Sam alone in the room.

"I'm really glad you're okay, Sam. Thanks for telling me. I'm grateful that we're best friends."

It occurred to Sam that she felt the same way. "Me too."

"It's been a crazy year, hasn't it?"

Sam laughed. "That's an understatement!"

The air seemed to buzz with electricity. A moment later, a nurse entered the room.

"Just checking up on her. Please give me a moment."

Kato nodded and waited patiently while the nurse checked Sam's vitals.

"Everything looks good. Actually, better than I expected." The nurse looked a little perplexed. "You'll probably be ready to go home in a day or so. You're a lucky girl. In all my years of nursing, I've never seen such a remarkable recovery after this type of trauma. It's truly a miracle."

When the nurse left, Kato spoke up in her normal voice. "Sam, there's something I need to tell you."

"What's that?"

"I wanted to tell you when you were awake."

It was hard to read Kato now. She had a serious expression.

The words sped out of Kato's mouth. "Well, the government decided to close down the TitusTech operations until their buildings are upgraded to meet the new standards. They've been ordered to cease all operations at several sites. Some say it'll take a year to upgrade them to meet the new specifications."

"That's really great news!" Sam replied, thinking about the implications. Her initial tension dissipated as Kato continued.

"It's only been a couple of weeks, but people are talking and the scientists are hopeful about an improvement in the water quality over time," she said, perking up in her chair. "Also, they're planning to hire more people back at the fisheries, and...my dad said he's coming home! His old employer wants him back, and they said they'll pay him double what they were before!"

"Wow!" Sam exclaimed, unable to contain her delight. "That's awesome!"

Kato's tone became more serious as she lowered her voice. "I want to thank you, Sam. I don't think things would be the way they are if it wasn't for you."

"What?" Sam suddenly felt awkward and self-conscious. "No! It was a team effort!"

Kato grinned and stood up. "By the way, I'm helping myself to some of your chocolates and candies," she said as she headed over to the windowsill.

Sam looked around at the treats piled high in different parts of her room. "There does seem to be a lot. How long was I out for?"

"I don't know. You were in a coma for like, a couple of weeks," she said as she popped a handful of jelly beans into her mouth, and then held out the box to Sam. "The nurse was right. You're really lucky."

Sam took a few jelly beans. "I know." She felt grateful to be back and exhilarated by the seemingly infinite amount of amazing news.

Kato opened a box of chocolates. "Yeah, I think it's definitely too much for one girl. But don't worry, I'll help you lighten the load," she said as she ate a chocolate and offered the box to Sam. "It will be a team effort."

They both laughed.

* * *

The next day, Sam took some time to answer the police's questions. It went by quicker than expected, only because she mostly pretended not to remember what had happened and made sure not to give them too much information. The nurse came in to check on her again while the officers questioned her. The nurse was annoyed by their presence.

"The recovery process can take a long time and it's important not to interfere with it. Her memories are still fragile. Dissociative amnesia is quite common in these types of traumatic events," the nurse explained. The two officers' expressions changed swiftly to bewilderment. "I suggest you leave her your card, and if she remembers anything, she can contact you. In the meantime, she needs time to rest and recover."

The officers weren't happy, but respected the nurse's wishes. They gave her their business cards and left.

Sam relaxed. "Thank you."

"Of course," the nurse replied, and set a cup of tea on her bedside table. "Now, depending upon how you're feeling, we'll likely discharge you this evening. Your vital signs are good, and your scrapes are healing much quicker than I expected. How are you feeling?"

"Much better. It'll be nice to go home soon."

"Yes, of course. Well, in the meantime, I thought you might like some books and magazines to read, so I brought you a few. Take your pick. I'll leave them on the table here."

"Thank you. I really appreciate it," Sam replied as she took a sip of tea and let her tensions melt away.

Once the nurse left, she looked through the pile. She noticed a local newspaper had been left too. She opened it up to the front page and began reading a recent story.

TitusTech Founder Dead at 48

Mr. Titus Dyaderos, CEO and founder of TitusTech Industries, a multi-billion-dollar company with offices worldwide, is presumed dead after an explosion at his Shediac, New Brunswick laboratory late Tuesday evening.

The cause of the explosion is unknown at this time. Three casualties have been reported, including laboratory staff. Mr. Titus Dyaderos's body has not yet been recovered. Police are still searching the area for clues. All security tapes were destroyed in the fire.

Taylor Dyaderos, the daughter of Mr. Titus Dyaderos, has presumed acting CEO of TitusTech Industries in the interim period. The family requests privacy at this difficult time. More details to follow.

* * *

It didn't take long to adjust back at school. Sam's friends and teachers greeted her warmly and were supportive. Only a few more days and they would be on summer vacation. Sam couldn't wait. She needed a break from everything that had happened, especially over the past month. She was just glad to have finished her first year of public school and to have made some friends, including a best friend.

Kato looked in better spirits lately. During lunch one day, Kato asked Sam, "So, my dad, brother, and I are going kayaking next weekend. I was wondering if you wanted to join us?"

"Sure, that sounds fun!"

Sam felt more confident these days in so many aspects of her life. It felt good to be able to help her friends. Kato seemed especially grateful.

And of course, she felt a great sense of accomplishment, of awe almost, at being able to help the Krygians strengthen the light of their sun using the Hopewell Star's energy. She now knew the secret of its power and how to sustain it. Nevertheless, she thought about the second part of the prophecy. Earth remained wracked with disease, overpopulation, and violence, and global warming also presented a real threat to its stability. Sam had much more to do to save Earth. At least she felt more self-assured now, and could stand up for herself and others. Maybe that was the first step. She looked forward to seeing her parents again, and to the next part of her journey.

* * *

In the evening, Sam thought about Onnisa and how things were unfolding on Kryg. It wasn't long before she drifted off to sleep. Her visions became clearer and images flashed in front of her as she moved from one location to the next.

She observed Krygians busy dismantling the megastructures surrounding the Hopewell Star, piece by piece. It didn't take long. She watched as Kryg's sun grew brighter, and how nature now thrived. The population looked physically stronger and healthier compared to what she remembered.

When she woke up, the morning sunshine filled the room, and she felt a sense of relief. She felt inner peace and happiness, and looked around. At first, she thought it was a dream.

Only, it wasn't.

On her dresser, the kylie flower, which had looked sickly over the past few months, now miraculously thrived, and had sprouted smaller flowers along its stem.

After watching the kylie flower for a while, Sam went to the window and opened it a crack to take in a breath of fresh air. The sunlight poured through, filling her with warmth, like the familiar warmth of a star.

It felt good to be home.

THE END

Acknowledgments

There are many people I wish to thank who helped bring this project to fruition. First, thank you to my father, for encouraging me to turn my short story into a novel, even though it meant much more effort than I'd initially anticipated. Thank you to Robin, who helped me recognize its potential and provided positive feedback, and thanks to Nancy and Paul, for your support and encouragement during the early draft. Thank you to Sandi, for giving me hope and confidence to see this project through to completion, and for your words of wisdom in helping me let it go and not be afraid of failure.

Thank you to my mentor and writing coach, Terry, for sharing your knowledge and wisdom in the writing process, for your genuine and insightful feedback, and for helping me to explore and improve my writing without making me want to quit. Many thanks to Erika, my copyeditor, whose keen eyes, thoroughness, and professionalism greatly contributed to the final product. Thank you to Lee, for taking on the proofreading task within short timeframes, for noting the finer details, for sharing your knowledge and expertise, and for providing sound advice.

Special thanks to my novel writing group at the University of New Brunswick, who provided helpful, constructive criticism and thoughtful suggestions: Cathie, Angela, Jeff, Mary, Donna, and Michael.

Lastly, a BIG thank you to Brent, who read and reread countless drafts, who offered great ideas and suggestions (even though I sometimes didn't take them all), for recognizing and bringing important details to light (when I didn't always see them myself), and for believing in me and this project.

Thanks again—it's been an exciting journey!

About the Author

Hannah D. State is a Canadian author. She graduated from McGill University with a BA and earned her MPL from Queen's University. Hannah is bothered by inequality, violence, greed, complacency, snakes, entering a dark room, and not getting enough sleep. She enjoys writing about strong-willed characters who don't fit the norm and who overcome great obstacles with perseverance, self-discovery, and help from others. Sometimes Hannah can't keep up with her characters' ideas and plans, so she takes breaks, drinks coffee, does yoga and tai chi, and takes nature walks to calm her mind and really listen. *Journey to the Hopewell Star* is her first novel. You can find her author page on Facebook.

CPSIA information can be obtained
at www.ICGtesting.com
Printed in the USA
BVHW031328291121
622790BV00013B/106